JUL 2003

a.k.a. SHEILA WEINSTEIN

Also by Pat Jordan

a.k.a. Sheila Doyle
Black Coach
A False Spring
Suitors of Spring
Broken Patterns
Chase the Game
After the Sundown
The Cheat
A Nice Tuesday

a.k.a. *Sheila Weinstein*

PAT JORDAN

An Otto Penzler Book

CARROLL & GRAF PUBLISHERS
NEW YORK

A.K.A. SHEILA WEINSTEIN

Carroll & Graf Publishers
An Otto Penzler Book
An Imprint of Avalon Publishing Group Inc.
161 William St., 16th Floor
New York, NY 10038

Copyright © 2003 by Pat Jordan
First Carroll & Graf edition 2003
Interior design by Sue Canavan

All rights reserved. No part of this book may be reproduced in whole or in part without written permission from the publisher, except by reviewers who may quote brief excerpts in connection with a review in a newspaper, magazine, or electronic publication; nor may any part of this book be reproduced, stored in a retrieval system, or transmitted in any form or by any means electronic, mechanical, photocopying, recording, or other, without written permission from the publisher.

All of the characters in this book are fictitious, and any resemblance to actual persons, living or dead, is purely coincidental.

Library of Congress Cataloging-in-Publication Data is available.

ISBN: 0-7867-1191-4

Printed in the United States of America
Distributed by Publishers Group West

For Alice K. Turner

and

Otto Penzler

a.k.a. SHEILA WEINSTEIN

Part One

1

"Ess, mein kind!" his mother said. "Eat! Eat!"

Barry ate. A little nosh before work. Scrambled eggs, lox, a bagel with a schmear.

"You need your strength, *bubbeleh*."

Barry "The Bear" Berenson sat hunched over the little table in his mother's kitchen on the nineteenth floor of her condominium in Hallandale Beach, Florida, his face low to the plate as he ate slowly, methodically. His huge bulk loomed over the table like the shadow of a predatory prehistoric bird. He was six-foot-five, over 300 pounds, mostly fat. His small-featured face was puffy, doughy, with a grayish cast to his reptilian features. He was as bald as an egg, except for a little tuft of hair that ringed his shiny dome and fell in long, feathery wisps to his shoulders. He wore thick-lensed tinted eyeglasses that concealed his tiny flat-black eyes, like a dead bird's. He was already dressed in his chauffeur's uniform.

"My poor *bubbeleh*. Schlepping your *tuchas* all hours of the night." Rose Berenson stood over her son, watching him eat, hugging herself in her old purple silk nightgown that smelled of her stale sex that made her son sick to his stomach when he ate, if he didn't breathe through his mouth. Rose was as tiny as her son was huge. She had a lacquered bouffant metallic orange hairdo, eyes made up to look like Elizabeth Taylor's in *Cleopatra*, and frosted orange lipstick that spilled over her lip line and coated her sharp teeth. Her nightgown fell to the tops of her gold lamé stiletto mules. She kissed the top of her son's head.

"Ma!"

"You're never too old for your *mammeleh's* kisses." Barry was forty eight. He had lived with his mother these last ten years, ever since his father had died in a wrestling ring in Pensacola, Florida. His father was known as "Harry the Hun." He entered the ring wearing a black mask and one of those World War I German officer helmets with the little spike on top. On the night he died, his opponent, a muscle-bound, ex-Florida Gator lineman known as "The Brick," was in the throes of a wild-eyed steroid rage. The Brick was supposed to let Harry the Hun catapult himself off the ring ropes, fly through the air, and. land on top of The Brick, smothering him to the mat to the count of three. Harry the Hun was flying through the air according to the script, his arms outstretched like airplane wings, when The Brick caught him in midflight. The Brick held Harry the Hun over his head, Harry's arms flailing helplessly, the muscles in The Brick's arms bulging. Then The Brick slammed Harry the Hun, a fat, old man pushing sixty, headfirst into the mat, breaking his neck.

After sitting shiva for his father, Barry paid a visit to The Brick. He broke his arms and legs and his back with an aluminum baseball bat, left him crying like a baby, crippled for life. Now the only time The Brick appears in a wrestling ring is when he is wheeled out in his motorized wheelchair to an ovation from the crowd at a benefit for the once-promising World Wrestling Star. Barry liked to be in the audience at those benefits. While The Brick's former fans cheered and applauded him, and some women even cried, Barry just sat there with a small smile on his lips. The Brick's once-muscular arms were white and flabby now, his once-thick legs like white sticks. It was the right decision, Barry thought, sitting there, better even than whacking him.

Barry checked his watch. Almost midnight.

"I suppose you'll be home late again," Rose said.

Barry shrugged. "I never know, Ma."

Rose shook her head. "What these people do all hours of the night. Shiksa whores and Cuban gangsters. You'll never find a *hamisha maidel* driving shiksa whores, *bubbeleh*."

Barry sighed, pushed his plate from him. "Ma, I'm not looking. I would never leave you." Rose smiled at her son. She loved the idea of her son bringing home a nice Jewish girl, and then some grandchildren. She also knew she'd hate any girl he actually *did* bring home. So did Barry.

"I gotta go, Ma," he said, standing up, his bulk filling the small kitchen. He put on his chauffeur's cap, went to the kitchen cabinet where his mother kept the canned goods, and reached in behind them. He withdrew a chrome-plated Colt .45ACP semiautomatic pistol and stuck it into the back waistband of his pants while his mother averted her eyes and busied herself with the dishes.

Without looking at her son, Rose said, "Which limousine tonight?"

"The Hummer."

Rose scrunched up her features while she scrubbed dried egg from her son's dish. "Such an ugly thing. Mr. Kressel couldn't let you take the Cadillac?" She smiled. "Such a nice man, Mr. Kressel. Tell him from Rose he shouldn't be a stranger."

"Sure, Ma." Barry leaned down to kiss his mother's cheek.

Barry waited for the elevator in the lobby that smelled of herring and onions. When the elevator door opened, he stepped in alongside a bent, white-haired old man holding himself up with an aluminum walker.

"Good evening, Barry," said the old man. "Driving tonight?" Barry nodded. He took off his horn-rimmed eyeglasses that pinched the bridge of his nose. He squinted at the harsh elevator lights that hurt his eyes. The old man looked up at Barry with big watery-blue eyes, like Tweety Bird's. Barry massaged his sore eyes with his thumb and forefinger, then looked down at the old man and said, "Cataracts, Mr. Mandelbaum?"

"What?" Mr. Mendelbaum cupped a hand to his hairy ear and tilted his head toward Barry.

"Cataracts!" Barry shouted.

"I thought you drove a Lincoln."

Barry drove his Lincoln Town Car north on I-95, got off on Sunrise Boulevard and headed east toward Fort Lauderdale Beach. When he reached the big glass showroom of Paradise Auto Works, the showroom crowded with the dark, humped shapes of exotic cars—Porsches and Ferraris and Lamborghinis—he turned right, down the side street that ran alongside the high concrete wall, topped with razor wire, that surrounded the car dealer's back lot. He came to a metal gate, buzzed himself in in the darkness, and parked his Lincoln next to a black stretch Hummer limo.

Barry drove the stretch Hummer east on Sunrise, past the Gateway Theater, Big Louie's, Cary Keno's jewelry store, over the canal bridge, and turned left on Bayview Drive. He drove slowly down Bayview until he came to 15th Street. He took a right that ran parallel to a canal and drove to the end of the street that fronted the Intracoastal Waterway. He parked the Hummer in front of a new two-story, Spanish revival town house on the point lot. Maybe half a mil, maybe more, he thought. Sucking cock paid. He slipped his .45 from his waistband, racked the slide to chamber a round, flipped on the safety, and stuck the piece into the back of his waistband. Then he beeped his horn, lit a cigarette, and waited for the hooker.

"It's cancer, Mrs. Roberts. Bone marrow. There's nothing I can do." He saw a look cross her face for a split second, and. then it was gone. No tears, nothing but that cold look in her blue eyes. "I'm so sorry, Mrs. Roberts."

She gave her head a quick little shake—once—as if to dismiss his sympathy. "How long?" she said.

"A month, maybe two, three at the most. The last few weeks will be bad for him. A lot of pain. I can give you something for it, but I'd advise you to consider putting him down before it gets to that."

"Don't worry, I'll never let him suffer. Right, Hoshi?" She smiled at the muscular little dog with the reddish fur, pointed nose, prick ears, and curled tail, who was standing unsteadily on the metal table in the veterinarian's examining room. She pressed her cheek against the dog's cheek, and hugged him. She breathed in deeply his musty smell. The dog let her hug him for a moment, then pulled away and shook off her hug. She looked at him. "Always the hard guy, eh, Hosh?" The dog looked back at her with an eerily human expression in his almond-shaped eyes. It was a look of pity, not for himself, but for her. He knew where he was going soon. She didn't.

"It happened so fast," she said, forcing back a catch in her voice. "He was eating, going for his walk, and then yesterday he wouldn't eat, wouldn't walk. He just sat there, like Queequeg, as if he'd rolled the bones and they'd come up. . . ." Her voice trailed off.

"That's the way it happens with Shibas," said the veterinarian. He was a slight Asian man in a white doctor's smock and. wire-rimmed eyeglasses. He smiled at her, this beautiful American woman in her forties, tanned, slimly muscled in her T-shirt and cutoff shorts. She had close-cropped, ash-blond hair that stood up like spring grass. He took off his glasses. and said, "You know, I'm Japanese also, Mrs. Roberts. Like Hoshi. In my native country, Shibas are a National Treasure. They're very revered as noble creatures, more noble even than man,we believe. They know things we don't know," He stroked the fur behind Hoshi's ears. The dog turned his head and licked the man's hand. "He knows, Mrs. Roberts. It's time for him to go to another life, a better life. He's not afraid."

The woman burst out angrily, "But *I* am! I'm afraid! I'll miss him so! He's all I've got now!" She bit her lower lip and forced back her tears. "I'm sorry, Doctor."

The little man reached up his hand and placed it on her shoulder.

"That's all right, Mrs. Roberts. You're entitled."

"I still can't understand it. He was always so strong. He's only fourteen."

"A lifetime for a dog."

"Somehow I feel it's my fault. I should have done something. Brought him for more check-ups. Changed his diet. Exercised him more."

"There's nothing you could have done. Cancer is only a physical manifestation of emotional stress. In dogs, like humans, it's often brought on by a breakdown of the immune system caused by a terrible loss." The woman looked stricken. "Has Hoshi suffered a terrible loss lately, Mrs. Roberts?"

The woman lowered her head and stared at the linoleum floor dusted with little clumps of her dog's reddish fur. "I knew it," she said softly. "I *did* cause it."

"I beg your pardon?"

She looked up at him, her eyes half-lidded. Without emotion, she said, "Bobby left a month ago. He left me, not Hoshi, but he knew . . . so he left Hoshi to take care of me. We woke up one morning, Hoshi and I, and Bobby was gone. Because of me. What I did." She exhaled a great breath. "I can't blame him. But I did it for him. I told him I'd never let anyone hurt us. So I did it. I don't regret it. But it scared Bobby off. What I'd become. And now this. Hoshi, too." She gave the little man a thin smile. "You see, Doctor, *I'm* the fucking cancer."

Bobby hitched a ride to Key West with the two fags he met at Warsaw a few nights after he'd left Sheila and Hoshi. He'd stayed as long as he could after Sheila told him what she'd done in South Beach. She'd picked up Medina at The Anvil. The fucking spic wouldn't get off their backs, wouldn't stop until he killed them all—Bobby, Sheila, even Hosh—for what, nothing, except his own crazed need for revenge. And then she'd taken Medina into the Cuba Room at The Anvil, where it was nice and dark, private, and while they waited for their dinner at a banquette against the wall, Sheila had dipped her head below the table and begun to suck Medina's cock. Medina lay back and closed his eyes to Sheila's expert blow job (that Bobby had taught her), and then she shot him between the eyes with her little Seecamp .32 ACP, the same Seecamp Bobby had given her on a whim.

It was all his fault. He'd started something with Sheila that got out of control. He never thought she'd go as far as she did. His mistake. He should have known. She was always smarter than he was. They both knew it. They just didn't know how far she'd go when pushed. Once Bobby knew, it changed him, what she'd done, but mostly what she'd become, the way he saw her now, scary, dangerous, out of control. As long as he was with her, she was crazed to protect him.

So he left her—not for him, but for her, because he still loved her. With him gone, he hoped she could find her way back to that other woman she had been when he met her; sweet, scared, trusting. He slipped out of their rented wood-frame Key West house in Victoria Park in Lauderdale one night while Sheila and Hoshi slept. He drove to Warsaw, the fag dance club in South Beach, to look for a job as a bouncer, and to lose himself in the South Beach scene of transients, spics, fags, hip-hop niggers and slumming celebrities like that spic broad with the big ass and her nigger boyfriend, Puff Doggy Snoop or whatever-the-fuck the nigger's name was. He sold his car—big, black SHO that he loved—for getaway cash, and then he spent his nights at Warsaw, sizing up the scene, waiting for a chance to make his move. He'd hang there for a few months, waiting for Sol to surface again, hoping Sol *would* surface again, and then they'd both go back into business, without Sheila, the way it had been with them for years.

He was sitting on a sofa on the second-floor balcony that looked down over the dance floor at Warsaw, all the fags with their shirts off, their bodies glistening with sweat Bobby could. smell all the way to the balcony as they danced manically to the deafening thump-thump-thump of that head-splitting music only fags loved, when two fags sat down beside him. They smiled at him, a big muscle-beach-looking dude in his thirties with a bleached blond ponytail. Bobby smiled back.

"You must be from Lauderdale," said one of the fags, with a spic accent.

Bobby looked down at his clothes, an aqua Hawaiian shirt dotted with pink flamingos, O.P. shorts, and flip-flops. "You should be on *The Millionaire*," Bobby said.

"It wasn't hard," said the other fag with a preppy East Coast accent. They were both dressed in black mesh T-shirts and black leather pants they got from The Male Catalog.

The spic fag reached over his hand and put it between Bobby's legs.

Bobby looked down at the fag's hand. The spic fag said, "It's not hard yet, but the night is young."

"The night's gonna be over for you pretty quick, you don't take your hand off my dick."

The spic fag pulled his hand away and squealed like a teenaged girl. "Aiiiee! So macho! I luff tough boys."

The preppy fag said to his friend, "René! Can't you see he's straight? He's just slumming."

René pouted. "I supposta know?"

"He probably had a fight with his girlfriend," said the preppy fag.

"Oh, don't tell me!" said René. "One of those *gringa* strippers with the fake water-balloon *tetas*. Sooo sordid."

Bobby shrugged. "What can I say? You got me nailed."

The preppy fag smiled and reached out a slim white hand toward Bobby. Bobby shook his hand. "I'm James. My friend is René."

Bobby said, "I'm Bobby. Robert Roberts." He grinned. "But my buddies call me Bobby Squared."

"Bobby Squared?" said René, confused. "Whassat?"

"Bobby with a little two over it," said James. "Like in algebra, René."

"Aiiieee! I was *terrible* in algebra."

James shook his head and rolled his eyes. Bobby smiled and said, "Can I buy you boys a drink?"

Over drinks they told him they were driving to Key West for Fantasy Fest the minute Warsaw closed at six in the morning. Bobby said, "Can I hitch a ride?" He didn't know why he said it. He had never liked Key West. It was worse even than South Beach, and not because of all the fags. Bobby had no problem with them. It was the tourists off the cruise ships, gawking at the fags, cam-cording them like they were exotic birds so they could show their friends back in Ann Arbor, and the writer wannabes searching for Hemingway at

Sloppy Joe's—not even the real Sloppy Joe's where Hemingway once drank—the wannabes sitting at the bar, looking around, and then writing something in their journals for the novel they would never write. And then there were the crazies, who only wanted to be noticed for being crazy, like the Iguana Man who put on a show at the pier every day at twilight so he could be filmed by some Midwest local-TV news crew to show the folks back home how colorful Key West was, the Iguana Man and the Chainsaw Man and the fags and the warm reddish-orange sun setting over the pale blue-green waters of the Gulf, while back home, in Duluth, the locals were freezing their asses off in the dead of winter. If the Midwest film crew was lucky, they might find a tourist from their hometown they could film, too, for their reactions to all the craziness they saw in Key West. It was like that red-haired chick who used to be married to Tom Cruise said in that movie: "You're not anyone unless you're on TV."

But, what the hell, Key West was even farther from Lauderdale than South Beach, more isolated, the end of the line. Bobby could vanish there. He wouldn't stand out, a big, muscular dude with a bleached blond ponytail to hide the fact that he was really just Robert Redfeather, a Cherokee pot grower from the hills of western North Carolina. So he decided to go even farther south, as far south as he could go and still stay in the U.S. Why not? He couldn't think of a reason not to go to the end of the line. How ironic, he thought. That's what Sheila told him the day she had decided to live with him, to change her life in ways neither of them could ever know.

"At first, Bobby," she had said, "I thought people had to have a reason to change their lives. Then I realized some people change their lives because they don't have a reason *not* to."

Sol ordered a pastry from the guinea chick with the blue eyes standing behind the glass display case. "I'll take dat one, honey." He pointed at a fruit tart in the case.

"*Mi dispiace,*" she said. "*Non parlo inglese.*"

Sol jabbed his finger at the case. "Dat one, honey. Wit da strawberries on top."

She shrugged, a beautiful guinea chick in her late thirties, with that strong Anna Magnani face.

"Jesus fuckin' Christ! Don't no one speak English in dis fuckin' country?"

"*Scusi, signore,*" said a little guy looked like an accountant standing beside Sol. "Maybe I can help. I speak *inglese.*" He wiggled his hand. "*Piccolo.*" The little guy pointed at the tart and said something in Italian to the broad. She reached in for the tart and put it on a piece of waxed paper. She said something in Italian to the little guy. "The signora wants to know if the signore would like anything else," the little guy said.

Sol looked at the woman, her big tits straining against her white apron. Real tits the way they hung a little bit, like cantaloupes, not like those fuckin' strippers' tits in Lauderdale looked like the bullet bumpers of old Buicks. Sol smiled at her and said to the little guy, "Yeah, you can tell her the signore would like to get laid, too."

The little guy blinked. The broad said, "I'm sorry, signore. I can't help you there."

"I'll be a sunuvabitch!" Sol said, grinning. "You been puttin' me on all dis time." She smiled at him and shrugged. "Well, if you can't help me get laid, baby, maybe you can help me wit dis." He showed her a photograph of him with a much younger girl, maybe twenty-five to his forty-eight. They were seated close together at a banquette in what looked like a fancy French restaurant. The girl had thrown her arm over Sol's shoulder and was hugging him. Sol looked a little embarrassed, a bald, fat, older guy with a neat goatee and blue-tinted contacts. He wore a lot of gold chains around his neck, gold bracelets on his wrists, a diamond-studded Rolex, and diamond-encrusted pinkie rings on each hand.

The girl looked fresh-faced, scrubbed, with short sandy-colored hair that fell over one of her pale blue eyes.

"Her name is Delphine," Sol said to the woman.

The woman looked at the photograph, narrowed her eyes, then looked at Sol. "Is your niece?"

"Yeah, my niece. You seen her?"

The woman smiled, then shook her head.

"Her parents been worried about her. Sent me to bring her back home, ya know, tell her all's forgiven."

"Forgiven? For what?"

"It's a long story." An old story, too, Sol thought. A young chick scammin' a wiseguy outta his 300 large drug money, the wiseguy shoulda known, he didn't get careless, he must be gettin old not to see it comin'.

Sol put the photograph back in his pants pocket. "I'm stayin' at da Pensione Al . . . Al. . . ."

"Alberghi," said the woman.

"Yeah, you know it? If she comes in maybe you could give me a call." Sol grinned at her. "If she don't, maybe you could call me anyways we can discuss dat other thing, ya know."

The woman threw back her head and laughed. When she stopped laughing, she said, "Oh, *signore*, I *do* love American gangsters. They are like children, no?"

Sol went outside to the little cobblestone square and sat on the stone bench that encircled a little fountain of a kid pissing. He ate his pastry and drank his cappuccino while he tried to figure out what the broad meant by "children."

It was early morning in the Santa Croce section of Florence in the square the guineas called San Piero Maggiore, a fancy name for a dirty little square Sol called "Scuzzi Square" because of all the derelicts and druggies who congregated there. "The *drogati*," the guineas called them. They sat nodding off on the cobblestones, their backs against the salmon-colored buildings, their discarded needles scattered around them in the sunlight slanting between the buildings. A one-armed man hurried into the square, peered around nervously through his wire-rimmed eyeglasses like a frightened bird, clutching to his side a slim leather briefcase as if it contained his drawings for today's art class at the Pitti Palace. The "drogatti" looked up, alive now, and when the one-armed man hurried off, his empty white shirt sleeve pinned up to his shoulder, they shuffled off after him one by one.

The fruit and vegtable girls, two hard-looking chicks, one a blonde, the other brunette, began opening their boxes of fruit and vegetables in their corner of the square. They stacked the boxes just so, like stairs, and stuck in the hand-printed price tags. "*Albicocche. Al chilo.* Cinque Lira." A fat old lady with a broom began sweeping off the little corner of the square under her osteria sign where she set up her table for lunch.

Tourists began to come through the square in groups, plodding under the weight of their backpacks, and then the merchants, the cheese sellers and the bread sellers and the meat sellers, all stopping for a few minutes in Bar Daria, where Sol had gotten his pastry. They threw back a quick espresso laced with amaretto and then went to their shops.

A beautiful little girl, maybe six, in a dirty white communion dress, whirled into the square, dancing in circles as if in a dream. She had thick black hair that framed her fat red-cheeked face in ringlets. She whirled and whirled and then spun herself out of the square and was gone. A moment later a young woman rushed into the square. She was wild-eyed, frantic. She stood in the center of the square and screamed out, "Lucinda! Lucinda!" And then she ran off.

Sol sat there, watching all the traffic pass through the square, remembering what the cabbie had told him when he dropped him off here. "Signore, if you're looking for someone, sooner or later everyone in Florence passes through the square of San Pietro Maggiore." Like Fort Lauderdale Beach, Sol thought. You sit on the beach wall and sooner or later you'll see everyone you ever knew when you were a wiseguy sitting on your stoop in Brooklyn. Now, if Frenchie would only pass through the square. McCraw had tracked her from his P.I. office in Palm Beach on his computer. Then he called Sol at "Uncle Sol's Title Loans, A Friend InDeed in Time of Need."

"Solly," McCraw said, "the French chick was in London for a few days, then Paris. She's in Florence now, Italy, but I got no address."

So Sol had gone to Florence, had been here a week now, hitting all the places he thought Frenchie might visit, showing her photo at the Belle Epoque Bar to the fag owner with rotting teeth and straight white hair like Andy Warhol. The fag shook his head, and then insisted on showing Sol all his Belle Epoque memorabilia on the walls, the old, sepia-tinted photographs of turn-of-the-century soldiers and plump opera singers in their bustle dresses, and letters from fans to their favorite singers. Sol showed her photo at Donatello's, the workingman's bar that was always crowded at lunchtime. The old *nonna* with a few gold teeth, shook her head and hustled back to the kitchen for more food. An old man peeled a tomato carefully, sliced it, sprinkled salt on it, then fed it to his mangy dog sitting patiently at his feet.

Sol walked across town to Harry's Bar along the Arno and ordered a Cuba Libre, explaining to the bartender just what was in it. Then he sat there in the fancy bar and restaurant, all dark wood and red velvet, watching all the American businessmen come in in their guinea suits and order lunch, tomato soup and hamburgers, like they were back home in Tuscaloosa. It was the only place in Florence where everyone spoke English. Sol moved through the room, stopping at tables to show the photo, but no one recognized her. One guy smiled at him, and said, in his shit-kicking drawl, "Y'all find that little lady, let me know. I sure as shoot'd like to meet her." His friends all laughed.

After dinner, Sol walked across the street to a bar–pool hall for a drink. The place was too dingy for Frenchie and he was about to leave when he noticed the two broads shooting pool. They were dressed in '50s prom dresses, red and royal blue, their full skirts puffed out with crinolines. They were husky broads, with thick, hairy arms covered with tattoos. They had deep voices and a faint shadow across their faces that no amount of pancake makeup could hide, not that they cared. Sol showed them the photo anyway. They shook their heads, then smiled at Sol, showing him their missing teeth. They said something in Italian, pointing to his glass of scotch, and then each one grabbed his arm in a grip like a stevedore's and tried to lead him to the bar.

Sol said, "Thanks, girls, but I ain't that thirsty." He tried to pull away from them, but they pulled him toward the bar anyway. He pulled back, the three of them in a tug of war until the bartender said something to them in Italian and they let go of his arms. Sol hurried to the door, was outside in the darkness, walking fast away from the bar when he heard the two broads call out to him in falsetto voices. He glanced over his shoulder and saw them waving at him, giggling girlishly. Jesus Christ!

Sol went to the Red Garter late at night, squeezing his fat body between all the young kids, Aussies and Swedes and Americans, drinking beer and dancing to '50s and '60s American rock-'n'-roll music. He showed the photo to a stumpy, unshaven guy who looked like he done time checking the IDs at the door, but he just shook his head and waved Sol away from the door.

The *drogati* drifted back into the square by early afternoon. They sat down on the cobblestones, their backs against the building walls, and nodded off again. Sol watched them, thinking how he could make a nice living here after he chased off the one-armed guy, if only he could find Frenchie and get his 300 large. It wouldn'ta happened if Sheila was around. Sheila woulda spotted Frenchie right off for what she was, a scam artist. "Oh, Solly, for Crissakes!" Sheila woulda said. "Sweet, my ass! Your brains in your dick these days?" Sol smiled to himself. He hadta admit, Sheila was a piece a work. But she knew things him and Bobby didn't. Jeezus, I wish they were here. He tried to phone them before he left for Florence, but they didn't answer. Then he was on the plane, reading the *Miami Herald,* when he saw the photograph of Medina on the front page, under the headline: "Cuban-American Patriot Assassinated." Which made Sol laugh, "Patriot," until he read that the heat was looking for a "statuesque woman in her thirties, with sharply cut black hair," and he knew it was Sheila, one of the Sheilas anyway, there were so many of them Sol couldn't keep track, the broad able to change her spots on a whim. But he knew it was her. Sheila did things hadta be done. Bobby didn't have the stomach for it—they all knew that. Sheila was a broad who could convince herself to do anything. Guys draw a line in the sand and never cross it, not even for their broad. Broads draw a line in the sand and when they have to, when they convince themselves there's no other way to get what they want, they move the line.

The one-armed guy came back into the square. He looked around, and then left quickly, like someone was chasing him. Then Sol heard a funny-sounding siren, like one of those high-pitched, honking horns on those clown cars in a circus. A little white car, with *Polizia* in blue on the side doors, roared into the square, stopped, and four cops carrying machine guns hustled out and began rousting the *drogati*. They pulled the nodding *drogati* up and threw them into the back of a van that pulled up. Then they were gone in only a few minutes, and the square was quiet again. The one-armed guy came around the corner of a building, glanced around the square, and then walked through the square and was gone.

Sol was ready to leave for lunch, when he saw a guy walk into the square who looked familiar. A slouchy guy in his forties, in a wrinkled brown suit. He had a droopy mustache and bulgy eyes like that Italian actor who always played comic lovers of Sophia Loren. The guy walked right past Sol without recognizing him and went into Bar Daria. Sol waited, grinning to himself, remembering how the guy, Paolo, had helped Sol, Bobby, and Sheila scam the Jew owner of Paradise Auto Works out of 50 large each. A nice little score. When the guy came out of the bar, Sol walked over to him. "Signore Fortunato, you need maybe a limousine, someone to find you a nice companion can show you sights in Paradise."

"Signore Sol!" The guy's face spread out in a smile. He grabbed Sol in his arms and hugged him like the guineas do, and kissed him on both cheeks. He held Sol at arm's length, and said, "Signore Sol, your friends are with you, no?"

"No. I came alone. A little business maybe you can help me with, you know Florence."

"Anything for you, Signore Sol, but first we go to lunch, and then we talk business." The guy threw his arm over Sol's shoulder, and as he led him out of the square, he said, "So tell me, Sol, how is Signora Sheila? Well, I hope."

2

CAROL JENKINS, PART DAVIE, FLA. REDNECK, PART CHEROKEE, PART CUBANA, a.k.a. Candy Kane, part-time stripper at The Booby Trap, Home of Stylish Nude Entertainment, and full-time hooker for the Celebrity Dream Dates Escort Service, was sitting at her makeup table in the bedroom of her $700,000 Spanish Mediterranean town house off Bayview Drive in Fort Lauderdale. She was putting the finishing touches to her makeup when she heard the limo driver beep his horn. "A Hummer," she said to herself. So fucking uncomfortable in the backseat. How did the service expect her to work on those hard, cramped seats? The limo driver beeped his horn again. Fuck him. Let him wait.

When she was finished, she stared at her reflection in the mirror, brightly lighted by the theatrical makeup bulbs that surrounded it. Her long burgundy-tinted hair fell over one violet eye to her shoulder. She had perfect, if undistinguished, features and creamy white skin. She never went in the sun, partly to protect her skin, now in her thirties, but mostly because she worked all night and slept all day.

She stood up and struck a stripper's pose, hands on hips, back arched, and checked herself out. She was wearing a gauzy, black see-through blouse and no bra. She hefted her $7000 tits with each hand, then let them drop. They fell naturally. She needed the extra heft to balance herself out because she had wide hips and a big ass that stuck out behind her like a porch in her short, flouncy black skirt. What'd Sol call it? A hamster ass. She smiled, remembering the days when Sol owned the Trap and a girl could make a living there. Then Solly went away for a year on an old smuggling charge and the new owner, a yuppie with a bleached blond ponytail, made the girls kick back 20 percent each night, which was why she had to join the service, to pay the nut on her $700,000 town house. Actually, the little prick did her a favor. She was getting too old to throw her big ass around the Trap eight hours a night, for what, $500 a night. She made five times that with the service for each date. It was easy work. A blow job in the backseat of the limo on the way to a restaurant. Then drinks, a nice dinner, and back to the john's pad for a full session on the black satin sheets of his black-lacquered king-size bed on the twentieth floor of a Galt Ocean Mile condo that looked out over the ocean below. He stood close to the side of the bed while she kneeled on all fours on those black satin sheets and he fucked her from behind, his stomach slapping against the cheeks of her big white, dimpled ass, her hands cupped under her chin as she stared out the sliding glass doors of his bedroom at the stars against the black velvet sky and below the colored lights of the ships passing in darkness. He came quick, with a strangled cry, and fell, soaked with sweat, on the sheets. He lay there for a moment, catching his breath, and then, determined to get his money's worth, he made her suck his cock again until finally he got it up after an hour and his salty cum spurted down her throat and he was asleep. This was the time she liked best, lying there alone, looking out at the soft, dark Florida night until finally, exhausted, she, too, drifted off. He woke her a few hours later as the sun was coming up.

Half-asleep, she rolled over between his legs and began sucking his cock, almost gagging on the smell of his dried sweat and his stale cum and the taste of her own pussy, until he came one last time and then threw her out. They all said the same thing, like they invented it. "I pay you to go, bitch, not come."

They were mostly older guys, fat, hairy, not like the young, good-looking guys that came to the Trap. But the young guys didn't like her body much. They preferred their strippers lean, tanned, and toned, with abs and big tits that didn't fit their bodies. But older guys, the kind who could afford to pay $2500 for a piece of Carol Jenkins's big ass—they looked at Carol Jenkins, a.k.a. Candy Kane, and they remembered the young Ann-Margret.

Candy Kane stood beside the rear door of the Hummer limo in the darkness, and waited. The driver was smoking a cigarette. She tapped on his window with her knuckles. He lowered the window.

"Well, asshole, you gonna open the door for me, or what?"

"You think you're going to a fuckin' prom? Get in." He blew cigarette smoke out the window.

Candy flapped her hand in front of her face. "Not until you put that thing out." She waited there, in the darkness, until finally he dropped his cigarette out the window. Then she got in.

She arranged herself in the backseat, flouncing up her little skirt so he could see through the rearview mirror she wasn't wearing any underwear. He didn't seem to notice.

They were driving south on Federal Highway toward the airport, when she said, "So what's the deal?"

"The guy's birthday."

"And I'm his present?" No answer. "Who paid?"

"What do *you* care?"

They passed the exotic car dealers and then Searstown and headed for the cheap motels that lined Federal all the way to the airport. She saw a black hooker walking on the sidewalk, looking back over her shoulder at passing cars, smiling.

"What's the guy do?" she said.

The limo driver didn't answer.

"I don't do freaks, you know. And no anal. He gets out of hand I expect you to be there for me."

The big guy in the chauffeur's cap shook his head.

Candy settled back into her seat and looked out the window at the deserted storefronts in darkness. She said, "Where we going to dinner? Someplace nice, I hope."

The driver slowed the big Hummer as they approached the Dolphin Delight Motel, rooms by the month, week, day, or hour. The motel office was painted pink. A blue dolphin—the fish—was leaping out of its roof. The Hummer turned into the Dolphin Delight's parking lot, passed the office, and moved slowly past each of the motel's six rooms, all of which were numbered for a retired Miami Dolphin. No. 39 was the Larry Csonka Room. No. 21 was the Jim Kiick Room. When they stopped at No. 42, the Paul Warfield Room, Candy said, "Whoa, big boy, this shit hole can't be it."

The limo driver said nothing.

"I ain't going in there! I'll get the crabs just opening the door." She waited for the limo driver to say something. Finally, she said, "I ain't getting out of this fucking limo until you tell me who this guy is and what's he doing shacked up at this shit hole." She folded her arms across her massive chest and settled back in her seat.

Barry "The Bear" closed his eyes behind his tinted glasses and muttered a Yiddish curse. He should listen more to his ma. Finally, he turned around in his seat to face the shiksa whore. "You're getting paid is all you gotta know."

Candy sat there for a moment, remembering that her mortgage was due in a week, and then she snapped, "Oh, for Crissakes! The fucking things I do!" She opened the door, got out, and went up to the Paul Warfield Room door. She knocked, once, twice, more loudly a third time. The door opened slowly.

A big guy in a cheap JCPenney suit stood in the light of the doorway. He wasn't bad looking, Candy thought, and smiled at him, her smile fading when she saw the pistol in his hand held down at his side. She opened her mouth to speak but the big guy clamped his hand over her mouth and grabbed her arm hard. He looked over her, then left and right, yanked her into the room and shut the door.

"What the fuck you think you're doing?" Candy yelled, pulling her arm free.

The big guy smiled at her and opened his suit coat to put his gun into the holster at his hip. Candy saw a badge clipped to his belt. United States Marshal.

"Lennie," the big guy said. "Your birthday present from Uncle is here."

Candy turned around to see two guys playing cards on a bed. One was wearing a cheap suit like the big guy. The other one was younger, muscular, handsome, with a pouty baby-fat face and short black hair. He was all dressed up for a night out: black silk T-shirt, black jeans, red and black embossed cowboy boots. The room around them was littered with junk-food wrappers, plastic cups, ashtrays overflowing with cigarette butts and cigar butts.

The guy in black slapped his cards down on the bed, and got up. He went over to Candy, looked her up and down, her massive white tits showing through her blouse, her big ass, her clunky low-heeled shoes.

"Is this all Uncle thinks of me?" he said to the big guy. "I got a reputation. I fucked Madonna." He shrugged. "Not that she was that good, but still, it counts for something, fucking Madonna."

"Not anymore it don't," the big guy said.

Candy said, "Hey, wait a minute assholes! I got better things to do than—"

The big guy talked over her as if she wasn't there. "Well, Lennie? It's up to you. You rather stay here, play cards with me and Ronnie, we can order out a Domino's."

Candy hated the way guys talked about her when she was standing right in front of them. But the $2500 gave them the right, they thought. She'd learned that over the years, so she kept her mouth shut.

"Fuck it," Lennie said. "Let's go, baby." He grabbed her arm. She pulled it away.

"I ain't moving until I get my fee up front." She stared hard at Lennie, his short black hair tight to his head like Julius Caesar, his small black eyes, his full lips that were smiling to hide the meanness behind them. It was then she recognized the guy from a photograph she'd seen in the *Miami Herald* a few months ago. She was going to say something, Hey, you're Lennie Pacco, the guy they call "King of South Beach Nightlife," but she didn't, remembering the captions that went along with his photograph. "Owner of Club Drip, hottest dance club in South Beach, arrested for money laundering." And then, a few weeks later, "Pretty boy who dated Madonna turns state's evidence against the Brooklyn mob that bankrolled his clubs." And finally, a few weeks ago, "Pacco under protection of Federal marshals until trial. Awaits new home in Federal Witness Protection Program."

The big guy slipped an envelope out of the inside of his jacket and handed it to her. "Is this what you want, honey?" he said.

The envelope was sealed. Candy slit it open with her long nails and fanned out the contents. Twenty-five crisp new $100 bills. She looked at the big guy, "These better be real. They don't feel real. The fucking ink's still wet."

"It should be, honey." The big guy grinned. "Uncle printed them just for you."

"We going, or what?" Lennie grabbed her arm. Now she let him lead her to the door.

The big guy called out, "Stay in the limo, Lennie. No stops, you hear?"

"I thought we were going to dinner," Candy said as she stuffed the envelope into her purse.

Lennie grabbed his crotch with one hand. "I got your dinner right here, bitch." The two guys in the room were still laughing when Candy slid into the backseat, followed by her date.

Barry "The Bear" drove the shiksa whore and her guido west on State Road 84 at 3:00 A.M. He heard the shiksa trying to make small talk with Pacco, asking him what Madonna was really like, but he wasn't buying it.

"I ain't got all fuckin night!" He unzipped his fly and pulled out his cock. Barry pressed the button to put up the dark-tinted window that separated the driver from his passengers. Lennie, smiling, said, "Hey, that's all right, dude. You can watch." Barry shrugged.

The shiksa whore shifted in her seat, then kneeled on the floor, her face over Lennie's cock. She tossed her hair off one side of her face so she could work better, and then she began to suck his cock. Lennie grinned at Barry's face reflected in the rearview mirror. He reached over the shiksa's bobbing head for a bottle of Dom. He opened it, the champagne bubbling over, spilling on the shiksa's hair. She pulled her head up.

"Hey, I just had it done," she said. Lennie put his hand on the back of her head and forced her mouth back down on his cock. He sipped his Dom from a fluted glass while she worked. She made a lot of slurping noises, mixed with groans, like she was loving it, jammed down there on the hard floor, scraping her knees, which was probably what made her worth her 25 Cs.

Barry turned the big limo west on Alligator Alley. He drove for a few miles past the muddy canals in darkness and, beyond, the marshy grasslands of the Everglades. He glanced in the rearview mirror. The shiksa was still working while the guido rested his head on the back of the seat, his eyes closed. Barry pushed the button that locked the doors and pulled off the road at a deserted rest stop close to a canal. He waited until the lights of a big semi passed. Then he slipped his .45 out of his waistband, flipped off the safety, turned in his seat, and shot Lennie Pacco in the shoulder, the sound of the gun firing like an explosion in the car.

Lennie's eyes opened wide, like he couldn't believe it. The shiksa's head yanked up and she started screaming. Barry shot Lennie again, the bullet grazing his forehead. The shiksa, clutching her purse, pushed herself away from the guido and began tugging at the door handle that wouldn't open.

Barry shot Lennie again, this time in the thigh, and then again and again, cursing his bad eyesight until finally he got lucky and put his seventh bullet between the guido's eyes. Lennie slumped down in his seat and was still. Blood was splattered everywhere—on the seat, the windows, all over the shiksa's clothes and face. She looked like that broad with the great tits, Tony Curtis's daughter, in one of her slasher movies.

"Jesus Christ! Jesus Christ!" the shiksa was screaming. "What the fuck?"

Barry aimed the .45 carefully now, trying to put one right between her tits. "No, please don't!" she pleaded, pulling up her purse in front of her chest like that would stop a .45 hardball. "Please!" Barry hated it when they begged. He pulled the trigger. Nothing. He pulled it again—nothing—and noticed the slide was locked back and the .45 was empty. The shiksa was yanking at the door handle with both hands now just as Barry lunged half over his seat and wrapped his, big hands around her neck and squeezed. The shiksa's eyes bulged as she gasped for a breath, her legs kicking spastically at the back of Barry's seat. Barry squeezed harder until he could feel the bones in her neck snap and she stopped kicking and went limp, pissing all over herself and the floor.

Barry let go and looked at the puddle on the floor. "Serves you right," he said to the lifeless body. "Teach you to wear underwear."

Barry unlocked the doors, got out, and went around to the back door closest to the canal. He opened it and dragged out the guido's body and dumped it into the canal. A gator up ahead stirred in the muddy water, but waited. Barry dragged out the shiksa, still clutching her purse. Before he dumped her in the canal, he took the envelope out of her purse.

By the time Barry "The Bear" drove back to Paradise Auto Works, the sun was starting to come up. He parked the limo beside his Lincoln, got in his Lincoln and drove to Dunkin' Donuts. Mr. Kressel would have the limo cleaned up before his crew arrived, and an hour later it would be on a flatbed truck going to Vegas.

Barry bought a coffee and a dozen jelly doughnuts and drove to the beach. He parked next to the retaining wall that separated the sand and the ocean from the sidewalk. The white wall had a plastic tube running through it that was fed some kinda liquid that changed colors from pink to blue to green all night long. But it was getting light and the tubing was no longer turning colors. Barry liked watching the colors change, trying to figure how they did it as he sat there, sipping his coffee and eating his jelly doughnuts. Instead, he settled for watching the sun come up all pinkish orange over the pale blue-green water. What he didn't like was the people passing by, the tourist couples and the old power walkers and the joggers who spoiled it. People always spoiled it, the peaceful time after he'd done a job. He stuffed a doughnut into his mouth and took a bite, the jelly running down his chin. He wiped it off with a finger and sucked his finger clean. Some guys couldn't eat after a job. Some guys even threw up. Not Barry. He always felt good, like that Polack broad with the WASP name always said "It's a good thing." That's how Barry saw it. He'd done a good thing because like that actor who played a hit man in a movie said, "If I show up at your door, you must have done something to bring me there."

But it was too bad about the shiksa. Ma mighta liked her, she wasn't a shiksa. She had a great body, and that face, who'd it remind Barry of . . . Liz Taylor?

3

They drove south through the Keys in René's red '69 Eldorado convertible with body rot and ripped white-leather seats. René had put the top down and they had all taken off their shirts to get some color. Bobby was sprawled in the backseat, staring up at the blue sky and hot sun. René drove. James sat beside him, his arms spread over the back of the front seats like fragile wings. They both wore nipple rings.

Bobby took a swig from a fifth of Jim Beam and handed it up to James. He said, "Those things hurt? Your nipple rings."

James took a swig of Beam and handed it to René. "It's supposed to hurt, Bobby," said James. "That's the *point*." Bobby shook his head. René took a swig of Beam and handed the bottle back to Bobby.

"Did you get your bra fitted?" James said.

"Just barely in time," René said. He was shorter and pudgier than James, with olive skin, big black eyes like a Kewpie doll, and sleek, long black hair pulled into a ponytail. "Did you shave your legs?" René said.

"No," said James. "I'm going to wear two pairs of panty hose under my mesh stockings. My legs will look as slick as glass." James was slim and pale with a sunken, hairless chest. He had short blond hair and a young boy's blue eyes.

"I'm beginning to wonder if this was such a good idea," Bobby said, taking a swig of Beam.

James turned in his seat. "Oh, Bobby, for Crissakes, relax. It'll be fun. A drag ball in Key West. It'll be good for you to explore your feminine side."

"You can even wear a dress," said René.

"Trust me," Bobby said. "I'm never gonna wear a dress."

"Never say, 'Never,'" James said, turning back to the front.

Bobby remembered something Sheila had told him once. Once a philosopher, twice a pervert. He was beginning to get the idea what she meant. Still, he said, "Never."

"So, just watch for Crissakes," James said. "You can be our chaperon like at a high-school dance, make sure no one takes advantage of us."

René giggled. "Aaaiieee, I hope so."

James turned in his seat and stared at Bobby. "What else do you have going for you anyway? Nothing, that's what you told us."

"You got a point there."

"Besides, we know everyone in Key West," James said. "We can get you a job at one of the clubs."

"Oh, they'd luff you," said René. "You hafta beat off the little boys with a stick."

"Except I'm into pussy, not cock," Bobby said.

René flapped a limp hand at him. "No difference, Bobby. Cock only pussy on a stick."

"Most straight guys are so boring," said James. "They work so hard at it, all that macho posturing. You don't even work at it. I don't know how you do it. I tried it once when my father came for a visit from Short Hills. That's in New Jersey. It was so exhausting, I had to sleep for a week after he left."

"You need practice," Bobby said.

"I suppose so," James said. He turned back to the two-lane blacktop that shimmered up ahead in the sun, and then, far off, began to rise up into the sky.

"Oh, look!" René said. "The Seven Mile Bridge."

Bobby sat back and sipped his Beam. There was nothing on either side of them now but a little patch of grassy land, the powdery white sand, and then the clear, pale blue-green waters of the Atlantic to their left and the Gulf to their right.

"By the way," Bobby said. "I got no place to stay."

"You can stay with us," James offered.

"Just the three of us? In one room?"

"And a few friends," said René.

"How many?"

"Three or four," James said. He turned again to face Bobby with an evil grin. "Not to worry, Bobby. No one's going to molest you . . . if you don't want them to."

"I'm not worried," Bobby said. "I just don't like to sing in chorus . . . Especially when the chorus is a buncha fags in dresses like those dancers from Monaco."

"Oh, Les Ballets Trockadero de Monte Carlo!" squealed René. "Aren't they wun-derful?"

James said, "I just love Ivana Cumova."

"It'll be such fun," said René. "All of us in the same room."

"Yeah, like a slumber party," Bobby said. He reached down to the floor and took a cigar out of his fag bag, and lighted it.

James sniffed the air and made a face. "Ugh! Disgusting! That thing stinks!"

René glanced over his shoulder and smiled. "I luff it. It reminds me of my grandfather in Santiago de Cuba."

"Well, I don't," said James.

René flapped a limp hand at James. "Oh, Jimmy, behave. Bobby's our guest." Then he grinned at James. "Besides, you've had big brown things in your mouth before."

"Yes, I have," said James. "But they weren't lit."

"This is my chastity belt," Bobby said, grinning. "Like Mace, to scare off your friends, they get fresh."

"Why do you need a cigar?" said James. "When you've got that big gun tucked into the back of your shorts."

Bobby didn't say anything for a moment. Then he said, "You noticed?"

"Puh—leeze!" James said. "We may be faggots, but we're not idiots."

"You don't hafta tell us you don't want to, Bobby," said René.

Bobby thought about it for a long moment, trying to figure it out, but then he decided to just go on instinct, an old Cherokee habit he couldn't break.

"Some people might be looking for me," he said. "The kinda people you don't wanna know."

"That why you're going to the end of the line with us?" said James. "You figure they won't look for a big, macho straight dude like you in a city full of faggot queens."

Bobby smiled. "I couldn'ta put it any better myself, Jimmy."

They started to cross over the Seven Mile Bridge. At the top, Bobby looked out at the water below and, far off, little white boats that seemed to be still. A little later they entered Key West.

They cruised slowly down Duval Street past the old wood-frame Key West houses painted Caribbean blues and greens and pinks, like the house Bobby and Sheila had rented in Lauderdale. René had shifted in his seat so he could throw one arm insouciantly over the seat like James had. The sidewalks were crowded with pairs of men in tank tops, cutoff jeans shorts, and construction boots, and tourist couples who stared, grinning, at the men, and a few tough-looking men with long, stringy hair and sunburned faces who did not grin at the gay men.

"Sooo many boys," said René. "I hope I find a nice boy tonight."

"Some a them don't look so nice," said Bobby.

"That's why we haff you, Bobby," said René.

"And your big black gun," said James.

They passed a pink rocketship float parked on a flatbed truck in front of the La Te Da Club. There was a sign over the door: "Tea Dance and Miss Galaxy Pageant. Cash Prizes." They passed the Medical Aids Rexall Pharmacy and the army-navy store with its display window filled with mercenary T-shirts that had printed on their front: "Kill 'Em All, Let God Sort 'Em Out." They passed a novelty shop that specialized in SM gear, like the little penis whips that were "perfect for away-from-home punishment."

"I never did get the pain thing," Bobby said.

Without looking back, James said, "It's all about guilt, Bobby. Are you a Catholic?"

"No. I was never into guilt. My girlfriend . . . ex-girlfriend . . . she useta say guilt was the most destructive of human emotions."

"What she mean?" René said.

"I'm not sure. She was a lot smarter than me."

"Is that why you broke up?" René asked.

"Maybe."

They passed the Copa, an old movie theater. James let out a little sigh of pleasure. "Oh, look! Gracie's performing tonight." In a window to the right of the ticket booth there was a big photograph of Grace Jones. She looked like a dark, primitive half-human, half-animal, androgynous creature.

"I met Gracie once, ya know," Bobby said.

René gasped. "Oh, my God! You didn't!"

"I was dancing at this club in Miami."

"You were a stripper?" said René. "I knew it. That body of yours."

"Dancer," Bobby said.

"But you took your clothes off," said James.

"No. I came onstage with my clothes already off. I didn't see the need for all that teasing shit."

"For boys or girls, Bobby?" said René.

"Girls. Women, actually. That's how I met—"

"Your girlfriend?" said James. Bobby didn't say anything. James said, "Maybe we can get you a job dancing here. But for boys." He turned and looked at Bobby. "Would that bother you?"

Bobby shrugged. "Why should it?"

"So tell me about Gracie," said René.

"She was really very sweet. Nothing like her macho image onstage. Except the way she eats. She polished off two dozen oysters at dinner one night, and then leaned over toward my girlfriend and whispered, 'They're wonderful for your sex life, honey.'"

"That's soooo Gracie," said James.

"Then we went back to her dressing room and she stripped naked in front of us like it was nothing. She used burnt cork to darken her skin which is really a light coffee color."

"I would haff given the world to be with you," said René. "We luff Gracie."

"What a body!" said James.

"Small tits," Bobby said.

"Oh, Bobby," said James. "What is it with you straight guys and tits?"

Bobby grinned. "If you don't know, I can't tell ya." Then he said, "But they were perky, Grace's tits. She had the body of one of those fourteen-year-old nigger boys always play basketball at Holiday Park."

René began flapping his hand in front of his face as if to cool off a hot flash. "Enuff! Enuff, Bobby! I can't stand it."

"You're a racist, Bobby?" said James. "I never would have guessed."

"Homophobic, too. And anti-Semitic. I don't like professional victims."

"Whass he mean by that?" said René.

"He means he doesn't like people who think they're special," said James.

"You got it," Bobby said.

They turned onto Fleming Street and parked in front of Colours Guest House, a typical coral-pink, wood-frame Key West house.

"Let's check out the pool before we sign in," said James.

They walked around the guest house to a small backyard so thick with palm trees and elephant palms and lady palms and arecas that it looked like a mini rain forest. Two men and two women were sunbathing by the small kidney-shaped pool. They were all naked. The sunbathers glanced at the three men without interest, then closed their eyes to the sun.

A man came out through the back door. He was naked, except for a G-string. His body was painted from head to toe with colorful stars and sunbursts like a Peter Max poster from the '60s.

René squealed, "Michael!" and threw his arms around the man and kissed him on the lips. "You look wun-derful!"

"It's for Gracie," said Michael. "I hope I get to touch her tonight. She probably won't even notice me. Gracie's so into herself." Then, sotto voce, he said of the sunbathing couples, "The two women are lovers and so are the men. But they're all married to each other. Isn't that cute?" He sighed. "Oh, I can't wait for tonight. I'm going to party like there's no tomorrow." Then he noticed Bobby standing behind James and René. "And who is this?" he said lasciviously. He let his eyes roam over Bobby's body, his muscular arms and chest, and his flaring thighs in his shorts. "You brought your own boy-toy—isn't that sweet?"

"Watch yourself " said James. "He got a big gun."

"Oh, I bet," said Michael.

They signed in at the front desk, with a paddle-wheel fan turning slowly overhead, and went up to their room. It was already crowded with James's and René's friends. They all greeted each other with hugs and kisses and squeals of delight.

Then James introduced them to Bobby. "This is Karl, a hairdresser from Long Island. And Donald, a window artist from Lauderdale. And David, a realtor from South Beach. And this is Bobby, girls. You can't kiss him because he's straight. So far, anyway. You'll just have to shake his hand like men."

Karl, Donald and David shook Bobby's hand. James said, "Sooo boring."

René said, "Time to put on our costumes, girls."

Bobby sat down in a wicker peacock chair and watched them get dressed.

They showed each other their costumes, squealing with delight—"To die for!"—and tossed them into the air. Feather boas, lace panties, sequined G-strings, textured nylons, a feathered headdress. The frilly things hung in the air for a brief moment like colorful leaves and then floated to the floor. The room was littered with frilly things and high-heeled pumps and costume jewelry and wigs and curlers and hair dryers and cosmetics and makeup brushes. It looked like the backstage dressing room of a French farce, except for the occasional pair of sneakers and jeans and boxer shorts.

They began dressing in earnest now that it was fast approaching "the bewitching hour," as Karl put it. He wore pink curlers in his hair and a bra. He went into the bathroom, singing "Hello, Dolly," and began to shave.

"Carol Channing," said René with a toss of his head.

James was putting on makeup in front of a mirror near the door. Donald, in Kabuki whiteface, stood over him, adjusting his tiara.

"Fun, fun, fun!" Donald said. "Anything goes tonight."

James put on lipstick and said, "I hope it's windy tonight so my skirt will blow up."

David was dressed in a sort of Darth Vader–Mad Max costume. He stood in the center of the room with his legs spread, like a warrior. René kneeled at his feet like a slave. He ripped holes in David's black panty hose. "It looks very macho this way," Rene said.

David called into the bathroom. "What are you going as, Karl?"

A falsetto voice trilled, "A *maaan!*"

"That's a switch," said James, staring at his face in the mirror.

"How long is that going to take, Karl?" David asked.

"For-*ever.*"

Karl came out of the bathroom with his hands on his hips. "Ta-da!" he trilled. He was a big, soft-looking, hippy man dressed in a gold lamé pantsuit. He smelled of cheap perfume.

"Karl!" James said, glancing over his shoulder. "You look like a Long Island housewife going out on New Year's Eve."

"Precisely," Karl said. Then he cried out, "My God, René! I could never wear *that!* I'd be aroused all night."

René was dressed as a French whore in a lacy pink-and-black corset, garter belt, fishnet stockings, and stiletto heels. His sequined G-string exposed his ass. He gave it a yank.

"My sequined basket is ready," he said.

Finished dressing, James turned to face René. "Well, my dear?" he said.

"You look gorgeous, niño," Rene said. James puckered his lips and blew him a kiss. James was dressed as a French maid in a costume not quite so risqué as Rene's. Lace panties covered his ass. Rene and James struck a pose together. René, hands on hips, looked haughty and lascivious.

James bent over at the waist so the ruffles on his short skirt showed around his lace panties. He pouted, then announced: "The Transformed Illusion."

When they all left the room and walked down the hall, other men in costume peeked their heads out of their rooms and exclaimed, "I *love* it!" James and René glanced over their shoulders and blew them kisses.

"If I meet a nice boy tonight," James said, "Maybe I'll let him take off my garter." He pinched his blouse off his shoulder. "With his teeth."

Bobby walked behind them all in darkness as they flounced down Duval Street toward La Te Da. People shrieked and laughed at them. One woman saw René's naked ass and cried, "Oh, my God!" Tourists pleaded with them to take a picture with them. Only a few tough-looking men did not smile at them.

"Don't worry," Bobby said from behind them. "I'm watching your asses, girls."

When they reached La Te Da, the courtyard in front was packed with men in drag. They milled about, complimenting each other on their costumes. Two men in '50s satin prom gowns had beards and chest hair curling over their low-cut gowns. A camera crew from a Miami TV station was filming everyone. When they saw the bearded men in prom gowns, they bathed them in a bright light and filmed them. A woman reporter stuck a microphone in their faces and asked them questions.

"Well, Bobby," James said. "What do you think?"

"Not one of my usual stops." He looked around at all the men in dresses. "But, whatever. . . ."

James looked around. "Where's René?" Bobby pointed to him, standing in the darkness on the sidewalk, talking to a girl in jeans and biker boots. René was saying something to the girl. She shook her head and walked away.

"What was *that* all about?" James said.

"She was very nasty at first," René said. "She called me a faggot and said I had AIDS. I said, 'Why do you say that? I'm not doing anyone harm. I'm just having fun.'" He fussed with his strand of pearls and put his hands on his hips. "You know what she said then? She said, 'The things you do are disgusting.' I said, 'You do the same things, honey.' She said, 'You know, you're right,' Then she smiled at me and said, 'If you were straight I'd love to bite you on the ass.' I said, 'It's too late, honey. Maybe in another life.'"

The front doors of La Te Da opened and two bouncers, who were trying to look like Marlon Brando in *The Wild One,* began ushering everyone inside. Bobby hung back in the darkness as René, James, Karl, Donald, and David flounced toward the open doors. They had forgotten him now. He waited until everyone was inside, then began walking up Duval Street.

Sloppy Joe's was dark and crowded with tourists and straight couples having drinks at the mahogany bar and at tables against the darkwood walls. There was a bandstand against one wall. Three guys in Hawaiian shirts, O.P. shorts, and flip-flops were playing a medley of Jimmy Buffett's greatest hits.

"Wastin' away in Margaritaville. . . ."

Bobby sat at the bar, ordered a Jim Beam, and lighted a cigar. The bartender brought his drink and put it down on a napkin with a drawing of Ernest Hemingway's face on it. There were black-and-white photographs of Hemingway all over the walls: Hemingway on his boat, the *Pilar*, reeling in a huge swordfish. Hemingway kneeling in the tall grass with a hunting rifle beside a dead lion. Hemingway standing at a lectern in his bedroom, peering over bifocals as he wrote with a nubby pencil. There were Hemingway posters everywhere. Hemingway T-shirts. Hemingway ashtrays. Hemingway coasters. They could all be bought at a counter near the front door.

A few hours later, Bobby paid for his drinks and left. The streets were still crowded with tourists as he walked past Jimmy Buffett's restaurant, Cheeseburger in Paradise, and then, farther down Duval Street, Buffett's T-shirt shop where all his Parrothead fans could buy gifts with his picture on them. When he reached the courtyard of La Te Da, it was deserted. He heard loud, thumping disco music inside. He went through the front door and looked inside. He saw a dance floor crowded with men in dresses, all of them dancing wildly, and up on the stage, three men stripped down to G-strings gyrating to the cheers and shouts of the dancers.

This was as good a place as any to start again, Bobby thought. Tomorrow he'd come back and get a job dancing at La Te Da. Sheila always hated his dancing, all the hysterical women stuffing bills in his G-string. He smiled to himself. He wondered how she'd take it with men stuffing bills in there, trying to cop a feel. "Oh, Bobby!" she'd say. "It's still the same thing. I don't want anyone touching that body of yours. It's mine." That was the thing about Sheila he both loved, and now feared. She took possession, quick, total, and was fierce in protecting her own. It was a good feeling to have someone watching your back, for the first time, but it got out of control. *She* got out of control.

Bobby stepped back outside and sat down on a little bench under pineapple palm and waited, in darkness, for the boys.

Sol sat at an outdoor table at a little bar on Via de Pepe in the early morning. He sipped his cappuccino and read *USA Today* while an old woman washed the sidewalk around him with a brush-broom. Young shopgirls zoomed up the cobblestone street on their little Vespa scooters that sounded like zippers, the girls dressed sharp for work, their hair still wet from a shower, the wind from their speeding Vespas drying it off.

Sol put down his paper and looked at the old apartment building across the street. No. 44 red. Every so often someone would come out the front door. A young art student with a scruffy beard. An older guy in a suit and tie looked like a banker—a teller, not a manager. A sturdy little guy with his sleeves rolled up over his muscular arms on the way to a construction site. By 7:30 A.M., the traffic from the apartment building stopped and the street traffic slowed to one or two Vespas, a small car, every few minutes. Sol went back to his paper.

He missed the States. But he hadta admit Florence wasn't bad—different, not like he'd expected. The guineas were better than the guineas he'd known back in Brooklyn, wiseguys he never trusted because they never trusted him, a Jew in a guinea crew. The thing was, the guineas in Florence were like real people, even Paolo couldn't wait to help find Frenchie, getting the word out on the street, and never expecting anything back from Sol. "For friendship," Paolo said, when he handed him the slip of paper with a street address on it. It surprised Sol. When guineas he knew in the States did things for you, they always expected more in return and you never came out ahead. They had all their fucking rituals, family, loyalty, but it was alla piecea shit they didn't believe in, they just used to get what they wanted. There was nothing real about them, like they were living out their lives from some movie they'd seen showed wiseguys. It was just the opposite what straight people thought. The movies didn't get their wiseguys from real life. It was the other way around the wiseguys studying guys like DeNiro and Pacino and that kid with the bad skin in *Goodfellas* and

Sonny in *A Bronx Tale* so they'd know how to act trying to get it right that thing Sonny done with his fingers but not getting the real thing right because they didn't feel all that stuff Sonny had inside him made him Sonny. The real wiseguys didn't have nothing inside them, like they were made outta straw, like the kid he was reading about right now, here in the papers some wiseguy wannabe outta South Beach took money from some Brooklyn crew and when he gets rousted he can't wait to start pointin' fingers at everybody so he can beat the rap and live out his life in some Federal Witness Protection Program mud hut outside Phoenix, always 110 degrees in the shade. Like the wise guys didn't have long arms, long enough to pay off two U.S. marshals to let the kid take a ride in a limo on his birthday so some guy in a chauffeur's hat could whack him in the backseat with a hooker. Sol remembered the guy, Pacco, the paper was right, a pretty boy more interested in fuckin' South Beach models than doing the right thing he got money for. "The Rise and Demise of a South Beach Playboy"—the paper got that right.

Sol stopped reading. "Oh, shit!" he said out loud. "Jesus Fucking Christ!" He went back over the last paragraph, hoping he didn't read it right.

"Along with Pacco's body that was found, half-eaten by alligators in a muddy canal west of Fort Lauderdale, the police found a second body they identified as Carol Jenkins, a.k.a. Candy Kane, a part-time dancer at a local adult nightclub, and reportedly a high-priced call girl."

Sol put down the paper. He remembered Carol from The Trap when he owned it. A hardworking kid, trying to save her money for a better life than she come from outta trailer camp in South Dade with her boozing old lady and six or seven half-brothers and sisters from so many men, alla them different except they all tried to get a piecea Carol before she was even eleven and still she managed to fight them off before she could finally split at fifteen. Sol respected that, her making the choice who she was gonna fuck and when and for how much. She was a tough broad kept her mouth shut like Sol liked and never complained when he asked her to do things. "You sure you can do this thing, kid?" Sol said to her one night.

"I can do it," she said. "I trust you, Sol."

She didn't deserve that, Sol thought. They coulda just whacked the pretty boy and let her go she woulda kept her mouth shut. It musta been some hard case liked his work, whacking a broad 'cause he'd never have her even with a fistful of G-notes. I meet the cocksucker, he'll wish he was in that mud hut in Phoenix.

Sol looked up and saw Frenchie and a guy leaving the apartment building across the street. Frenchie still looked good, her sandy-colored hair falling over one of her pale blue eyes, her small tits with the big nipples showing through her T-shirt, a short swishy skirt that showed her muscular thighs. The guy with her was muscular, too, in his white T-shirt that showed his big arms. He had curly black hair and a face like Michelangelo, black eyes and broken nose and full lips. He looked like a second-rate club fighter, Sol thought. A problem.

Sol watched them walk up the narrow street toward Scuzzi Square, arm in arm, like two lovers. Sol threw some of that guinea monopoly money on the table and followed them from a distance. He watched them enter Scuzzi Square and go to the bank on the corner. He leaned against a building and watched them through the bank's big window. Frenchie went to the teller, filled out some forms, and the teller handed her a stack of guinea money. *My* fuckin' money, Sol thought.

They came back out and went into a cheese store. A few minutes later they came out, Frenchie carrying a wicker basket with something in it. Then they stopped at the bakery. When they came out, the guy was carrying two long loaves of bread. Then they stopped at the deli, probably for some cold cuts, Sol thought, getting hungry. He wondered if Frenchie would invite him for lunch. On their way back through Scuzzi Square they stopped at the outdoor fruit market, haggled with the dark-haired chick over some apricots and peaches, bought some of each and then a bottle of wine at the liquor store, and began walking back to their apartment building for a long lunch, then an afternoon fuck, and a nap, the way guineas do. Sol smiled to himself. A short nap, but they didn't know it, the guy groggy from pussy and wine and sleep. Sol could handle him then. Maybe. He looked down at his big belly. Maybe not.

Sol walked through the Santa Croce section to Borgo dei Greci, and turned right down the narrow cobblestone street lined with tiny storefronts that sold gold and silver jewelry and leather goods. Groups of tourists, sipping bottled water, with backpacks, moved up and down the narrow street like swarms of bugs, jabbering in foreign languages. Sol came to a big leather store, with a sign in Italian he couldn't read, except for the name of its owner, Paolo Fortunato. He went inside. It smelled of fresh leather, wallets and those guinea fag bags behind glass cases, and, on the walls, racks of leather jackets. A pretty blond chick, maybe twenty, came up to him.

"Can I help you, sir?" she said in English, with a Brit accent.

"How'd ya know?"

"Americans have a certain look," she said, staring at his gold necklaces and Rolex and diamond-encrusted pinkie rings.

"Yeah, I forgot," Sol said. "I'm lookin' for Signore Fortunato."

"This way." She led him down a narrow winding stairway, the walls built of old stone, into a small room in the stone-walled basement where Paolo was sitting at a desk.

"Paolo, someone to see you," the chick said.

"Signore Sol, good to see you again." Then he frowned. "My information, it didn't help you?"

Sol looked at the chick until she got the hint, and went back up stairs. Then he turned to Paolo. "It was very helpful, Paolo, but now I need a little more help. Maybe you can, maybe you can't."

"I am at your service, Sol."

"It might be a little more difficult than I figured, ya know what I mean?" Paolo frowned. "I'm not so sure I can go in . . . naked, so to speak. It might be a problem."

Paolo nodded. "I see." He reached into his desk drawer and took out a Beretta 9mm, ejected the clip to make sure it was filled with bullets, slammed the clip back in again, and handed the piece to Sol. "This is maybe what you need."

Sol hefted the big pistol and smiled. "I probably won't need it, but still. . ."

"A precaution, of course."

Sol stuck the gun into the front of his pants at the belt and pulled his shirt over it. The big grip showed through his shirt.

Paolo shook his head. "That won't do, Signore Sol." He called upstairs on his phone and said something in Italian. In a few minutes, the blond chick came down with a leather, guinea fag bag, the kind all the guinea men carry thrown over their shoulders. "Now, you will look just like a Florentine," Paolo said, and laughed.

Sol pulled out a roll of guinea bills and began peeling them off.

Paolo put his hands up, palms out. "Please, Signore Sol, don't offend me. A gift between friends." Then he looked. very seriously at Sol, his thick brows over his big brown eyes chicks probably thought were seductive. "You could do me, maybe, a little favor."

"Just name it."

"You could tell Signora Sheila I was asking about her."

Sol felt stupid walking back to Frenchie's apartment with the fag bag thrown over his shoulder, the Beretta inside. But he had to admit, the guineas in Italy were all right. Paolo, at least. He smiled to himself. Fuckin' guinea's still got the hots for Sheila. I find her, I'll tell her. Bobby, too, see what he has to say about it.

Sol checked his watch, 3:30 in the afternoon. Frenchie and the muscle guy had probably finished their lunch, fucked, and were taking a nap now. Sol stopped at her apartment door, lighted a cigarette, and leaned up against the mustard-colored wall of the old building, and waited. After a few minutes, he heard the door buzzer, and then the door opened and an old woman carrying a shopping bag came out. Sol slipped in behind her before the door shut. There was a line of mailboxes on the foyer wall. He studied the names on them until he came to one that looked French. Delphine Trevail—5A. Sol pushed open the foyer doors.

Inside, the apartment building was all concrete that made it dark and cool, the yellow paint peeling off the walls, the stone stairs worn from centuries of people climbing up to their apartments with heavy loads of gas canisters and furniture. Sol began to walk up the narrow stairway, floor after floor until he came to an even narrower wooden stairway that led almost straight up to a small door and an apartment that used to be the building's bell tower. Sol waited a minute to catch his breath and then he started climbing the stairs that creaked under his weight. He had to hold onto the railing to keep from falling backward.

When he reached the door, he pressed his ear against it. Nothing. He knocked on the door. He heard someone moving inside. Sol put his hand into his fag bag and gripped, his Beretta. The door opened. The guy stood there, naked, rubbing sleep from his eyes, his big schlong dangling between his hairy legs. Jesus!

"I'm here for Frenchie," Sol said.

The guy stared at Sol, his gold jewelry, his pinkie rings, and then, without a word, he began to shut the door in Sol's face. Sol pushed it open and stepped inside the kitchen. *"Minchia!"* the guy said and shoved Sol with both hands, Sol staggering backward, pulling out the Beretta, the guy's eyes opened wide now, awake now, the big gun aimed at his hairy belly, the guy looking down at his belly as Sol swung the heavy Beretta hard against the side of the guy's head, the guy groaning, crumpling to the linoleum floor, losing consciousness. Sol shut the door behind him, stepped over the guy, and sat down at the kitchen table. He put the gun down on the table and waited.

It was a tiny apartment, just the kitchen and part of a living room Sol could see and, off it, probably, a bedroom. Frenchie called out something in Italian. When she didn't get an answer, Sol heard a door open and then Frenchie stood in the kitchen doorway, naked, her thick sandy-colored bush level with Sol's face. Fuckin' European broads, Sol thought to himself. Look like fuckin' Sasquatch they don't give it a nice trim. Frenchie looked down at the crumpled body of her boyfriend without interest and then at Sol. Without skipping a beat, she smiled and said, "Oh, Sol! Is you! I was so worried about you."

"Like you're worried about your boyfriend there?"

Frenchie didn't even bother to look down at the guy. "Is not my boyfriend, Sol. Is only someone who help me."

"Like me."

"Oh, Sol! Never like you." She came over to him and leaned down to hug him, her big nipples pressing against his chest. "Oh, Sol! I miss you so much."

"I figured," Sol said, "that why you never called from the hotel?"

"I did! I did, Sol! But no answer. I get scared and take plane to London."

"With the cash?"

"Of course. I save it for you all these months before I plan go back to Florida."

"Where is it, baby?"

"Is safe. But money later. How are you, Sol? I so glad you're safe."

"Me, too."

Frenchie stood in her tiny kitchen, still beautiful, her face so scrubbed-looking, fresh, innocent. "I make some espresso and we talk." She went over to the sink, poured water into a pot, put it on the stove, still naked, her back to him, Sol smiling to himself how at ease Frenchie always was with no clothes on. Like some broads had to be dressed fancy to feel in charge. Not Frenchie. Naked, she acted like she had a suit of armor on nothing could penetrate.

"I never got your call, baby. I was in my apartment waiting all night."

"Must be the hotel operator dial wrong number. But that over now. We together again." She put a cup of espresso in front of him and one in front of her as she sat down across from him. She reached across the table and put her hand on Sol's hand, stroking it lightly as if it were a cat she wanted to soothe.

"I thought maybe you was trying to run out on me," Sol said, "take all 300 Gs for yourself."

She frowned, as if her feelings were hurt. "Oh, Sol, never! I your partner, remember. You save my life. I could never hurt you."

"That's what I thought, baby." She smiled at him. "So where did you stash the cash?"

She looked at him with her big blue eyes. "I use my half to buy this apartment," she said. "Florence very expensive, Sol."

"And my half?"

She smiled. "Is safe . . . most of it."

4

Sheila loaded the car in the early-morning darkness in front of her rented house in Lauderdale. Her neighbor, a dyke known as "The Cat Lady," was already prowling through people's yards putting down cat food for every stray in the neighborhood. When she saw Sheila hoisting suitcases into the trunk of her rented Taurus, she walked over to her.

"Taking a trip, Sheila?" she said. She was a skinny blonde in a floppy sweatshirt and men's boxer shorts that hung off her skinny ass. She always reminded Sheila of Sandy Dennis if Sandy Dennis had fallen on hard times.

"A little vacation," Sheila said.

"Where are you going?"

"To the mountains in North Carolina. Hoshi loves the mountains."

"Isn't that where Bobby's from?"

"Yes."

"I haven't seen Bobby in a while."

"Oh, he's off on business. He'll join us soon." Sheila turned her face away from the blonde so she wouldn't see the tears welling up in her eyes.

"Well, tell him I said hello." She trudged off, hunched over by the weight of her backpack filled with cans of cat food.

Sheila went in the house she had painted and decorated so painstakingly for herself and Bobby. The walls were still painted all the colors of a box of Crayolas. But they looked barren without all the Haitian paintings she had hung on them, and all the Haitian carvings and tin figures she'd placed on the fireplace mantel and the dressers and the bookshelves to surprise and delight people when they discovered a little giraffe, a hippopotamus, a 1920s flapper kicking her legs in the air. She'd sold them all back to Krystal, the tin works and the paintings, *The Blue Lady–Erzulie,* and the harvest scene, and the market scene with all the black women carrying baskets of fruit on their heads. She'd sold all the furniture, too, so that she'd have enough money to rent the cabin in the mountains where she and Bobby and Hoshi had once stayed for six months on the run from Medina. Medina. He'd had the last laugh, after all. He'd hurt them all in ways even he couldn't have dreamed.

"Come on, Hosh!" Sheila called. In the darkness where he was lying by the fireplace, Hoshi stood up unsteadily. He walked toward her with the slow, stiff walk of a dog in terrible pain. But he didn't whimper.

"Poor baby. Come here." Hoshi went to her and sat down with difficulty. He looked at her with pleading eyes. "It won't be long now, Hosh." She went to the kitchen cabinet and took out a syringe and a little vial of clear fluid. She filled the syringe with fluid and then shot it into Hoshi's thigh. "There," she said. "That should lessen the pain for a while."

Hoshi followed her out to the car. She had to hoist him up into the passenger seat. He settled into a tight circle while she started the car and they drove off. Bobby had always driven the twelve hours to the cabin. Now Sheila was making the drive for the first time, alone.

Sheila was tense at first, hunched forward in her seat, and then she began to relax as she drove north on the Florida Turnpike toward western North Carolina. Bobby never liked the drive much. "Going back home, it ain't my thing." He'd grown up on the reservation in Cherokee and he had bad memories about being a Cherokee in a white man's world. Which was why he split for South Florida when he was twenty-one and became Bobby Squared, smuggler, with his partner, Solomon Billstein.

But Sheila loved it, the mountains, the cabin, the silence sitting on the front porch looking down a mountain to a valley and, beyond, the mountains that led to Tennessee.

She sat back in her seat and rolled her shoulders to loosen a crick in her neck. She drove with one hand, now, past the flat Florida scrub north of Palm Beach. She slipped in a tape, Mozart, and then ejected it and slipped in one of Bobby's tapes. Little Richard's shrieking filled the car. Hoshi looked up, his ears pricked, and then went back to sleep.

She reached the orange groves south of Orlando at daylight, and two hours later she was driving on I-75 north toward Gainesville. Hoshi whimpered. She looked over at him. "Just a little while, Mommy will stop so you can piss."

She had never realized what a monotonous drive it was because Bobby always drove. She read the *Miami Herald* to him to keep him amused. Crime stories about scams that had gone bad, like the black teenager who had robbed a guy at gunpoint at a bank teller machine at midnight. He wore a University of Miami T-shirt with an ibis on it, and sneakers that had colored lights in their heels. The cops just followed the colored lights until they cornered the guy up against a building.

"Just like a fucking nigger," Bobby said. "No wonder they get caught."

Hoshi was making breathy woofs now. "All right." Sheila pulled off the highway at a Mobil station and stopped at a pump. She filled the tank then went inside to pay. The black girl behind the counter looked familiar. She gave Sheila a big smile.

"Hey, girl, I been missing you."

Sheila smiled at her and handed her cash. "It's always cash," Bobby had taught her. "Credit cards can be traced."

"We haven't made the trip in a while," Sheila said.

The girl looked over her shoulder toward the car. "Say, girl, where's that big ole man a yourn?"

Sheila tried to smile. "He's gone. We had a . . . He left."

"Oh, girl, I'm so sorry. But don't worry, he'll be back. Mens always come back. They need us."

But Bobby didn't need her. He needed to be away from her to be safe. She knew that. That's why she never looked for him. She loved him too much. She wanted to let him save himself from her.

Sheila brightened. "It's all right. I'm over it now." Then she asked the girl for a cup of water.

"For the dog, huh? Well, at least you still got him. They's more loyal than mens, anyway."

"I suppose so."

Sheila went back to the car with the water, leashed Hoshi, and took him around back of the station to a grassy area. Hoshi wobbled unsteadily in the grass and then just stood, spread-legged, and pissed. It was too painful for him to raise his leg anymore. Sheila put the cup of water down for him, but he ignored it.

When they passed the horse farms of Ocala it started to get cooler. Sheila shut off the air conditioner and opened her window. Maybe the autumn leaves would still be on the trees, she thought. Maybe they had turned brown? Maybe they'd already fallen?

She was starting to get hungry, but she fought it. It surprised her. She hadn't thought much about food since Bobby left. She ate whatever was in the fridge. A piece of broiled chicken. A salad. It sustained her. But she'd lost a few pounds. Her body was less hard than when she and Bobby went to the gym every morning. She didn't have the heart or the interest to lift weights anymore. What the hell, she was pushing fifty, an old lady for Crissakes. Look at her hair. Her ash-blond was now tinged with black at the roots, and the sides were gray. She remembered what the little nail tech—hairdresser Lucrezia had told her that first day she had cut and bleached Sheila's hair. "You let yourself go, honey. But I can bring you back."

Now it surprised her that she was actually thinking about food lustfully. A big cheeseburger at Pop's. With spiral onion rings and crisp french fries. She and Bobby always stopped at Pop's in Valdosta on their way to the mountains. It was a college kids' place decorated like a soda fountain out of the fifties, with an aquamarine '57 Chevy on the dance floor, and the waitresses in poodle skirts and saddle shoes. The loudspeakers played only '50s rock-'n'-roll and every so often the waitresses would form a chorus line and dance down the aisles while everyone cheered and clapped. Bobby always flirted with the big waitress with the frizzy hair and huge breasts. The girl would blush and glance at Sheila. Sheila smiled and winked at her. "Give my old man a thrill," she said. But Bobby wasn't an old man, he wasn't her old man anymore. He was not yet forty and looked younger except for his narrow black Cherokee eyes, that could be hard at times.

Sheila pulled up to Pop's in darkness. There were only a few diners inside. She sat at a table by the window so she could keep an eye on Hoshi in the car in the parking lot. The big waitress stood over her.

"Hi, there." She smiled. "I missed you."

"We haven't been up in a while," Sheila said, then placed her order.

The girl didn't leave. She looked around. "What about your husband?"

"He's not with me."

"Oh." The girl looked embarrassed.

"We broke up."

The girl's round, small-featured face got flushed. She stammered, "I'm so sorry. I didn't—"

"That's all right. It's taken a while but I'm over it." Sheila smiled at her, thinking, the more I say it, the sooner it'll be true. But she knew it would never be true.

Her hamburger was delicious. She ate every bit of it, and all the onion rings, and drank two glasses of white wine. She left the girl a nice tip and went out to the car. It was colder now. She hugged herself for warmth and got in. She drove a few yards down the drive to the motel behind Pop's. She checked in with the old man behind the desk, who didn't recognize her.

"The handicapped room around back," Sheila said. They always got the handicapped room because Bobby said it was out of view of the road in case anyone, like Medina, might be looking for them.

After she took Hoshi for a piss, she put down his bowl of food beside the bed. He looked at it without interest and lay down. "You gotta eat, Hosh." She shook his dish under his nose. "For me, baby." Hoshi dropped his head over the bowl and ate a few bits of kibble. "Good boy."

She fell asleep to the light from the television and the sounds of gunshots from an action movie, soothing to her now that she was no longer in that life.

Sheila woke at midnight with a start. She didn't know where she was. She looked around the motel room, saw Hoshi sleeping on the rug, and remembered. The television was still on, an old black-and-white movie, *Casablanca*. She sat up in bed, wide awake now, and watched the movie. Bogart and Bergman. Unfulfilled love. Giving each other up to save each other. It was too fucking depressing. Sheila clicked it off and got out of bed. She went to the door in her T-shirt and panties and opened it. She leaned out and looked through the darkness toward Pop's. The lights were still on. She closed the door and put on jeans and sandals.

She looked down at Hoshi, still sleeping. "You gonna be all right, Hosh?" she said. He raised his head, looked at her, then went back to sleep. Sheila took a C-note from her purse, left her purse on the nightstand beside the bed, and went outside into the darkness. She walked past the other empty rooms toward Pop's bright lights. The parking lot was deserted, unlighted. She remembered what Bobby had told her, "It's better to have a gun and not need it, than to need a gun and not have it." She thought of going back to the room for her purse with the little chromed Seecamp .32 ACP in it, but she didn't. Those days were behind her now. She wasn't that woman anymore. Always a gun in her purse, always cash, always a phony name. Sheila Doyle. Sheila Weinstein. Sheila Royce-Jones. She slipped into the names and their personas as effortlessly as she had once slipped into that black slip when she had played Maggie the Cat, in summer stock one year. It had come in handy, her acting, when she met Bobby. Now, what good was it?

Most of the tables in Pop's dining room were deserted. Busboys were cleaning up the remnants of late meals. The bar at the far corner of the room was still open, a bartender with black-rimmed Buddy Holly eyeglasses and a skinny black tie was still serving drinks. Sheila sat down at the bar. The bartender came over to her. Jesus, he even had that skinny Buddy Holly neck with the protruding Adam's apple.

"What can I do you for, Peggy Sue?" he said, grinning.

She gave him that flat, cold look of hers. "Vodka rocks. And a pack of cigarettes. Marlboros."

He brought her drink and her Marlboros and waited for her to open the pack so he could light her cigarette with the lighter in his hand he kept flipping open and closing.

She looked at him, grinning at her. He was just a kid, he didn't mean anything. So she smiled at him. "I'll let you know," she said.

"Just holler." He went down to the end of the bar to two guys drinking beer from bottles.

Sheila sipped her vodka. She felt stupid. It was a habit left over from her time with Bobby. Always protecting herself because everyone she met was on the make, had a scam, couldn't be trusted. It had been so long since she had let her defenses down, just been herself . . . she smiled. Her self. Jesus. Who the fuck *was* she? She knew who she had been. A schoolteacher. The wife of a lawyer. A. divorcée who worked in a little theater in Fort Lauderdale. And then, Bobby's girl. Bobby's *girls,* really. A hooker. Art critic. Vegas Mob wife. Bobby's wife. Mrs. Roberts. She liked that role the best, except, like all the others, it wasn't real. She wasn't Bobby's wife, or an art critic or a hooker. She was just what he needed her to be at the time. So many different Sheilas, she forgot who she was. Well, she had time to find out now. Without Bobby. All the fucking time in the world. She wondered who she'd become. Someone new she didn't know yet, or maybe she'd just go back to being the scared divorcée she'd been when Bobby picked her up that night at the Crazy Horse, where he was stripping. No, she could never go back to that Sheila. She wasn't that scared anymore. Just tired, carrying the load for Bobby these past two years. And Sol. It was exciting at first, the power she had with men, over men. But now it wasn't so exciting anymore, just draining. She wondered how it would be to surrender her power to someone else. There might be a peace in that surrender, a kind of emotional release that, in a way, would be just as exciting as having the power. She opened her pack of cigarettes and tapped one out. She put it to her lips and was about to call over Buddy Holly when a hand reached in front of her face and a match flickered and lighted her cigarette. She turned on her bar stool and smiled.

"Thank you," she said, and knew immediately she'd made a mistake.

Two men were standing behind her, grinning at her, staring at her big tits in her T-shirt. One of them was big, beefy, like a football lineman gone to fat in his late thirties. He had tousled, sandy-colored hair, small blue eyes, and freckled skin. The other one was small—twitchy, dark-haired, with the simpering smile of a perpetual hanger-on. His good fortune now to be buddies with the ex-football star, who wouldn't have given him the time of day when he was a star. They both wore cheap dress shirts from Kmart, and Kmart ties loosened at the neck after a day's work . . . selling cars? real estate? computers? whatever? It didn't matter. It only made them more pissed off at the end of every day, especially the big jock. And now, here she was.

"Y'all shouldn't be drinkin' alone," said the big one.

"I just stopped in for one," Sheila said, still smiling, trying not to give them an excuse. "I have to be on the road early tomorrow."

"Hey, Buddy!" the big one called out to Buddy Holly. "Another one for the lady here."

"No, really. Thank you, but—" The big guy threw his meaty arm over her shoulder and crushed her to his side. The little one grinned at her.

"You ain't goin' nowheres, honey, so relax, enjoy yourself."

Buddy Holly brought her another vodka. Sheila tried to pull away from the big guy's grip, but couldn't budge. She thought, you wanted to surrender your power, so how do you like it now? She didn't like it. She wondered why. Because *she* didn't make the choice.

Finally, the big guy loosened his grip, and Sheila turned to the bar and sipped her drink.

"What's your name, honey?" the big guy said.

She smiled over her shoulder at him, and slipped right back into it. "Sheila," she said. "My name is Sheila Doyle."

"Well, this here's Ronnie, and I'm Bigger Johnson." He grinned. "My friends just call me 'Big.'"

"I can see why. You *are* a big one."

"Big all over, baby," he said.

She forced herself to keep smiling at him. "I'll bet."

"What room you in?" the big guy said.

"How do you know I'm staying here?"

"Drinkin' this late, a foxy lady alone." He eyed her up and down. "You ain't no Valdosta girl, that's for sure, or I'd know it. You must be passin' through, couldn't sleep, maybe got a twitch, ya know what I mean?" He flashed his best seductive smile that must have melted all those UGA belles when he was a star, but wasn't melting many of them now that his best days were behind him and those belles were hard-case divorcées.

"You've got me," she said. "I just stopped for the night. I've got to be on the road early in the morning."

"So what room ya'll in?" the big guy said.

"Oh, way in back somewhere. I forget the number."

"Just look on your key," the little one said.

She dug the key out of her pocket—room 329—and said, "429." The little guy grabbed her hand and looked at it.

"It says here, 329, sweetheart. Can't you read?"

"I must be tired," Sheila said. She stood up and reached into her jeans for her C-note and dropped it on the bar. The big guy picked it up and dropped a twenty on the bar.

"Your money's no good with us, honey."

"That's awfully kind of you," she said. "Thanks for the drink, but I really have to be going. I need to get to bed."

The two men grinned at each other. The big one said, "Us, too, sweetheart, but we ain't got a room."

Finally, Sheila stopped smiling, wasting her time. "Well, then, go book one at the front office, asshole, and leave me the fuck alone." She brushed past the two startled men and walked out the door into darkness. Through the window, she saw the two of them staring after her. She started to walk quickly through the parking lot, past the deserted motel rooms, every so often glancing over her shoulder, until she got to her room, opened the door, stepped inside, closed the door, and latched it with the chain.

Hoshi was still sleeping. He was so weak now, from the cancer, he could barely lift up his head. All he wanted to do was sleep in preparation for his eternal sleep. I don't blame him, Sheila thought. There was a knock on the door. Jesus Christ! She knew who it was. She went to the door and looked through the little peephole. The big guy was standing there, not grinning now, looking chastened.

Sheila called through the door, "What do you want?"

"Jes' to apologize, little lady. We didn't mean to scare you."

"You didn't."

"And to bring you this," he said. He held up her C-note to the little peephole. "You left it on the bar."

"Oh, Jeez, thank you," she said. She opened the door a crack as far as the chain would allow and waited for him to reach in with her C-note. Instead, she felt the door slam against her, knocking her back, the chain ripping off the door. The big guy and his friend came in and shut the door behind them. Hoshi raised his head and growled weakly.

"That's all right, Hosh," Sheila said. "I'll take care of it."

The big guy held out the C-note in front of Sheila's face. "This oughtta take care of it," he said. Sheila reached for the C-note, but he snatched it away. "Not so fast, honey. We ain't got what we come for yet."

Sheila stared at him with a thin smile. "You guys don't take no for an answer, huh?"

"That's right," the little one said.

"Well, there's no point in saying no then, is there?"

"That's more like it," the big guy said.

Sheila went over to the bed and sat down on the edge of the mattress. She pulled her T-shirt over her head and tossed it on the floor. The two men stared at her massive tits. She smiled at them.

"Jeezus Keerist!" the big guy said. "You got some set on you, honey."

"What about you?" she said. "Both of you. Come here."

They went over to her and stood close to her, her face level with their crotches. She reached out with both hands and unzipped their flies. "Hmmm! Let's see what we've got in here." She reached her hands into their pants and pulled out their cocks. The big guy's was limp, the little guy's was as hard and skinny as a pencil. They both grinned down at her.

"What you waitin' fer?" said the big guy.

"Just a little precaution," she said. Sheila reached toward her purse on the nightstand, searched inside it, and pulled out her chrome .32 ACP Seecamp. She jammed the gun against the big guy's balls. His eyes bugged out.

"Jeezus, lady, don't!" the big guy cried. "We didn't mean nuthin'." The little guy's cock spurted cum down the leg of his pants. "Oh, man . . . please, lady. . ." he cried.

"Back up, both of you," Sheila said. They both backed up, their hands fumbling at their fly. "Not yet," Sheila said, aiming the gun at the big guy's cock. "Wait until you're outside."

"Yes, ma'am," said the big guy.

"Now, get the fuck out of here." The two guys ran toward the door and were gone. Sheila went to the door and looked out. She saw their shadows running through the parking lot. She closed the door and went back to the bed. She sat down on the edge of the bed, smiling. I'll never lose it, she thought, as she unzipped her jeans. and began to pull them off. "Oh, fuck!" she said out loud. "The fucking C-note!" She pulled off her jeans and threw them across the room. She may not have lost it all, she thought, but she'd lost some of it.

She woke the next morning in darkness, took Hoshi outside for a piss, then put him in the car and headed north on 1-75. The road was deserted at 5:00 A.M. except for a few trucks. Bobby liked to hit the road early, beat the traffic, and make up 100 miles before he even woke up. She remembered one time they were driving north on I-75 in 4 A.M. darkness. Bobby came up on an old truck in the right lane and pulled his big black SHO into the left lane to pass at 80 mph. Suddenly a pair of headlights were coming straight at them going south in the wrong lane. Bobby snapped awake, jerked the wheel to the right, almost hitting the truck he was passing, and then as the speeding car shot past them on the left, he yanked the wheel to the left, barely missing it. The wheels chirped and they slid sideways onto the grassy divider.

"Are we gonna make it?" Sheila said calmly.

"I think so," Bobby said even more calm as he fought the steering wheel, trying to keep the SHO from tipping over. They did make it. Bobby eased the car back onto the highway. "Well, baby," he grinned. "I guess our time ain't up."

When she passed through Macon, she hit the backroads of north Georgia, two-lane blacktops through small antebellum towns like Gray and Madison and Eatonton, with their little rotting shotgun shacks where the blacks lived, and the big white columned Civil War mansions where the whites lived. It was cool and sunny in the afternoon when she drove through Homer, past the dilapidated junk-furniture store where she had made Bobby wait in the summer heat one afternoon while she dickered with the old owner over a breakfront that had only three legs. "A hundred dollars!" Sheila said. "It's junk!" But the old man in bib overalls held firm, and they left without it. Bobby was laughing in the car. "What'd you expect, baby? He seen our Florida plates, thinks we're Floridiots will buy anything."

She crossed into North Carolina in the afternoon, and immediately Hoshi sat up, his ears pricked. "Almost home, Hosh." She went a few miles until she came to the Otto Post Office and Joe's Country Kitchen, and she turned right onto Tessentee Road. She passed a mobile home on cinder blocks, drove across a rickety bridge, passed a falling-down shack where an old man sat on the porch, cradling his single-shot rifle. She waved, and the old man waved back. Bobby had told her once, "That's their entertainment in the mountains, waving at cars. It gets old."

And then she was in the valley that never failed to take her breath away, the rolling valley to her right and the steep, forested mountains to her left. She followed the twisting road, slowing at each curve, and then speeding up at the straightaways past cows and horses and tin-roofed barns and stacks of hay and the big Cherokee burial mound and then the white-frame Baptist church and then a few turkeys and their chicks walking across the road as if they owned it out of turkey season. She turned left at their mailbox, and started climbing a gravel road up and up a mountain, the road getting rougher and narrower, branches scraping the side of the car, until she reached the cabin almost at the top of the mountain. It was surrounded by trees on three sides. She pulled into a small open space and stopped. She leashed Hoshi and let him out for a piss. When he was younger, he used to run along the edge of the open space, raising his leg and pissing every few feet to let the wild animals in the woods know he was back in town. But now he just spread his legs and pissed like a bitch.

She brought Hoshi into the cabin and then went back to unload the car. She opened the trunk, looked at all the bags, took out only her travel bag with her change of underwear, and the pistol Bobby had given her a few years ago. "You just point it, pull the trigger, and it'll do the rest," he told her. So she did.

Sheila opened the kitchen cabinet to get a bottle of vodka, but changed her mind, and took out Bobby's Jim Beam instead. She poured some Beam, with a splash of cold water, into his tin cup and took a sip. Then she went into the living room and sat down. The cabin was as they had first rented it, all yellow pine floors and walls and thick, exposed beams that still had bark on them and, what she loved the most, the family photographs of the previous owner, his wife, his kids, and his grandkids, spread throughout the house. They reminded her of a home that she and Bobby would get one day, or so she had thought.

It was getting cold in the house as night fell. Sheila went out to the porch and gathered up some firewood. She threw the logs in the black Franklin stove and lighted them. Soon, the cabin was warm and cozy. Hoshi lay close to the blazing fire to keep warm. She closed the stove doors to protect him from sparks.

She ate a can of soup at the dining-room table looking out over the darkness below. She sipped from her third bourbon, then brought her dishes to the sink. She didn't bother washing them. She went back to the living room, threw a few more logs on the fire, watched the wood ignite, flame up, and shoot sparks onto the rug. She left the stove doors open and straightened up. Her head was spinning from the bourbon. She heard Hoshi woofing by the front door. She got his leash and went to him. He was looking up at her with that pleading look. She bent down and kissed his muzzle. "I love you, Hosh," she said, tears in her eyes. "We both do." Then she opened the door to let him out into the darkness. He waited a minute, as if confused, and then he walked out onto the porch and down the steps into the woods. She stood there with the leash in her hand, then closed the door.

She went upstairs to the bathroom with her travel bag. She opened it and took out her flannel nightgown, a change of underwear, her toothbrush and toothpaste, but decided not to bother. She went to bed fully dressed. She lay there in the darkness listening to the sounds of the woods, the animals thrashing through the brush, the rushing stream, a stray hound dog far off in the distance. She reached over for her travel bag on the dresser and took out her pistol. She laid it on the dresser and rolled over. The pistol was only a reach away. Bobby said it would always be there for her when she needed it.

Part Two

5

Barry the Bear stood in front of La Donna Bellicósa on Las Olas, reached out a meaty hand to open the door, then took it back. People passed behind him on their way to lunch or shopping. He just stood there, sweating, his breathing labored, and then, finally, he opened the door and stepped inside the beauty salon. He was immediately disoriented by all the shrill chatter of broads having their nails painted and their hair bleached and cut. The bright artificial light; the dizzying colors; the smell of chemicals and perfume; the buzzing of clippers, whining of blow dryers, snapping of scissors like shark's teeth tearing at flesh; it all made his head spin, his ears ring, his stomach queasy. From the backroom he heard little yips from broads getting their pussy fur waxed off for their bikinis. Jesus! The things broads do to themselves! Pouring hot wax on their skin, sticking needles in their ears, burning their scalp with chemicals, pulling out their eyebrows, *then* drawing them in again, frying their skin under hot lights in those little beds reminded Barry of coffins, cutting up their faces to get rid of loose skin, injecting that poison shit into their faces to get rid of wrinkles, sticking those silicone bags into their tits, paying some quack to suck out globs of fat from their ass and hips. Jesus Christ! Barry was glad he wasn't a broad. It was a fucking full-time job, no wonder they didn't work.

Squinting behind his tinted eyeglasses, Barry looked around for Angel. So many fucking broads! Finally he saw her cutting some old broad's hair in a chair in the middle of the room. He walked over to her, the room momentarily quiet now, the broads staring with their mouths open at the sight of Barry the Bear in his chauffeur's hat and sleeveless white undershirt that showed the hair on his back and under his arms, the broads trying to calculate exactly how much it would cost *him* for a wax job. Barry stood behind Angel and waited for her to acknowledge him. The broads began chattering again. Angel acted like he wasn't there while she snipped at the old broad's pinkish gray hair that looked like cotton candy. The old broad smelled of flowers. Angel smelled of Paco Rabanne.

"This is the perfect cut for you, Mrs. Weiner," Angel said. "Sooo youthful."

The old broad touched a skeletal hand to her hair that was so thin Barry could look down and see her scalp. "You think so, Angel?"

"Absolutely!" Angel said like she believed it. Jesus! Barry thought. The old broad looked like a bleached prune with a slash of red spilling over her shriveled lips. How did Angel stand it, lying all the time to these broads like they never looked in a mirror.

"Not that you need it." Angel smiled into the mirror in front of them. "You're so youthful anyway."

The old broad smiled, showing her teeth with lipstick on them.

Angel looked in the mirror and stared at Barry without expression. He took off his hat and lowered his head, fingering his hat in his hands. She was a hard-looking broad with coarse skin that looked like her face had been beat up with a bag of nails. She had small black eyes and thin lips she tried to make look bigger with lots of eye makeup and lipstick.

Her hair was bleached a metallic white-gold and cut like a boy's, shaved around her ears and in back, and long on top so a lock of it fell across her forehead. She was dressed in black, like she always was, a black turtleneck sweater, black pants, and men's black shoes with laces.

Finally Angel said, "Why, Mr. Berenson! I didn't notice you. How rude of me." She smiled into the mirror at Barry the way broads do, not meaning it, meaning the opposite. "Maybe you'd be more comfortable waiting in my office."

"Yes, ma'am," Barry said and walked toward the back of the salon. He went through a door and walked past the little cubicles where the yips were coming from. He stopped at a receptionist's desk beside the big metal door that led into Angel's office. The receptionist, chewing gum like a cow, looked up.

"Hiya, Barry," she said. She was a tiny, dark little guinea chick looked like a rat except her face was slathered with makeup and lipstick. She wore feather earrings and a fringed suede vest and matching fringed miniskirt like she was that broad in the *Dancing with Wolves* movie Kevin Costner had the hots for and not just a tough little guinea chick named Lucrezia Santucci, who carried a Smith & Wesson 9mm loaded with CorBons in her saddlebag purse she knew how to use.

"Angel told me to wait in her office," Barry said.

"Natch, Barry." Lucrezia buzzed him in.

Barry sat in the chair facing Angel's desk, and waited. The room was small, with no windows, no doors, except the big metal door that locked behind him. There was a telephone with a dozen lines on the metal desk, and a big computer, and, on the wall behind the desk, a print of that old-timey painting of a naked broad with funny shoulders stepping out of a clam shell. Barry waited, his hat in his hand.

Fifteen minutes later, Lucrezia buzzed Angel into her office. She sat down at her desk and, without looking at Barry, began typing on her computer. She stared at the screen while she typed and said, "That was nice work you did, Barry."

"Thank you, ma'am."

"I'm being facetious, Barry. What I mean is, you made a fucking mess, all that blood, all those bullet holes in the upholstery. Sonny Kresnel was very pissed off, Barry, because now he has to redo the upholstery of his Hummer before he can ship it to Vegas."

Barry said, "The guy wouldn't sit still."

Angel looked at Barry with her eyes opened wide, her eyebrows raised. "Oh, I get it," she said, "you expected him maybe to pose for you, like for a portrait, only you were pointing a Colt .45 at him, not a Canon Rebel. Christ, Barry! You were supposed to put one between his eyes, not spray the backseat." Barry didn't say anything. Angel went back to her computer. "And did you have to ice the chick? She was one of my best earners."

"I didn't want no witnesses."

"I told you she was a stand-up chick, didn't I? She knew how to keep her mouth shut, the money I'm paying her . . . *was* paying her."

"She started screaming."

"Of course she started screaming with all that noise."

"She was rude to me."

Angel exhaled deeply and shook her head. She looked at Barry and said, "If I knew you were so fucking sensitive, Barry, I would have given someone else the contract." Barry was silent. Finally Angel stood up, turned around, and pulled the print of the naked broad away from the wall like it was a door. There was a metal safe in the wall. Angel started turning the dial on the safe, first one way, then another. Her phone buzzed, and Lucrezia's voice said, "Angel, Tamara and Ingela are here."

Still turning the dial, Angel said, "Send them in."

The buzzer sounded and two girls walked in. One was a tall black chick with white features and skin the color of a brown eggshell. The other one was just as tall, but as white as milk, with long, straight blond hair like corn silk. The black chick had one of those Afros out of the '70s. They wore matching outfits, tube tops that exposed their navels, each with a belly ring, and miniskirts and six-inch-high stripper's pumps. The black chick's outfit was white, the blonde's was black. They stood behind Barry and waited until Angel opened the safe. She took out an envelope and handed it to Barry.

"Your compensation, Mr. Berenson," she said. Barry stared at all the cash in the safe, neat stacks of C-notes with little bands around them. Then Barry opened the envelope and started counting the bills one by one. Angel closed her eyes and shook her head again. Then she said to the girls, "How did it go last night?"

The blonde, looking bored behind her half-lidded blue eyes, said, "O.K. Mostly he had me and Tammy perform together." She smiled lasciviously at the black chick.

"I eat any more a Ingie's pussy last night, my jaw be locked," said Tamara.

"Oh, Tammy," the blonde pouted, "I thought you liked it."

Tamara glanced at her, "Don't flatter yourself, baby. I ain't no dyke." The room went silent. Tamara's face jerked toward Angel. "Oh, Miss Angel, I didn't mean . . . you know . . . I . . ."

"It's an acquired taste," said Angel, smiling. "Isn't that right, Ingela?" Ingela smiled at her. "Well, you have something for me?"

Each of the girls reached down into the front of their miniskirts and pulled out a wad of bills. They handed the bills to Angel. She counted out ten bills for each girl.

"Thank you, Angel," said the blonde.

"Thank you, Miss Angel," said the black girl. Angel put the rest of the bills in the safe and closed the door. Barry finished counting the bills in his envelope and stood up.

"Is it all there, Mr. Berenson?" said Angel.

The two girls laughed. Barry's face got red. "Yes, ma'am," he said.

Angel buzzed him out of her office. She called after him, "And the next time, Barry, go directly to my office. I don't want you scaring my clients."

Barry was halfway out of the salon when he remembered where he'd seen those two chicks before. The black one with the Afro looked like that actress broad in those '70s black gangster movies, Coffee, Tea, Hot Chocolate, whatever. The white chick looked like that Kraut model was paid millions to be seen on the arm of that fag magician always dressed in black.

Sheila woke, fully clothed, with a splitting headache on the four-poster bed in the cabin in the mountains of western North Carolina. She lay there for a moment, remembering the drive from Lauderdale, all the Jim Beam she drank, the gun on the dresser beside her that she didn't have the courage to use, Hoshi. She remembered letting him loose last night into the woods. It was her final gift to him. She hoped he went quickly. Tears welled up in her eyes.

She got out of bed and went downstairs. She made some coffee and drank it at the kitchen counter. What would she do now, without Hoshi, without Bobby? What she always did. Go on. Her gift and her curse. She washed her cup at the sink and suddenly realized how cold it was in the cabin. She went into the living room to check the fire in the old Franklin stove. It was nothing but warm embers. She went to the front door to go out to the porch to get some wood. She tried to open the door, but something was blocking it on the other side. She pushed against the door, heard a whimper, got it half open, and saw Hoshi lying up against it on the porch.

"Hosh!" she screamed, and bent down to him. His eyes were open, his breath coming in little gasps. She hugged his half-lifeless body to her chest. "Oh, Hosh! I'm sorry!" His fur was greasy and matted, and it smelled of something dead he'd rolled in. He licked her face.

"You're welcome, Hosh. I knew you'd have fun. One last time." Tears rolled down her cheeks. "Go out on your shield, like Reverend Tom said." But he hadn't gone out on his shield. He'd come back, and now it was up to her. She scooped him up in her arms. He whimpered in pain as she carried him to the car and laid him down on the passenger seat. His head hung limply off the seat.

Sheila drove out of the mountains, down through the valley, past wheatfields and cows and a dilapidated cabin with two baby goats and a pig standing on the sagging front porch. When she reached 441, she turned south toward Georgia. She talked to Hoshi all the way as she sped past cars. "Hang in there, Hosh. It'll be all right soon."

She burst into the vet's waiting room holding Hoshi in her arms. An old man in overalls and his droopy-faced hound dog lying beside him both looked up, startled. The girl behind the counter said, "Can I help you, ma'am?"

Sheila charged past her toward a line of examining-room doors. "Which one is he in?" she said.

"He's with a patient," the girl said, moving toward Sheila. "I'm afraid you'll have to wait—"

Sheila kicked open one door. The room was empty. She kicked open the second door. The vet, examining a tiny white poodle, looked up. An old woman with blue-rinsed white hair clutched her purse to her chest as if Sheila were going to take it.

"My dog," Sheila said. "He's dying."

The vet looked at her as if he was about to say something, something reassuring, but then he saw Hoshi in her arms, his head hanging limp, the look in his eyes changed. He was a tall, hunched-over man in his early fifties, with a pencil-thin mustache and slicked-back, wavy hair.

Sheila heard the receptionist's voice behind her, "I'm sorry, Dr. Keith. I couldn't stop her."

"That's all right, Becky," he said. Then, to the old woman, he said, "If y'all excuse me, Mrs. Woodrow, I'm afraid this is an emergency."

The woman picked up her little poodle off the examining table and left. Sheila kicked the door closed behind her.

"He's got bone-marrow cancer," Sheila said. "My vet in Florida said he had only a few weeks. That was two weeks ago."

"Jes' put him on the table and I'll check him out."

"No. I'll hold him." She looked around, saw a little plastic chair, and sat down with Hoshi in her arms. The vet bent over to examine him. He pulled back Hoshi's lips to check his gums. They were white. Sheila could see the look in the vet's eyes—first shock, then recognition, and then, as his eyes turned to her, pity.

"I'm sorry, ma'am. I'm afraid your vet was right. I could do some blood work on him to be sure, but—"

"He's had enough blood work. He's suffering, Doctor. I don't want him to suffer anymore."

The vet looked at her, this slim, tanned, blond woman from Florida in her tight jeans, with her dying dog and not a tear in her eyes, just that cold look that didn't want sympathy.

"Do it," she said.

The vet nodded and left the room. When he returned he had a syringe in his hand. He tapped it with his fingertips, squirted a bit of liquid out of the needle, then bent over the dog.

"What's his name?" he said.

"Hoshi. It's Japanese for 'Little Star.'"

He stroked Hoshi's cheek with the back of his hand. "This won't hurt, Hoshi. I promise you, boy." Hoshi's eyes fluttered open. He looked into the vet's eyes for a brief moment, and then, satisfied, he closed his eyes. The vet inserted the needle into a vein in Hoshi's front leg, plunged in the clear fluid, then withdrew the needle and stood up.

Sheila pressed her face against Hoshi's cheek. She breathed in his musty, leathery smell. Her arms were wrapped around his body, holding him tight. She could feel the beating of his heart in her hands. She whispered in his ear, "Shhhh, Hosh, go to sleep. I love you. Bobby loves you." She felt the beating of his heart grow slower, fainter. "We both love you, Hosh." And then it stopped. Hoshi's head fell limply over her arms. His lips were slightly parted as if in a snarl that didn't look like any expression Hoshi had had in life. His eyes were slightly open. Sheila tried to close his eyelids over his eyes, but they wouldn't close.

"His eyes are still open," she said.

"He's gone, ma'am."

"Are you sure?"

"I'm sure."

The woman burst into hysterical sobs that wracked her body, like a convulsion. Then, just as suddenly as the sobs had come, they were gone and she was still, gasping for breath. She stared up at the vet with her cold blue eyes open wide. "But where?" she said. "Where has he gone?"

"He's at peace, ma'am."

"But where? I have to know. Don't you understand. I have to know where he is now. If he's safe."

The vet reached down and tried to take the dog's lifeless body from her, but she held the dog tight to her chest. The vet tried to ease the dog out of her grasp as he said, "Not to worry, ma'am. God doesn't make things for us to love and not reward them for it." He felt her hold on the dog loosen. He took the dog from her and held it for a moment.

"Are you sure?" she said.

He nodded. "God only gives 'em to us for a little while. They're His, ma'am, not ourn. They break our heart, but that's proof that God exists." And then he was gone, with Hoshi, and Sheila was alone. She sat there for what seemed like hours, and then he came back holding a mason jar filled with a white liquid. He pulled up another plastic chair close to her and sat down. He unscrewed the top of the jar and handed it to her. "Jes' a small sip," he said. "It's 150 proof. A hobby of mine." He smiled as if embarrassed.

She took a sip. It burned her throat for a moment, and then it diffused her body with a warmth that tasted like strawberries. She took another sip.

"Whoa, there!" He smiled, and took the jar from her, then screwed the top back on.

"Aren't you having any?" she said.

"I have to work today. I don't like it much anyway. I jes' keep it for my patients." He smiled. "I mean, the owners of my patients. For times like this."

Sheila nodded. "Thank you, Doctor."

"Do you have someone who can be with you today?" She shook her head. "Are you married?"

"I live alone. In a cabin in the mountains."

He smiled at her. "You don't look like no mountain girl."

"No, I guess not. I'm a Florida girl."

"I already figured that out."

"It shows?"

He smiled and shrugged. Then he said, "The mountains can be lonely if you don't have no one."

"I *want* to be alone." She laughed. "Jesus, I sound like Greta Garbo."

"Maybe now. For a while you might. But you can't hide forever.

Whatever you're runnin' from, ma'am, sooner or later it'll find ya, even here."

"You're here."

"I was born 'n' raised here. I never left 'cept to go to Vietnam. I was a medic. After that"—He shook his head once—"well, I lost any desire I had to see the world. I seen more'n I cared ta."

"Do you have someone?"

He laughed. "Now, who would have me, ma'am, a hangdog country vet loves animals more'n people. That's not someone ladies are lookin' fer."

"Some women might."

"Well, they ain't livin here."

"You haven't given up hope, though."

"How can you tell?"

"That Clark Gable mustache and that slicked-back hair."

He lowered his eyes and grinned in a way that made Sheila think of him as a boy. "Maybe I haven't, ma'am. It's jes' . . . some people expect less outta life." He looked at her. "You ain't one a them." He stood up. "Take my advice, ma'am. After you're through your grievin', go back to Florida. The mountains get old after a while."

She looked up at him. "That's what Bobby said."

A week later, Sheila picked up Hoshi's ashes in a reddish-tan ceramic urn the same color as his fur. His name, Hoshi-o, was printed in black on the front. She put the urn on the cupboard in the kitchen. She had thought of burying it in the backyard. but the thought of Hoshi being in the ground was too much for her. She wanted him near her. In the morning, when she sat out on the front porch in the damp, foggy, cold mountain air to drink her coffee, she brought Hoshi with her. Late at night, after dinner, when she put on her down vest and took her glass of Jim Beam to the porch and sat in a rocking chair looking down over the valley and beyond to the mountains of Tennessee, she brought Hoshi with her, too. She took him with her everywhere she went in the house, from room to room. She put him on the dresser beside the four-poster bed on the second floor when she went to sleep. After a while, she stopped sleeping in the bed. It was too much of a hassle to make it every morning. She began sleeping on the couch in the living room so that the television would put her to sleep, with Hoshi beside her on the end table. After a while, she didn't bother to change into her nightgown before she went to sleep. She just lay down in the sweatpants and sweatshirt she had worn all day, and slept in them, and when she woke, she didn't bother to change her clothes.

She began to smell. Her hair grew out, like unruly Brillo, the blond only tipping her brown hair flecked with gray. She ate what was in the cabinets and the refrigerator; a bowl of canned soup, some eggs, a can of tuna fish out of the can. She could feel herself losing weight, her skin growing slack like it had once been before she met Bobby and he had dragged her to a gym to pump iron. Those days seemed to be from another lifetime, when she was another person.

One cold, clear night, she took her supper out on the porch with her glass of Jim Beam and Hoshi's urn. She had found some canned ham and crackers, and she ate the ham out of the tin, cold. She looked out over the valley in darkness and saw little lights, plumes of smoke, and, in the sky, diamond chips tossed over black velvet. She heard the animals in the woods, the heavy grunting of a black bear, the screeching, like a woman's scream, of a bobcat, the howl of a pack of coyotes, and then the mad, hungry yipping of coyote pups. It didn't even frighten her now that Hoshi was gone. He was beyond the reach of those coyotes now. He was beyond the reach of everything, now, just as she was.

She heard the sound of animals' feet scampering up onto the porch. She turned and saw three ratty-looking puppies running toward her.

They looked like golden retriever puppies, except they were emaciated, their fur filthy and stuck to their protruding ribs. The puppies stopped beside her chair, their tails wagging, their stomachs growling, their tongues hanging out. She cut off three pieces of her ham with her fork and tossed one to each puppy. They wolfed their morsels down without even chewing them. Then two of them ran off. The third one didn't move. He just sat there, looking at her with his big, eager chocolate eyes.

"What's the matter, pup? No place to go?" Her voice seemed to soothe the puppy and he lay down beside her rocking chair. She took a sip from her drink and forgot about him. She must have dozed off because when she woke it was starting to get light the way it did in the mornings in mountains, a hazy grayish light, without the sun. She hugged herself against the cold dampness and stood up. Time for coffee, she thought. When she turned to go inside, she saw the puppy still lying beside her chair, his eyes open now, his tail sweeping back and forth against the floor. She picked up Hoshi's urn and went inside. The puppy followed her.

Bobby woke at noon in his rented room in Colours Guest House in Key West. Sunlight slanted through the gauzy, window curtains, across the pale-yellow hardwood floors, over the bamboo chair shaped like a huge fan, and over the bamboo dresser up against the pale peach colored wall. A fag's room, Bobby thought. He lay there a moment, staring up at the slowly churning paddle-wheel fan over his bed. A delicate wrought-iron bed. His calves were sore from dancing last night at La Te Da. He was out of shape. It had been awhile since he had danced all night long, almost a year. Sheila had made him stop dancing in nothing but his leopard G-string in front of hundreds of women screaming out his name, "Bobby Bobby! Over here," their hands reaching out for him, touching his muscular arms, his thighs, trying to cop a feel at what was inside his G-string. Sheila hated him dancing at The Crazy Horse in Miami. He smiled to himself in bed. I wonder if she'd mind me dancing in front of fags at La Te Da, the fags screaming out my name now, the fags trying to cop a feel now. Probably. What'd she say? "That's my body now, Bobby. Nobody touches it but me." And made him quit dancing.

Bobby got out of bed, slipped on his leopard G-string bathing suit, grabbed a towel off the dresser that was littered with dozens of crumpled bills, and went downstairs. Michael was standing behind the receptionist's counter, reading the *Miami Herald.* Without looking up, he said, "Morning, Robert."

"Yeah." Bobby took a copy of the *Herald* off a stack on the counter and then poured himself some coffee from the pot on the bamboo coffee table against the wall. He took a sip. He made a face. "Jesus, Michael, when you gonna get some Bustelo? This tastes like piss."

Still without looking up, Michael said, "When we can afford it, Bobby. When the tourists come back. You're our only guest, or haven't you noticed?" Michael looked up, grinning, showing his rotting teeth. He had a gaunt, sallow face like he was rotting from the inside out, and greasy long hair that curled behind his ears and at the nape of his neck. He wore a tie-dyed, sleeveless undershirt over his emaciated chest and tiny cutoff jeans shorts.

"Actually, Robert, that's not entirely true. We had a new guest check in last night. Oh, he's *gorgeous,* Robert! You're gonna love him. He's just your type. Muscular, but slim, and dark like you, too. But without the blond ponytail." Michael made a face. "When are you going to get hip, Robert, and stop bleaching that ponytail yellow? You look like a fucking Fort Lauderdale smuggler."

Bobby smiled at him. "Yeah, well, it's worked for me so far."

Michael made a disgusted sound with his mouth and went back to his paper. "I'll bet. All those Fort Lauderdale strippers with the hot pants and cold brains, they must have loved you."

"A few of them did."

"I'll bet. Well, there's one less to choose from now. Some chick named Candy Kane." Michael looked up, grinning. "Isn't that a clever name?" He went back to the paper. "She got iced in the Everglades with that South Beach club owner, you know the one, the gorgeous Eye-talian with the bedroom eyes. They musta pissed somebody off." He shook his head. "Fucking Fort Lauderdale. It's still the Wild West." He looked up and smiled at Bobby. "No wonder you moved down here, Robert."

Bobby ignored him and went down the corridor to the back door and outside to the swimming pool. It was a tiny kidney-shaped pool with so much overgrown foliage around it, areca palms, lady palms, bougainvillea, elephant ears, hibiscus, that it looked like a pool in the jungle. Bobby found a lounge chair in a patch of sunlight and lay down. He began reading the *Herald*. Candy Kane's murder was front-page news, not because of her, but because of the john who was offed with her. Fucking guinea got what he deserved, Bobby thought as he read, ratting out his backers just to avoid doing time. No fucking concept of loyalty, like him and Sol had—once had—wherever the fuck Sol was now. The only person Bobby ever trusted, and Sheila, too, he couldn't deny that, wherever the fuck she was now, too. But this chick, Candy, she probably didn't deserve what she got, probably never even saw it going down out there in the backseat of a Hummer limo, sucking some john's dick alongside the swamp, already counting her money, enjoying how she was gonna spend it when . . .

"Candy Kane?" Bobby said out loud. Where had he heard that name before? Then he remembered. She was the fat-assed, red-haired chick, what was her real name, yeah, Carol Jenkins, danced at the Booby Trap, helped him and Sol take down those two coons in the parking lot, Sol capped them both. Jesus! Poor fucking broad.

Bobby heard a voice with an English accent. "And you must be Robert." Bobby put down his paper and stared at a long black cock dangling in front of his face. He looked up to its owner standing naked over him. A slim coon with a mouthful of gold teeth, eyeliner and false eyelashes, and a small, tight Afro bleached orange. "Michael told me you were gorgeous," the coon said, grinning.

"He tell you I don't like people pointin' their thing at me it might go off get me mad?"

"Oh, I thought this was a clothing-optional pool? Michael said—"

"I don't give a fuck what Michael said."

"Don't be so testy. I'm just being friendly." He reached out a slim hand, black on top and pink underneath. "My name is Samson. It's really not. It's just my stage name. I'm a makeup artist and hair designer." He smiled, flashing his gold teeth. "Presently unemployed."

Bobby looked at the coon's hand waiting for him to shake it, maybe kiss his fingertips, they could lay in the sun together, rub oil on each other's back, have a nice chat, maybe Michael'd bring them a coupla mimosas, then go up to the coon's room for a tussle on the sheets see who gets to bite the pillow, put an end, finally, to Bobby's unbearable loneliness.

Bobby said, "Fuck off, Sambo," and went back to his paper.

Bobby dozed off in the sun. When he woke, late in the afternoon, the coon was gone. Bobby went downstairs to the cellar where Michael kept a few rusted weights, an incline bench, a Smith machine. It was hot and damp in the cellar as Bobby began to do squats with the Smith machine. He began to sweat as he worked, adding more and more plates to the bar after each set. When his legs got wobbly and he couldn't squat anymore, he did incline presses for his chest. He felt his chest begin to swell with each succeeding set. He was soaked with sweat now, breathing heavily, as he began to do biceps curls with dumbbells, and then a few French presses for his triceps. He finished off with a few hundred incline sit-ups for his abs, and then went to his room, took a shower and dressed for work; shorts, flip-flops, a Colours Guest House muscle T-shirt with the gay-pride flag on the back.

He walked up Duval Street at twilight, only a few tourists now, past Sloppy Joe's, Jimmy Buffett's joint, Cheeseburger in Paradise, past La Te Da until he came to the little Cuban coffee stand. He ordered a *café con leche* and a Cuban sandwich from the cute teenaged Cubana with the big black eyes.

"Always the same thing, Roberto," she said, as she wrapped his sandwich in wax paper. "Why you no try sometheeng e1se—plantains, some *frijoles negros,* and *pollo?*"

"I ain't that hungry."

She looked at him, his muscles, his blond ponytail. "Aaaiiee, Roberto, you need food to make that body, no?" She fluttered her dark eyelashes at him, trying to be sexy, but still just a kid.

"You flirtin' with me, Carmelita?"

She blushed. "Maybe."

He turned around so she could see the gay-pride flag on his back. "You're wastin' your time, baby."

She flapped a limp hand at him. "I not that young, Roberto. I know a *maricón* when I see one, and you no *maricón*—just faking it."

Bobby laughed. "You're a smart little chick, ain't you?"

"Smart enough."

"Well, don't get any bright ideas, Carmelita, I might take you up on them, call your bluff."

"Promises, promises, Roberto. How long I wait?"

"Until you grow up."

Bobby walked to the end of Duval Street, to the sign that read: "The Southernmost Point in the United States." The end of the line, that's what the sign should read, Bobby thought. Where the garbage washed up from Miami, Lauderdale, Daytona, points north. He found a bench facing the ocean and sat down to eat his sandwich and drink his coffee. He ate slowly, staring out at the water as far as his eyes could see. Then he went to work.

Bobby got back to his apartment at 2:00 A.M. He was exhausted. He peeled off his clothes and fell, naked, onto his bed. He was asleep in seconds, dreaming. . . . Sheila and Hoshi and him were back together again, with Sol, all of them at The Mark on the beach on a sunny day, drinking and eating and laughing, Hoshi sitting beside them, waiting for his dish of water, Sheila in her G-string bikini, smoking a cigarette in that limp-wristed, ladylike way that always amazed Bobby, Sol grumbling, muttering, complaining about something or he wouldn't be Sol, someone groaning, crying out in pain or pleasure, the groaning so loud it woke Bobby from his dream.

"Jesus Christ!" he said, and sat up. It was 3:00 A.M. The groaning was coming from the wall behind his bed. Bobby pressed his ear against the wall and listened. He heard the coon cry out, "Oh, man, it's so fucking big! It hurts! Owie! Don't stop. Fuck me! Come on, harder! Harder!" And then the sound of someone grunting and the slap of flesh against flesh, the coon's bed banging against the wall, the coon crying out again, "Come on, harder!" His voice had an edge on it now, "Whassa matter, cowboy, that all you got?" the grunting getting louder and the slapping faster and then the coon's voice again, "Is that all you got, man, you ain't got shit." Bobby wondered what happened to his English accent. And then the noises stopped, except for the heavy breathing, and Bobby heard a slap and the coon cry out, "Man, Jesus, don't . . ." and another slap, and another, and then the sound of the coon's voice, but not a voice, just a gurgling sound like the coon was drowning.

Bobby got out of bed and went out into the hall. He walked down to the coon's door and listened. He heard the sound of someone grunting hard, and then a different voice "That hard enough for you, nigger cocksucker?" Then the gurgling again, only fainter. Bobby tried the door. Locked. He lowered his shoulder and slammed it against the door, the door swinging open, revealing the coon on his back on a bed, a white guy sitting on his chest, the white guy's hands wrapped around the coon's throat, strangling him. The white guy looked over his shoulder at Bobby, glaring at him through bloodshot blue eyes, his face burned from the sun, his dirty blond hair hanging to his shoulders. He wore only a leather vest and biker's boots—nothing else.

"This is none a your business, asshole" the guy said. "Fuck off." He turned back to the coon as Bobby walked across the room, reached out a hand, grabbed a fistful of the guy's hair, yanked it back hard, the guy falling on his back on the floor, screaming, "Man, Jesus!" until Bobby slammed his head hard on the floor, once, twice, three times, and the guy was quiet. The coon was coughing, holding his throat, gasping for a breath.

Bobby dragged the biker by his hair out into the hall, down the stairs, the biker's unconscious body bumping down each stair until they got to the lobby where Michael, rubbing his eyes, was standing behind the receptionist's counter, "Bobby, for Crissakes! What was all—Jesus, what the fuck—Who's that?"

Bobby dragged the biker across the lobby floor to the front door. "Go back to bed, Michael," Bobby said. "It's taken care of."

"Jesus, Bobby! What the—"

Bobby opened the front door, dragged the biker out into the street and dropped him. Then he went back inside. Michael was still standing behind the counter. Bobby said, "I told ya, go back to bed."

Bobby went back to the coon's room. The coon was sitting up in bed breathing normally now, feeling the burn marks around his neck.

"You all right, Sambo?"

"Samson," he said. He rotated his neck. "Yeah, I think so."

Bobby grinned at him. "That's why they call it 'rough trade,' ya know."

The coon, grimacing, said, "*Now* ya tell me." He looked at Bobby, his grimace fading, replaced by a smile. They both laughed. The coon shook his head. "Fuckin' dude got him no sense a humor. I just be play actin' with him."

"Fag drama, huh?"

"Yeah, that be it. I just be tryin' to inspire him, ya know, like a director, to get a better performance."

"You done good. You inspired the shit outta him."

"Man, that oughtta teach me a lesson, no more fuckin' straight dudes they all alike find out they like cock they be fuckin' mean like it be your fault makin' 'em do the nasty."

"I coulda told ya that, too."

The coon glared at him. "You so fuckin' smart, cowboy, maybe you wanna be my guru or sumthin'?"

"Maybe, you answer me one question."

"Whassat?"

"What happened to your English accent?"

The coon laughed again. "That, man, that jes' be part of the drama be a fag. You know everything you must know that."

Bobby nodded. Then the coon said, "Man! What'd my momma teach me? I'm sorry, where are my manners. Thank you, man. You saved my dumb black ass."

"Yeah, well, I always been partial to coons."

"I know. I could tell by the pool you be a sensitive, brother-lovin' type." Then, serious now: "How can I repay ya, man? I gotta do sumthin' for ya."

The coon looked down at Bobby's cock, then flashed him a lascivious gold-toothed smile. "I give awful good head, cowboy, give you a blow job put you right to sleep."

"Jesus! You coons really that fuckin' stupid? Ain't you had enough for one night?"

The coon shrugged. "Jes' tryin' to be grateful." Then he stared at Bobby's head, tilting his own head first to one side, then the other. "Man, who does your hair? That be the worst fuckin' dye job I ever seen."

"I do it myself. I can't see myself sittin' in no beauty parlor under a hair dryer surrounded by chicks, can you?"

"Naw, that ain't your style. Come on, let me straighten you out." Bobby raised his eyebrows. The coon said, "Aw, fer Crissakes, dude, relax, you white dudes so fuckin' uptight. I ain't gonna cop your joint, I'm jes' gonna do your hair." He grabbed Bobby's hand and led him into the bathroom.

"Sit down on the toilet," the coon said. Bobby sat down, his face level with the coon's long cock. The coon slipped Bobby's ponytail out of its elastic band and fluffed out Bobby's hair until it fell around his face to his shoulders.

"Man, you a Conan-lookin' dude with your hair down." He ran his fingers through Bobby's hair. "Split ends, bro, it be dry as shit." He opened the medicine cabinet and took out a bottle of bleach, some metal foil, a blow dryer, and a bottle of shampoo. "Lean your head over the sink, bro." Bobby did as he was told. The coon turned on the faucet and washed Bobby's hair, his fingers massaging Bobby's scalp, relaxing him. Then he toweled off Bobby's hair. "Now, sit up straight."

He began dabbing the bleach into Bobby's hair with a little paintbrush. "What's your name, anyway, bro?"

Bobby said, "Bobby. Robert Roberts, actually." He grinned up at the coon, his brows furrowed as he worked. "But my buddies call me Bobby Squared."

The coon didn't get it, or maybe he was just concentrating too hard on Bobby's hair. "My name's Reginald," he said. "Reginald Johnson, by way of Fort Lauderdale, Florida—Sistrunk Boulevard, to be exact."

"Me, too."

"Sistrunk? You lived in Black Town?"

"Fort Lauderdale. I look like I lived in Black Town?"

The coon stepped back to look at his work. Then he went back to brushing the bleach into Bobby's hair. He said, "What you look like, Bobby Squared, is a dude done things I don't wanna know."

"You done a few things, too, I'll bet."

The coon shrugged. "What I had ta." Then he stuck out his hand a second time. "Good ta meet ya, Bobby Squared."

Bobby looked at his hand, then shook it. "You, too, Reggie."

"How'd you like Italy?"

"Too many guineas."

"I heard." Gary McCraw, President of Deceptions Inc., Private Investigators, sipped his drink at the bar in Mango's on Las Olas. He glanced across the bar at two older broads flashing their fake tits at two older guys with painted-on tans and a lot of gold nestled in their chest hair. He tossed a head fake at the two guys. "Sol, you think they have hair transplants or what?"

Sol glanced across the bar. "The broads?"

"No. The two guys."

"They're fuckin' bald."

"Their chest hair. I don't know. It might be something to look into, a new market, chest hair." He was quiet for a moment, thinking. Then he said, "But where do you transplant it *from,* you know what I mean, the guys being bald and all?"

Sol turned sideways on his stool and looked down at McCraw. McCraw smiled up at him. He was a tiny, plump little guy, almost a midget, with a halo of golden curls, blue eyes looked like a light in them, and those Betty Boop lips. He always reminded Sol of one of them evil fucking elves in a Grimm fairy tale.

"Maybe you should go ask them," Sol said "In front of the broads—where they get their chest-hair implants, the guys really like that, maybe use you for midget bowling like I heard they do in the Midwest."

"I heard of that, too. I always wondered, do the midgets curl up in a ball and roll at the pins, or do they just slide down at them on their backs?"

"Maybe their stomachs, headfirst like Pete Rose useta done into second base."

"Do they wear helmets?"

"Pete Rose?"

"No, the midgets."

"Jesus Christ, McCraw!"

"They don't wear helmets, you wonder how many hits they can take into them pins. I'll bet you can't bowl a full game with just one midget."

Sol shook his head. "Don't you ever stop thinkin'?"

McCraw looked at him, not grinning now. "That's what you pay me for, isn't it, Sol, to do the things you don't like to do. Did you find the French broad?"

"Yeah."

"She have the cash?"

"She had it, only half, 140 Gs, Kept it in a fucking guinea bank you can believe it, so it'd collect interest, like it never dawned on her the guineas got a reputation for losing shady money from foreigners won't go to the heat to complain."

"That's a broad for you."

Sol slipped an envelope out of the inside pocket of his sport jacket and handed it to McCraw. "There's extra in there you got that other stuff for me."

"Let me see." McCraw took out a notebook he kept in the breast pocket of his plaid shirt along with a line of pens, and his reading glasses. He put on his reading glasses, low on his little upturned nose and flipped open the notebook.

"Bobby's dancing at a fag joint in Key West. La Te Da. He's trying to hide, but not serious about it." McCraw flipped over a page. "That other thing, I got most of it but not all the details. Candy was iced by Barry the Bear, that Hebe hitter works out of La Donna Bellicósa."

"Where?"

"That beauty parlor just down the street run by that dyke broad with the face looked like it been run over by a truck with snow chains. Her name's Angel. She runs a stable of high-priced hookers out of her back room, too. They look like celebrities, Madonna, Julia Roberts, broads like that. She calls it Celebrity Dream Dates Escort Service, you must have seen her ads in those fancy Palm Beach magazines about socialites and guys who play polo for a living." McCraw stopped reading his notes and looked at Sol. "She keeps a lot of cash in that back room, I heard. Unlike your French broad, Angel doesn't trust banks, it seems." He flipped over another page.

"But why Candy? She was a civilian."

"She got in the way, I hear. Maybe, too, Barry the Bear likes his work."

"That fuckin' Jew cocksucker!"

"You heard that, too?"

"Heard what?"

"Barry lives with his mommy, a real pain in the ass I hear." Sol looked at him, confused. "He's forty-eight-fucking-years-old, Sol. He works for a dyke he's afraid of and lives with his mommy who wipes his dick when he takes a piss."

"So?"

"Barry doesn't like broads too much, Sol. Maybe that's why he iced Candy while she was sucking a dick. Transference, they call it in those psych books."

"What the fuck you tryin' to say, McCraw, always beatin' around in circles?"

"Barry's a fag, Sol. He likes boys, mostly black ones, I hear."

"*Jesus* Fucking Christ!" Sol drained his drink in one gulp. He called out, "Bartender! Another scotch," and banged his glass on the bar so loudly the two old broads and old guys across the bar glared at him. "What the fuck you lookin' at?" he called across the bar. The two guys made believe they didn't hear him and went back to the broads. Sol said, "A fag! Jesus! That's fuckin' disgustin'."

"He's a hitter, Sol. *That's* disgusting."

"It's just a fuckin' job. Some people need to be hit, somebody's got to do it. But that other thing, suckin' a guy's cock, that's for broads not men."

McCraw shrugged. "Unless you tried it. . . ." Sol glared at him. "Just kidding, Sol." He flipped open another page in his notebook. "That last thing was a little harder, a lot harder, actually." He looked at Sol and smiled. "That Sheila broad, I've got to hand it to her, she don't want to be found you aren't gonna find her."

"I *gotta* find her."

McCraw grinned at him. "I said she was good, Sol, but I'm better." He ripped out a page from his notebook and handed it to Sol. Sol studied it. "It's a private prep school in Connecticut. Very fancy, the Kennedys went there. That actress with the big tits, Jamie Lee Curtis, who was in those slasher movies. Edward Albee. Adlai Stevenson. That cooking broad's daughter—what's her name—Martha Stewart."

"Big fuckin' deal. So what's the point?"

"She's a schoolteacher, Sol. Theater arts. Drama. She goes by the name Sheila Ryan."

6

The black four-door Lincoln Town Car moved slowly up N.E. Sixth Street in the predawn darkness, past old wood-frame bungalows in the Victoria Park Section of Fort Lauderdale. The houses were all painted different pastel colors, yellow and lime and coral, with white trim and a Greek blue under the eaves. The lights from the Town Car illuminated each house for a moment as it passed, then the next, and the next, but the driver in the Town Car didn't notice the pretty houses. He was leaning across the seat, straining to look out the passenger's window at the occasional figure walking along the side of the road close to the houses.

The figures in the darkness looked like boys although some of them weren't boys, but older men in their thirties, thin, wiry, with teenaged boys' bodies. They were all shirtless, their baggy shorts hanging off their asses to show they weren't wearing underwear. They had white T-shirts stuffed into their shorts back pockets, the T-shirts half hanging down over their ass like a flag. When they felt the lights of a car behind them, they turned and looked over their shoulder and followed the car with their eyes as it passed them slowly and then sped up.

The Town Car moved up on a skinny boy and slowed to his walk. The boy stopped, so did the car. The boy went to the passenger-side window and waited until the driver buzzed down the window. Then the boy leaned his arms on the window and looked into the car.

"Hey, man, you looking for a date?"

Barry the Bear leaned closer to the boy leaning on his window, Barry squinting behind his tinted eyeglasses until he could see that the boy wasn't a boy but a guy in his thirties, with rotted teeth, and a hairless, emaciated body. He was white.

Barry sped away from the guy, the guy's arms spinning off the window of the car, the guy screamin's after Barry "Fuckin asshole!" giving him the finger. Barry jammed on the brakes, threw the gearshift into reverse, and sped backward toward the guy, who began to run toward two houses and disappeared between them. Barry put the car in drive again and began moving west slowly on Sixth. After a few blocks he came alongside another figure walking in the darkness along the side of the road. He squinted across the seat through the passenger-side window until he was sure this time, then stopped the car. The skinny black boy, maybe fifteen, came up to his passenger-side window and stuck his head through it just as Barry's cell phone rang.

Barry looked at the number on his cell phone. "Shit!"

The black boy grinned into the car. "Hey dude, you lookin' for a date?"

Barry answered his phone. "Yeah?"

The black boy said, "You won't be sorry, man," and opened the passenger door.

"Barry, I got something for you," said Angel.

"I'm busy," said Barry.

"Busy!" Angel said. "Hey, Barry!"

The black kid was sitting in the car now. "Whaddaya mean, you busy, man? You stopped. You interested or what?" The kid pulled his cock out of his shorts and showed it to Barry.

Barry stared at the huge black cock, his eyes wide like a little boy who just opened a Christmas present. Barry said, "Yeah, I'm interested."

Angel said, "That's better, Barry. It's a small job won't take you but a few minutes. But it's got to be done right now."

"I said, I'm busy," Barry said.

The black kid threw up his hands in disgust. He stuffed his cock back into his shorts. "Fuckin' crazy white dude can't make up his mind wastin' my valuable time." He got out of the car and slammed the door.

"You're not interested now?" said Angel. "Hey, Barry, stop playing fucking games. You're lucky I'm giving you a chance to redeem yourself for that mess you made in the swamp."

The black kid was in front of Barry's car now, the kid illuminated by Barry's headlights, his leanly muscled body, his tight bubble ass half-showing above his drooping shorts. Another car had stopped alongside the kid, the kid talking through the window, nodding, getting into the car, the car speeding off.

"Shit!" said Barry.

"You want it or not, Barry?" said Angel.

Barry's shoulders slumped. Then he said, "What is it?"

"This guy is cheating on his wife. She comes into my shop, complaining all the time. I told her, 'Divorce the asshole,' but she says that's not an option,' she signed a prenup. She just wants to teach him a lesson, make him appreciate her more. I told her I might be able to help her out, but it'll be expensive. She was so thrilled she paid in advance. Here's the address. You got a pen?"

"Waita minute." Barry searched in his glove box until he found a felt tip pen, but no paper. "Go ahead." Angel gave him the address. He wrote it on the palm of his hand.

"Nothing permanent, Barry. Just teach him a lesson like I told her. And Barry, the guy works out a lot. With weights. That's how he met the chick, at the L.A. Fitness Center. They go jogging together and then fuck at her condo."

"So what?"

"So, he's a big guy, Barry, with lots of muscles. You should be careful, make it quick before he knows what's going down."

"Yeah." Barry clicked off. He sped up, passing boys alongside the road until he got to Federal and turned east toward the beach, muttering to himself, his meaty hands squeezing the steering wheel like they squeezed that shiksa whore's neck, his hands turning white, his palms beginning to sweat.

Barry drove past condos on the beach, squinting at the numbers in the darkness, then looking at his palm, the numbers a little blurred now. He stopped his Town Car at a duplex town house, two stories, two driveways side-by-side. There was a Porsche Turbo in one driveway, a red minivan in the other. He squinted at the numbers on his palm again, then opened the trunk and got out. He went around to the trunk, took out an aluminum baseball bat, and walked up to the front door of the town house with the minivan in the driveway. He rang the doorbell and waited. Nothing. He muttered in the darkness and pressed the doorbell hard, for a long moment, the doorbell ringing like church chimes. Finally, a light went on over the door and it opened.

"Jesus Christ, do you know what time it is?" said a bald little guy in silk pajamas. Barry saw a woman behind him, standing halfway down a stairway, clutching a faded pink nightgown to her chest.

"Marvin? Who is it?" the woman said.

The little guy looked back over his shoulder to say something, and as he did, Barry brought the bat out from behind his back, gripping it tightly with both hands, bringing it up over his head, the woman's eyes opening wide, the woman screaming, "Marvin! Marvin!" just as Barry swung the bat with all his might at the little guy's knees, the sound of his kneecaps breaking like a rifle shot. The guy went down in a heap, screaming in pain, clutching his broken kneecaps with both hands, tears of pain rolling down his cheeks, the woman running to him, screaming so shrilly Barry wanted to give her a whack, too, she deserved it, but didn't. Instead, he walked back to his car, threw the bat in the trunk, slammed it shut, got in and drove off. He felt better now.

Barry drove back to Sixth Street at twilight. The street was deserted except for cars driving to work. He drove slowly down the street, squinting across the seat toward the side of the road. His cell phone rang. "Yeah."

"Barry. What happened?" Angel's voice was so calm it momentarily frightened Barry.

"What do ya mean? I did the thing."

"You did the thing, Barry? You did the fucking thing!" Her voice was shrill now, screaming at him. "The fucking guy just got home! His wife sees him pulling up to their driveway in his Porsche Turbo and before he even gets out of the car she calls me, hysterical, demanding her money back, screaming at me, 'He's fucking *jogging* to the front door!'"

Bobby was dancing onstage under the spotlight in his leopard G-string, the fags in the audience screaming at him, "Oh, my God! Bobby, we love you!" He danced slowly, flexing his arms as he swept them across his chest so that his biceps looked as if they'd burst through his skin, then sliding sideways across the stage, flexing the muscles in his thighs and calves, too, then turning his back on the fags, clenching the muscles in his ass so that his cheeks jumped, the fags going wild now, "Oh, I'm gonna faint!"

And then he whirled around like a wild animal, stalking, and leaped off the stage into a sea of fags smelling of sweat and cologne, all reaching their hands out to him like he was a savior come down from a mountain with the power to heal them. He moved from table to table, stopping just long enough to let the fags slip bills into his G-string, but not long enough for them to cop a feel. He moved across the room, right to left, until he was almost to the last table in front of the stairs that led up to the dancers' dressing room. There was only one fag sitting at the table. Bobby danced over to him in the darkness. The guy was short, fat, bald, with a neat goatee, and a ton of gold jewelry around his neck, on his wrists, all glistening in the darkness. The fat guy reached out a hand with a C-note in it and stuck it inside Bobby's G-string. Bobby stopped dancing, stood still, looking down at the guy smiling up at him.

"A fuckin' C-note," Sol grinned. "That get me a peek inside that thing the fags die for?"

Bobby smiled at him. "You switch teams, Sol?"

Sol looked around, then back at Bobby. "It ain't me turnin' on a roomful a fags, Bobby." Then, not grinning now: "Meet me at the bar, you put on some fuckin' clothes."

Bobby watched Sol walk to the bar at the back of the room just as the fags started screaming at a new dancer, a slim black guy with a tight orange Afro. Bobby went upstairs to the dressing room, put on his flip-flops, shorts, and Colours T-shirt, and walked back across the room to Sol sipping scotch at the bar. He sat down beside him. "Marty," he said to the bartender. "Jim Beam, rocks."

"Whatever you want, Robert," said the bartender. He was wearing a black leather studded slave collar and no shirt.

Sal raised his eyebrows. "Whatever you want, Robert?"

Bobby shrugged. "Fags always liked me, Sol."

The bartender brought Bobby his drink. Bobby touched his glass to Sol's. "Good to see you, Solly."

"I know." They sipped their drinks. Then Sol said, "So, Bobby, you plan on makin' this your career?"

"Till something better comes along."

"It just did." Sol leaned toward Bobby. "I got something get you well. A piecea cake."

Bobby laughed. "Where'd I hear that before? A spic gangster by name a Medina? Remember him, Solly? Needed some guns fucked us all up."

"Yeah, I'm sorry about that, Bobby, was my fault settin' you up with him. But I'm gonna make that right."

"Sheila already made it right, Sol, maybe you heard."

"I heard, read it in the papers I figured she done him." Sol shook his head. "She's some kinda broad, Bobby."

"I know. You seen her?"

"No. But I will."

"Tell her hello from me."

"Tell her yerself when I bring her back."

"I wouldn't count on that, Sol. She might be pissed at me."

"That why she leave you?"

"I left her." They were both quiet for a moment, sipping their drinks.

"You gonna tell me?" Sol said.

"Not much to tell, Sol. She got scary. It was dangerous being with her."

"That's not your style, Bobby, runnin' to save your ass."

"It wasn't *my* ass I was worried about."

Sol nodded. "She understand?"

"I didn't tell her."

Sol shook his head in disgust. "Always the redskin hamster, eh, Bobby?"

"What can I say? I had a good teacher taught me to play things close to the vest maybe you don't remember."

"Some things. Not everything. Not the important things."

Bobby didn't say anything for a moment. Then: "So, what's this big score, Sol?"

Sol told him about Candy Kane and Barry the Bear and the dyke hairdresser with the stable of hookers and a ton of cash in the back room of her beauty parlor because she didn't believe in banks.

"The way I figure it," Sol said, "we make her a believer."

"She's just gonna let us snatch it we show her a withdrawal slip?"

"Bobby, how hard could it be, a roomful a broads?"

"Yeah, well, there's Barry the Bear, too, could be a problem."

"I'll take care a that Jew cocksucker what he did to Candy."

"She was a stand-up chick I remember. She deserved better."

"We just get someone inside the place workin' there everyday let us know when the cash's comin' in, who's watchin' it, how we can get to the back room without scarin' all the broads gettin' their hair done."

"What if she's got a security system?"

"To where? Hooked up to the heat so when they stop us from snatchin' her cash, they, maybe, look around at all that cash get an idea. 'Uh, excuse me, lady, but how did you say you acquired this money?' I don't think so, Bobby. What I think is, it's a beauty parlor nuthin' but broads she thinks no one'd guess what she's got stashed in the back room."

"I don't know, Solly. Broads are unpredictable, you never know what's gonna set them off. They start screamin' you can hear them all the way up Las Olas to police headquarters, the Broward lockup, and we go straight from one to the other without passin' go collect our $200."

"Bobby, you ain't been listenin'. We ain't goin' in on the muscle. We go in quiet, get whoever we got workin' inside open the back door for us, make our withdrawal the broads gettin' their hair done yakkin' in the front room never hear a thing."

"So who do we get to work inside?"

"I was thinkin' a broad, classy, got a lotta fugazzi names can change her look anyway she wants to."

Bobby smiled. "I think I know that broad. But she don't cut hair."

"I remember."

A falsetto voice called out from behind them. "Bobby!"

Sol and Bobby turned around on their stools. A black man with a tight orange Afro was walking toward them. He wore red satin hot pants and a black mesh see-through T-shirt. When he got to them he leaned over and kissed Bobby on the cheek.

"Thank God!" the black man said. "I was afraid you'd left and I'd have to walk home alone in the dark."

Bobby grinned at Sol. "Sol, this is Samson."

The black guy flashed Sol a mouthful of gold teeth and extended his hand. "Samson de la Plaine," he said. "Charmed, I'm sure."

Sol looked at the hand, and then the guy's face, the gold teeth, the eye makeup, the orange Afro. He turned to Bobby. "You gotta be kiddin'. A fuckin' faggot hamster?"

"Yeah, well, as you so eloquently put it, Sol, Reggie here is obviously 'a fuckin' faggot hamster.' Ain't that right, Reggie?"

Still flashing his gold teeth, Reggie said, "If your kike friend says so."

"More precisely," Bobby said, "Reggie, here—I mean, Samson de la Plaine—is a 'fuckin' faggot hamster hairdresser.'"

"Hair *designer,* I told ya, Bobby." He ran his hands through Bobby's ponytail, spreading the hair out like a fan. "I designed Bobby's hair," he said. "Got rid of that brassy orange and give it a nice, classy ash-blond tone." He frowned. "Fuckin' split ends took me all fuckin' night they be so dry." He narrowed his eyes and leaned his face closer to Sol's shiny, bald head. Sol pulled his head back. Reggie reached out a slim black hand and touched the little friar's tuft of hair above Sol's ear. Sol slapped his hand away.

"Now you got you some fine baby hair, massa, but Samson can do something with it. Give you a nice combover make you look like that New York dude owns all them hotels dates supermodels."

Bobby laughed.

Charles Cotton Mather IV, a descendant of Puritans and presently the headmaster of the Strawberry Hill Preparatory School in Essex, Connecticut, was sitting in the darkened back row of the school's drama theater on a rainy Saturday afternoon. He was watching his students' rehearsal of *Cat on a Hot Tin Roof* with the father of a prospective student, a Mr. Solomon Weinstein, an importer of rare objets d'art from Tel Aviv by way of Brooklyn, New York. Chas, as the faculty called him, was sucking on a cold pipe. He had both the rumpled look of a smelly, old man—he wore a wrinkled brown tweed jacket with leather patches on the elbows and an askew burgundy and navy rep tie—and the disheveled look of a prematurely aged boy—his thick, straight white hair fell over his wrinkled brow and sparkling blue eyes a la George Plimpton. In contrast, Mr. Weinstein, a portly man with a trim goatee, had manicured fingernails coated with clear polish and he smelled of expensive cologne. He wore a dove gray Turnbull & Asser double-breasted suit with wide chalk stripes and a canary yellow silk ascot tucked into the neck of his spread-collared shirt. Chas's clothes fit his body like an oversized garbage bag. Mr. Weinstein's suit was too tight for his portly frame.

"As you can see, Mr. Weinstein," Chas said. "It's a state-of-the-art theater your little Jacob would just love. It was designed after a Broadway theater by I. M. Pei."

"Yeah, Charlie, I hearda him," said Mr. Weinstein. "He's that slope designed that building in Boston all the windows blew out in a storm they hadta cover them with plywood."

"Well, yes, that was unfortunate. But he outdid himself for us."

They were quiet for a moment, watching the rehearsal. This is what I have been reduced to, thought Chas, sucking on his pipe. The Kennedys were bad enough, but now, this is too much. Being obsequious to Israelites to get them to send their little circumcised brats to a school that once boasted of our Founding Fathers as students. He sighed. The age we live in, I guess. He glanced at Mr. Weinstein. He wore a pinkie ring, for Christ's sake!

Onstage, a girl in a black slip was sitting cross-legged on a four-poster bed with a lace canopy under a spotlight. A boy in boxer shorts stood in front of her. She patted the bed beside her and smiled at him, her lips curling up into her cheeks in that pixieish Meg Ryan way. Then she spoke, her words drowned out by the pinging of drops of water hitting the bottom of a metal bucket placed beside the bed to catch the rainwater dripping down from the roof.

A woman's voice called out from the darkened wings. "No, Peggy! You're trying to seduce him for sex, not get him to join a slumber party." A woman walked out from the wings to center stage. She was tall, slim, with long brown hair flecked with gray. She wore a baggy black turtleneck sweater to conceal her large breasts, a pleated plaid skirt, navy kneesocks, and penny loafers.

The girl glared at her. "I thought that's what I was doing," she said. She was a cute little blonde with an upturned nose and blue eyes that were not as cold as the blue eyes of the woman lecturing her.

"No, it wasn't. What you were doing was being cute. Maggie is not cute. She's hot. The title of the play is *Cat on a Hot Tin Roof,* is it not? Maggie's in heat. You do know about sexual heat, don't you, Peggy?"

The boy standing there, fidgeting with his hands, began to giggle. The girl glared at him now. He stopped giggling.

The woman said to her, "You obviously know anger, Peggy. That's a kind of heat, isn't it? Now think of sex like that. A kind of angry heat that drives Maggie."

Chas leaned over to Mr. Weinstein and whispered. "She's wonderful, isn't she? We were so fortunate to find someone with her acting background."

"Yeah, Charlie. She looks like a broad can act."

"Now, shall we try it again, Peggy," the woman said. She walked back to the wings with the girl's eyes boring daggers into her back. When the woman got to the wings, she reached a hand down to stroke the fur of a large tan dog who was sitting in the wings. Then the woman clapped her hands sharply. "Once more!" she called out. "And, Peggy, try to get it right this time. Poor Edward hasn't even gotten a chance to turn down your advances yet."

The girl called out to her. "Yeah! And that's what I don't get. Why won't he have sex with me? I'm his wife." The girl arched her back to thrust out her small breasts. "I'm pretty."

"Yes, you are pretty, but not in a way Brick appreciates."

The girl frowned. "I don't get it."

"Brick doesn't like girls, dear. Not even little pretty ones like yourself. He's a homosexual. That's the point of the play, sweetheart."

When the rehearsal ended, the woman dismissed the girl and boy, the girl stomping off into the wings to let the woman know how furious she was. Chas and Mr. Weinstein walked down to the edge of the stage.

Chas called out, "Ms. Ryan! Could I see you a moment?"

The woman walked to the edge of the stage, the big tan dog beside her. She looked down into the darkness. "Yes, Chas. What is it?"

Chas and Mr. Weinstein stepped closer to the stage so that they were touched by the spotlight. "I'd like to introduce you to Mr. Weinstein," Chas said. "Mr. Weinstein, this is Ms. Sheila Ryan, the director of our drama department."

"Sheila Ryan," Mr. Weinstein said, stroking his goatee. "Ain't I heard that name before? Haven't we met?"

The woman looked down at him without expression. "I don't think so, Mr. Weinstein."

"Mr. Weinstein is thinking of enrolling his son Jacob at our little school," said Chas. "He's very talented in drama; isn't that right, Mr. Weinstein?"

"Yeah, the kid wants to be an actor," said Mr. Weinstein. He grinned at the woman. "You think you can teach him how to act, Miss Ryan?"

"I'm sure I could teach him a few things." She gave him a thin smile.

"I'll bet."

Chas looked at him as if confused. Then he looked at the woman. "Well, Ms. Ryan, why don't you tell Mr. Weinstein all about our drama department. I have some business to attend to." He turned to Mr. Weinstein. "I'll meet you back at the cafeteria, say, in an hour, for lunch, Mr. Weinstein."

"Yeah, Charlie, lunch'd be good."

The woman and Mr. Weinstein watched Chas walk back up the aisle until he was gone. Then Mr. Weinstein turned to the woman and said, "You look good, baby, except for the hair."

"They have a gym here, Sol. I terrorize the football players by doing heavier squats than them."

"I almost didn't recognize you, the hair, the clothes. Then I seen them big tits you hidin'."

Sheila hefted her breasts with both hands. "Yeah, Sol, I've been keeping them under wraps so Chas won't get any ideas."

"That little blonde give you a hard time she's got nice little titties."

Sheila laughed. "Jesus, Sol! You never change. Thank God!" She stepped down off the stage and threw her arms around his neck and hugged him. "God, I missed you, Solly."

"Me, too, baby."

She stepped back to look at him. "I see you got some use out of that suit we used for the art scam. I almost didn't recognize you without all your gold."

"Yeah, well, I figured I'd better be . . . how'd you useta say it . . . a little understated."

"Yes. Understated. That's always been your style, Sol." She was silent for a moment, looking down at the floor. Then she said, "How is he, Sol?"

"He's O.K. No smarter. Maybe a little bit smarter he learned his lesson. He misses you, baby. We all do."

"Things had gotten out of hand, Sol. I had gotten out of hand. I don't blame him for leaving."

"He left for you, ya know."

"You think I don't know that, Sol? At least he could have let me have a say in it."

"What, you live with him two years you don't know him? That's always been his weakness, baby, tryin' to save people from themselves. I told him for years you wanna be Mother Teresa go put on them nuns' outfits go to India."

"The funny thing is, Sol, he did save me. I'm O.K. now." She made a sweeping gesture with her arm to encompass the theater. "It's not very exciting, but it's safe."

"I never figured you for safe, Sheila."

"No. But without Bobby, safe is all I wanted."

"What's safe? Livin' like straight stiffs like Charlie there with a poker up his ass never took a chance. Safe's so fuckin' borin', Sheila, it ain't you, and it ain't me and Bobby. We're the same, that's why we hit it off even bein' different the way we are. We got things each other needed. I wouldn'ta got stiffed by Frenchie you were around. You wouldn'ta had to cap Medina I was around. Then maybe Bobby wouldn'ta left ya."

Sheila smiled at him as if at one of her students. "Very good, Sol. Impeccable logic. So Aristotelian."

"See what I mean? Always the bitch. I missed it. It kept me sharp even I don't wanna be. Bobby, too. He needs you. He ain't sharp without you, baby, trust me."

"I don't know, Sol. I'm too tired to keep anybody sharp, including myself."

"That's bullshit the old broad speakin' Bobby first met. You ain't that broad anymore whatever you think. You just gotta get in shape again, like doin' them squats Bobby taught you, you kept doin' them like you was keeping in shape for something else even you didn't know what it was. Now it's here. A little thing I got will straighten us all out like before. But we need a broad can act, don't mind takin' a risk, can think on her feet, not bad-lookin' either, with big tits she don't mind showin'."

"I still have the tits, Sol, but I don't act anymore. I direct. That's where the power is."

"Like you wasn't always directin' us, even I know that. You made us better, especially Bobby, baby, you and him together was . . . I don't know. . . ."

"More."

"Yeah, more. More than you was separate." He waited for her to say something. When she didn't, he said, "So? You comin' home? I told Bobby I'd bring you back you don't make a liar of me."

"Why didn't he come himself?"

"Come on, Sheila, you know him, He wanted to leave it up to you."

"That's the thing that used to drive me nuts about him. He was always . . . always so removed, elliptical. It was maddening."

"Ellip—what?"

"He had this way of always throwing things back on you, never answering the question, always making you come up with the answer so that when you did you felt good about yourself, like you discovered something and there he'd be with that shit-eatin' grin, 'My buddies call me, Bobby Squared,' and you knew you didn't come up with it yourself. He willed you to come up with it."

"He's a fuckin' Indian, what do ya expect? I told him that myself before I come. He shoulda told ya more, not always make you guess. You come back he don't open up more you tell Solly, I'll talk to him, beat him on the head I hafta."

She shook her head. "I don't know, Sol. Let me think about it." She forced a smile, then said, "God, Solly! It *was* good to see you." She kissed him on the lips. The tan dog at the edge of the stage began to growl low in his throat, the fur on his back standing up.

Sol looked at the dog, as if seeing him for the first time, and then at Sheila. "Where's the Hosh?"

"He died, Sol. He had bone-marrow cancer."

"Jesus, the Hosh! He was my main man."

"I know, Sol. Mine, too." Sheila looked up at the big tan dog with the floppy ears and round chocolate eyes and the long, wagging tail, like a flag with fringe on it. "This is Hoshi's gift to me after he died. I was up in the mountains in North Carolina. I was in bad shape, Sol, eating out of cans, and then one night Hoshi sent me Matthew to change my life." She called to the dog. "Matthew, come here." The dog leaped off the stage and stood beside her. "See, Solly. He obeys me. Hoshi never obeyed anybody. I think that's why Bobby loved him so much. He felt Hoshi was some higher being come back to earth for a reason, to show us something. I don't know what, but Bobby was right." She leaned over and. threw her arms around the dog and hugged him. "Matthew isn't Hoshi, Sol. He's just a dog, a good one, though. Isn't that right, Matthew?" The dog looked up at her and wagged his tail.

"He don't look like the Hosh."

"He's not a Shiba, Sol. He's a—how did the vet put it—he's of 'uncertain parentage.'"

"A mutt."

"Exactly, Sol." Then she said into the dog's ear, "Matthew, say hello to Uncle Sol."

Sol reached down a hand to pet the dog. Matthew stiffened and growled. Sol pulled his hand back. "Jesus fuckin' Christ!"

Sheila smiled at Matthew. "Good boy, Matt."

Bobby, Sol, and Samson de la Plaine were sitting at an outdoor table on the deck of The Mark's Chickee Bar under a hot sun looking down over Fort Lauderdale beach and beyond it, the pale blue-green ocean. The beach was littered with tourists turning pink, and locals, strippers in G-string bikinis and their bartender boyfriends, lying on blankets, their bodies glistening with coconut oil under the hot sun. The few tourists at the tables around the three men kept glancing at them, then giggling to themselves.

Bobby was wearing a Hawaiian shirt and O.P. shorts; Sol was shirtless, his big, hairy belly hanging over his baggy shorts; Samson was wearing his hot pants and mesh T-shirt.

"What those white dudes be starin at?" Samson said.

"Beats me," Bobby said, grinning.

"Like they never seen three dudes havin' lunch," said Samson as he took a bite of his cheeseburger.

"Maybe they don't see too many hamsters tryin' to get even blacker on the beach," said Sol. He sipped his scotch and water.

"Yeah, and maybe a fat, hairy white dude ruinin' their appetite?" Samson said. He sipped his white wine spritzer through a straw. He looked down at the beach at all the people lying under the sun, and shook his head. "White dudes always sayin' brothers be stupid, man, and here they be tryin' to look like a brother."

"You got a point there, Reggie," Bobby said. He lighted a cigar and exhaled smoke across the table. Samson flapped a limp hand at the smoke.

"Bobby, man, that thing stinks. It be bad for your health, too."

Sol, grinning, lighted a cigarette and exhaled smoke. "Oh, man," Samson said, "Boff a you gangin' up on the brother the way it always be."

"Yeah, well, life ain't fair, Reggie," Bobby said.

Sol leaned over the table and said, "What ain't fair is why we're here, some dyke pimp got a tonna cash in her back room, we gonna make it fair."

"White dudes always got the cash," said Samson. "And they always be pissed a brother try to get some for hisself they call the man."

"Nobody's callin' the man," Bobby said. "Not we do it right, get someone inside the beauty parlor help us out."

"Yeah, and the brother always be takin' all the risk, too."

"No risk," said Bobby. "We just gotta figure out how to get you in there."

"Barry the Bear," said Sol.

"Barry the Bear!" shrieked Samson. "Oh, man, I don't even like the sounda that name."

"A fellow bear, maybe you're related?" said Sol.

"How's Barry gonna help us?" Bobby said. He sipped his Jim Beam.

Sol tossed a head fake toward Samson. "Barry likes hamster boys, I hear, got the same tastes as him."

Bobby looked at Samson. "You got a problem with that, Reggie?"

Sol said, "Get Barry to fall in love with your black ass, maybe help you get a job you do him right."

"I do him," said Samson, "it be right. I never had no complaints."

"Seems to me," Bobby said, "I heard some complaints back at Colours."

"Aw, that, man, that be nuthin'. I jes' fuckin' with the dude he got no sense a humor. Besides, I told ya, Bobby, it only be straight dudes be a problem. They get mean find out they like cock."

"Jesus! I don't even like to talk about it," said Sol.

"No, but you don't mind *me* doin' it, Sol-O-Man, I get us inside."

"Just don't tell me about it," Sol said. "It's fuckin' disgustin'."

"What be disgustin' be the thoughta that fat, hairy belly bouncin' up and down on some skinny-assed white bitch can't even breathe."

"We don't get Reggie in there," Bobby said, "we'll need a broad." He waited for Sol to say something. When he didn't, Bobby said, "What about Sheila, Sol?"

"I'm sorry, Bobby. You musta really pissed her off."

"Sheila?" said Samson. "Who she be?" He looked at Sol, then Bobby, and then he said, "She be your bitch, Bobby, I bet."

"Yeah," Bobby said. "Sheila can be a bitch. But she can be other things, too."

"We don't need her," Sol said, "Reggie here get the job done."

Bobby and Sol looked at Reggie. He shuddered as if from a sudden cold. "Brrrr! Barry the fuckin' Bear! Jes' the name make my johnson go hide."

"Let us know now, or we'll forget the whole thing," Bobby said.

Reggie looked at Bobby for a long moment before he said, "All my life, Bobby, I be a faggot nigger from Sistrunk Boulevard ain't got nuthin' but what I know I should have but don't know how to get it. You two white dudes he'p me get it, I do what I hafta."

Bobby nodded. Sol stood up. He reached into his shorts' pocket and withdrew a roll of $100 bills fastened by an elastic band. He peeled off one bill and dropped it on the table. Then he peeled off five more and dropped them on the table in front of Reggie.

Reggie looked at the bills, and then up at Sol. "I said I ain't got nuthin', Sol-O-Man, but I never be on welfare, either."

"Don't be a fuckin' hamster all your life," Sol said. "That's just an advance'll come outta your end when we make the score."

Reggie looked at the bills, then put them in the back pocket of his tight shorts without saying anything.

"We make this score," Sol said, "them shortsa yours will be bulgin'."

Reggie reached down a hand and wrapped it around his cock. "My shorts *already* be bulgin', Sol."

"You just keep it that way for Barry," Bobby said.

"I gotta go," Sol said. "You comin', Reggie? I'll give you a ride in my Cadillac like a test drive you be buyin' one soon."

"I may be a faggot nigger from Sistrunk," said Samson, "but a Cadillac ain't my style, Sol-O-Man. That be for the brothers and old kikes. I'm a BMW man myself, get me an M5, triple black."

"You be stylin'," Bobby said, mimicking Samson. "How the brothers say it."

Samson looked at Bobby. "I didn't know no better, Bobby, I think you be a brother, too, halfa-brother anyways."

"You got that right," Sol said. "Bobby's a redskin hamster from the reservation you couldn't tell he's so fuckin' dark."

"Hey, Kemo Sabe!" Samson flashed his gold teeth and put out both hands, palms up. Bobby, grinning, slapped Samson's palms with his hands.

Sol rolled his eyes. "Asshole buddies, now, huh? Come on, Reggie, I got things ta do."

"Naw, man, I think I stay here chillin' with Bobby."

Sol glared at Reggie. "I think you should be comin' with me, Reggie, give me a scenic tour of Sistrunk, I always wanted to see it, like Monte Carlo."

"You wanna see Sistrunk, Sol?" Reggie said. "I drop you off at Omar's, where the brothers be drinkin' Thunderbird out front. You call them 'hamsters,' they show you how much they like it." He stood up. "You comin', Bobby?"

Before Bobby could answer, Sol said, "No, he ain't comin'. He wants to be alone, you so fuckin' stupid you can't see it."

After Sol and Reggie left, Bobby sat there, alone, puffing on his cigar, sipping his Jim Beam and staring out at the sunbathers on the sand and beyond them the pale blue-green ocean. People were swimming in the ocean. Two guys were playing paddleball on the sand where the tide lapped at their feet. A woman in a bikini was throwing a Frisbee into the ocean and her dog was leaping after it, plunging into the water and then swimming strongly toward the Frisbee before he caught it in his mouth and then swam back to the woman. She took it out of his mouth and patted him on the head. Hoshi always hated the water, Bobby thought, as the woman turned in the sand and began walking toward the wooden steps that led up to the Chickee Bar. The woman's body was in shadows, the sun at her back, so that as she approached the steps Bobby could make her out only as a dark form with sparks of golden sunlight outlining her body until she moved up the steps, the dog walking beside her, shaking off water, and she came out of the sunlight and Bobby saw it was Sheila, smiling, walking toward him. He stood up as in a dream. She was in front of him now, so close he could reach out and touch her, only he couldn't.

"Hello, Bobby."

"I didn't think—"

"That I was coming back? Bobby, I couldn't not come back to you."

"But Sol said—"

Sheila shrugged. "This was his idea. Always playing his little games. 'Let the sunuvabitch suffer just a little more,' he said. 'Teach him a lesson.' I made him promise to tell you I was coming back, but I guess he didn't."

"I don't care. You're here, that's all that matters."

"I know." They were both silent for a moment. Then Sheila said, "I'm sorry, Bobby. About everything."

"Me, too, baby. It was my fault."

"Both our faults. It was a waste of six months." Bobby nodded. "Jesus, I missed you so." She pressed the flat of her hand against her stomach. "I had this constant pain right here, like something inside me had been cut out."

"I had the same pain, baby, only it was lower."

Sheila laughed. "You still have it, Bobby? I think I've got the cure."

"You always did."

"Oh, Bobby!" She threw her arms around him and kissed him hard on the lips. "God, I missed your feel, your smell." She buried her face in his neck and breathed deeply.

The dog at her side began to growl. She looked down at him. "Not at Bobby, Matthew!" The dog stopped growling and sat down. Bobby looked down at the dog and then at Sheila. Before he could say anything, she said, "Didn't Sol tell you?"

"Tell me what?"

"Hoshi died, Bobby." She felt his body pressing against her body stiffen, his breath catch for a moment. She stepped back and saw that blank look in his black eyes that revealed nothing, and everything. "He was suffering a lot." She told him about the bone-marrow cancer and the vet who put him to sleep and how shortly after that Hoshi sent Matthew to her. "He died in my arms. I could feel his life slipping away. Just before he went, I told him that you loved him, and then he was gone. I have his ashes in an urn. I couldn't bear to put them in the ground."

Bobby gave his head a little shake as if to clear it from a blow.

"I'm sorry, Bobby."

Bobby forced a smile and looked her up and down. "You're looking good, baby." She was wearing the black G-string bikini Bobby had bought for her at Splish Splash two years ago. "It still almost fits," he said. She looked down at her huge breasts spilling out of the tiny top. Pushing fifty, she still had her faintly defined abs and the little flare to her thighs. "You been workin' out," Bobby said.

"Probably for you. Somewhere deep down I must have known I'd come back."

"You could use a little color," Bobby said, "and that hair—"

"I let it go on purpose so I'd look the part. Spinster schoolmarm, you know." She touched her long brown hair with streaks of gray in it. "But I was thinking of getting it done again. I heard of this *wonderful* salon on Las Olas."

"Sol told ya?"

"That's why I'm here, Bobby, isn't it? Sol said you needed a broad."

Bobby grinned at her. "Yeah, we could use a broad." Then he stopped grinning. "But it could be dangerous. This dyke is a mean cunt."

"Why, Bobby," she said with a thin smile. "You're worried about me!"

"I always worried about you, baby."

"I can take care of myself."

"Yeah. That was the problem, wasn't it?"

"No. It wasn't. The problem was me taking care of you, Bobby."

They were both silent for a moment, then Sheila, smiling, looked Bobby up and down, his huge, tanned, muscular body in a tiny, G-string bathing suit. "You're looking good, too, Bobby. You know, before you, muscles never turned me on. I never even thought of them as attractive, as something that made a man's body beautiful." She laughed, a breath. "Now, Jesus, I'm like a fucking cat in heat when I look at you. I guess you ruined me for any other man, Bobby."

"Is that bad?"

"No. It's good." She narrowed her eyes and stared at him. "But there is something different. I can't put my finger on it. It's . . . your hair! That's it. You finally got the color right."

A falsetto voice called out from behind Bobby. "That was me, sweetheart! *I* designed Bobby's hair."

Bobby turned around to see Samson and Sol walking toward him. Samson was flashing his gold teeth. Sol was grinning.

Samson came up to Bobby and ran a hand through his ash-blond ponytail. He said to Sheila, "Do you really like it, honey?"

"It's perfect," Sheila said.

Bobby said to Sol, "You prick!"

"What?" Sol said. "You want me to send her back, we get another broad?"

"You must be Samson," Sheila said. "Sol told me about you."

Samson put his hands on his hips and cocked his head. "I'll bet," he said. "Sol-O-Man always be puttin' me down, I almost think he don't like brothers." Sheila laughed. Samson reached out and took her hand in his slim black hand, bent over, and kissed it. "Samson de la Plaine at your service, honey."

"Why, thank you, Samson. Such a gentleman."

Bobby shook his head. "I'm glad you're back, baby, but if I gotta start kissin' your hand . . ."

Samson said, "Boffa these white dudes got no class between them, sweetheart."

"It's Sheila," she said.

"You got a family name?" Samson said.

"Of course. Doyle. McKenzie. Ryan. Take your pick."

Bobby and Sol laughed. Samson said, "You be Bobby's bitch, huh?"

Sheila smiled her 8X10 glossy smile, all eyes and bared teeth, and fixed her smile on Bobby. "Why, Robert?" she said brightly. "You told Samson all about me!"

Part Three

7

Sol was driving his black Cadillac Sedan de Ville slowly up Northeast Sixth Street at midnight, the headlights illuminating the pretty pastel houses and the occasional lone figure walking along the side of the road, disheveled, slouching, aimless, like the remnants of a defeated army, the figures looking back over their shoulder at the Cadillac coming up on them, the car's headlights illuminating their grinning faces for a moment before it moved past them.

"What they got to smile about?" Sol said. "Sucking cock all night."

Samson de la Plaine, slumped down in the passenger seat in his red satin hot pants and no shirt, didn't respond. He was pouting. Finally he said, "Sol, man, I be walkin' this street three nights in a row. My legs be cramped and still no fuckin' Barry the Bear."

"He'll show. You gotta have patience, somethin' hamsters don't have."

"I got patience, Sol-O-Man, I put up with your shit be proof."

Sol stopped the car by the side of the road. "Show time, Reggie."

"Aw, man, why don't you put on these hot pants walk up and down the road wait for a sick, scary white dude pick you up?"

"I don't look good in red. Besides, I ain't the color he's buyin', I hear."

"Thassa fact. I turn down so many white dudes these last three nights, the same ones be hittin' on me over and over think I'm playin' hard to get cause I be special."

"I heard you was special, Reggie, the way you said it."

"I shoulda kept my fuckin' mouth shut, always braggin' teach me a lesson."

"You gonna get out, or what?"

"How do I know it be him?"

"I told ya. He's a big ugly guy drivin' a black Lincoln Town Car. You wanna be sure, ask him his name."

"Man, what world you come from? Half these white dudes cruisin' be married don't give their real name like they wanna be buddies. Take me to their country club introduce me to their golf buddies, 'Hey, boys, this is my new best friend, Samson, the faggot nigger sucks my cock,' and then we all play a couple innings of golf or whatever the fuck they call it and I gotta carry all the bags being the only nigger and all, and then after the game we all go to the locker for a shower where they show off their tan lines and then maybe get Samson suck all their cocks before we go have martinis at the bar and that little finger shit white dudes love to eat don't taste like nuthin'."

"You finished? You're makin' me cry, Reggie, how tough it is to be a nigger cocksucker you don't hafta be."

"Yeah, and you don't hafta be no kike gangster either."

"I was born a kike, Reggie. I *chose* to be a gangster."

"See what I mean? You just like me, Sol-O-Man. I born a faggot, and I choose to be a nigger."

Sol grinned and shook his head. "You're a real smart-ass hamster, ain't ya?"

"Smart enough to know some white dude want me suck his cock ain't gonna tell me his name."

"He'll tell ya. He's too stupid not to tell ya. He's Barry the fuckin' Bear, Reggie. The way he thinks is nuthin' can ever hurt him 'cause he ain't afraid a nuthin', which is his weakness. He don't think because he don't hafta because he's Barry the Bear, you understand?"

Samson shivered. "Brrrr! Barry the Bear, what kinda name is that for a man."

"He ain't a man, Reggie, I just told ya. He's a fuckin' animal, you be careful."

Samson looked across at Sol. "You be worried about me, Sol, that's nice."

"I'm worried, about our *score* is what."

"No, you be worried about Reggie you can't say it don't change it." Samson opened the passenger door. "Pick me up in three hours."

"Good huntin', Reggie." Reggie got out and slammed the door. Sol drove off.

Reggie had walked up and down Sixth Street in the darkness for two hours, turning down one pink-faced fat white man after another who pulled up alongside him, when he felt the lights of yet another car coming up behind him. He looked over his shoulder, flashing his gold teeth, and the car stopped alongside him. The window went down and Reggie looked inside the big black Lincoln Town Car at the huge man in a chauffeur's uniform with the puffy, small-featured face and a little fringe of hair falling around his shoulders.

"Hey, man, whatcha be doin'?" Reggie said.

The huge man studied him through his tinted eyeglasses. Then he said, "Get in."

Reggie, grinning, said, "My name's Samson, bro, what be yours?"

"Who gives a fuck?"

Reggie faked a frown, and said, "Aw, bro, I just be friendly."

"It's Barry. Now you gonna get in, or what?"

Reggie got in the car and shut the door. Barry drove off with the lights of another car following at a distance.

"Man, you a big dude," Reggie said. "I love big dudes."

"I know what you love."

"Yeah, I love that, too, man."

Reggie ran the flat of his hand over the leather upholstery of his seat. "Real leather, man, that's chillin'." Barry said nothing. He came to the light at Federal, waited until it turned green, then headed east until he came to the entrance of Holiday Park. Reggie said, "What's that uniform you be wearin', bro, you a airplane pilot or sumthin?" When Barry didn't respond, Reggie flashed him his hurt frown again. "Jes' tryin' to be friendly, man."

Barry glanced at him. "I'm a fuckin' chauffeur, awright? Now shut the fuck up, I don't throw you out."

"Whatever. It be your ride, man."

Barry pulled the big Lincoln into the darkened parking lot alongside the baseball diamonds and directly in front of the little red railroad caboose where mothers brought their children to play in the afternoon, He parked facing the caboose and turned off the car lights. He didn't notice the black Cadillac follow him into Holiday Park with its lights off, and park in darkness far down the lot.

Barry pressed a button under the seat and the bench seats of the Lincoln moved back with a buzzing sound. Then he unzipped his fly. "Is this what you're lookin' for, boy?" He fumbled inside his pants and pulled out his cock.

Reggie stared at the smallest cock he'd ever seen on a grown man, and then he made his eyes get wide and said, "Oh, man, yeah, that be the biggest cock I ever seen."

Barry held his cock with his thumb and forefinger and aimed it at Samson. "Well, what you waitin' for, boy? Suck it!"

Reggie shifted in his seat until his head was over Barry's cock and then he went down on it, sucking it with his lips, not even having to take it down his throat, moaning while he slurped, groaning with pleasure, gagging every so often and pulling his head off Barry's cock as if to gasp for air, "Aw, man, you chokin' me," and then he felt Barry's meaty hand pushing his head back down on his tiny cock and he was sucking and moaning and gagging again all the while thinking to himself, I get outta this with my sorry black ass, make that score with the white dudes, that be the end of Samson de la Plaine nigger cocksucker forever.

Barry was leaning back in his seat, his breath coming in labored gasps, and then he came with a little spurt of cum and a weary grunt like a bear climbing a hill. He pushed Reggie away from him.

Reggie licked his lips and grinned at Barry. "You be sumthin' else, man, I musta swallow a gallon a cum."

Barry tucked his cock back into his pants, zipped them up, and reached into his back pocket. "How much?"

Reggie put a pained look on his face. "Aw, man, I ain't no hustler. I jes' be a brother doin' what he likes." Barry withdrew his wallet from his back pocket, took out a twenty, and tossed it at Reggie. Reggie handed it back to him. "I told ya, man, I ain't a hustler, I be a brother lookin' for real work." Barry looked at him. "You drivin' this fancy car, maybe you need some hep drivin' rich peoples."

"My clients don't want a nigger chauffeur."

"Thas not all I can do, man. I be a hair designer, too, got me a certificate an' everything got my name on it, Samson de la Plaine. I worked in a salon in Key West, nuthin' but faggots, so I come to Lauderdale work on rich white women's hair but I don't know nobody, maybe you can hep me out, you must drive a lotta rich white ladies around get their hair done." He waited, but Barry said nothing. Reggie furrowed his brows and said, "I be grateful, man, you hep me, I be your regular boy," grinning at Barry now, showing him his gold teeth, thinking, Sol be right, this scary white dude be the stupidest fuckin' white man I ever seen.

Barry stared at the nigger, his slimly muscled body, his fat nigger lips, and then he slid his hand down to his crotch and began to rub his cock. He reached his other hand over the seat and put it on the nigger's neck, forcing the nigger's head back down toward his cock again. Barry unzipped his pants, and said, "We'll see."

Two days later, Samson de la Plaine walked through the front door of La Donna Bellicósa. The receptionist looked up and stared at him. Samson was wearing tight red leather pants that showed off his cock and a black silk dress shirt open to the navel to show off his many gold chains against his black skin. Sheila had bought him the pants and shirt. Sol had loaned him his gold jewelry. "Aw, Sol, man," Reggie moaned. "I look like Sammy Davis, Junior, be wearing a Star of David."

"Can I help you?" the receptionist said.

"I have an appointment with Miss Angel," Samson de la Plaine said.

Without turning her head, the receptionist called out, "Angel! Somebody to see ya!" and went back to the book she was reading.

Angel stopped cutting hair at her chair in the middle of the room and walked over to the receptionist's desk. She looked down at the receptionist with her small black eyes, and said, "I almost didn't hear you, Maya. Scream louder next time."

The receptionist blushed. "Sorry, Angel."

"Now, what is it?" Angel said.

"This . . . gentleman says he has an appointment with you."

Angel turned to Reggie, looked him quickly up and down without expression, and said, "Yes?"

"Barry said—"

"Oh, Barry. Yes. He did mention something about a boy who needed a job."

Reggie smiled at her, not giving her too much gold teeth, and said, "I am Samson de la Plaine." He held out his hand. She ignored it.

"Do you have any experience in a salon?"

"I did makeup and designed hair in a salon in Key West and—"

"Key West? I'll bet they loved you there . . . Samson. Listen, I don't have all day. I run a busy salon as you can see. What I need is not a . . . hair designer, but a boy to clean up, sweep around the chairs, throw out the garbage, wash and dry towels, fold them and place them by each of my cutter's chairs, all the while making sure he's fucking invisible. Do you understand?" Reggie, trying to keep his smile, nodded. "Good. Now you ditch the Shaft outfit and come to work tomorrow morning at nine sharp in a white dress shirt buttoned to the neck and a pair of neatly pressed kahki pants."

"Yes, Miss Angel."

"Good boy. And . . . Samson, keep your name to yourself or get a new one."

"Yes, Miss Angel."

"If you work out and I get shorthanded, one day I might give you a shot at a chair." She turned and walked away.

Sheila was putting on her makeup in the bathroom. Bobby was sitting on the white leather sofa in the living room of the apartment on Bayview Sol had rented for them. It was the same apartment they had had when they first met. Bobby sipped from his glass of Jim Beam and looked around at the white walls, the glass and chrome furniture, the sliding glass doors that led outside to a deck shaded by a palm tree and beyond it the canal lined with sailboats and gofasters rocking in their moorings on a soft, warm evening.

It was like nothing had changed, Bobby thought. He left and he came back. Sheila called it his "sabbatical." She said, "I don't blame you, Bobby, everybody needs a break from reality." This life with Sheila that he was living was real. It was like they had never been apart. That's the way it must be with two people who fit like him and Sheila. They just slipped effortlessly into the life they had once lived. They woke in darkness in the morning, had their Cuban coffee on the deck, read the papers, Bobby the *Miami Herald,* Sheila the *New York Times,* then went to the gym to lift weights. When they got back home they had a protein shake and went to the beach. Sheila tanned again. Then at night they went out to dinner. They came home and fucked themselves to sleep. Not a bad life, he thought. Even the score was a part of it. They both had to admit that no matter how dangerous the score was, Barry the fucking Bear and that dyke Angel, it excited them, gave their life meaning, possibility, danger. That was it. Danger. Proof they were alive. Bobby didn't know whether they could ever live without it, even as Sheila planned for that one big score that would allow them to live without it, would let them live what she called "the quiet life, Bobby, just me and you and Matthew."

Bobby looked down at Matthew sitting by his feet, the dog's plumy tail sweeping back and forth across the white tile floor, his big, round, expressive chocolate eyes staring up at Bobby. Matthew was the only part of their life that had changed. Hoshi was gone. Sheila said he was always with them, that's why she kept his urn with Hoshi's ashes in it on top of the glass bookshelf against the wall. Bobby looked across the room at the urn, the color of Hoshi's fur, with his name written on it, and the date he died. It was so small, not much larger than a coffee mug. Bobby thought it would have been so much larger to hold the ashes of such a big dog, not in size, but in spirit, with a heart so big you would think nothing would ever be big enough to hold his ashes.

Bobby kept staring at the ceramic urn sitting by itself, like a shrine. Hoshi was inside it but Bobby knew he wasn't, just as his Cherokee ancestors knew that when a warrior died his spirit left his body to be with the gods and his ancestors, hunting game in the forests, blessing everything they killed as one of the Great Spirit's creatures. Hoshi was one of the Great Spirit's creatures. He was with the Great Spirit now, Bobby thought, with my ancestors, running with them through the forests in the afterlife, chasing deer the way Bobby could never let him do on earth.

Finally, Bobby felt the tears in his eyes. He turned away from the urn. He didn't see Hoshi in it. He saw Hoshi in his mind's eye, when Bobby was alone as he was now. He saw Hoshi as a puppy, chasing geckos on the deck, catching them in his soft mouth and bringing them to Bobby before he let them go. He saw Hoshi in a fight to the death with Reverend Tom's pit bull, a fight that saved all of their lives. He saw Hoshi lying beside Sheila on the beach while Bobby made a deal for guns with Machine Gun Bob at a table in The Mark's Chickee Bar. He saw Hoshi everywhere at odd moments, passing in front of his eyes, so real and yet a dream, Hoshi with his slanting, inscrutable almond-shaped eyes and his long nose like a wolf, his pricked ears and his bushy tail curled over his back like a scythe.

Bobby looked down at Matthew. Matthew wasn't like Hoshi. Sheila was right. He was just a dog, a good dog, but still, just a dog. When Matthew looked into Bobby's eyes it was always with a question. What can I do to please you, Bobby? What do you want from me? Bobby smiled. Hoshi never looked at him like that. Hoshi didn't need to ask questions. He knew everything without thought because he just was. The Hosh. When he looked at Bobby, it was to tell him what he expected Bobby to do. Sheila used to say, "When you're in doubt, Bobby, just think what Hoshi would do." It was good advice, even now, with Hoshi gone, but somehow not gone, never would be.

Bobby drained his drink and stood up. He called out, "Baby, I'm gonna take Matty for a walk before we go to dinner."

Sheila called back from the bathroom, "Go ahead, Bobby, bond with the big guy."

"Come on, Matty." The dog jumped up and followed Bobby out to the deck and then down the stairs to the dock and up the dock to the little grassy area between the canal and Bayview Drive. Matthew roamed back and forth in the grass, sniffing scents, pissing, while Bobby watched him. He was so much bigger than Hoshi, but less substantial. Matthew was tall and long and. rangy, like a distance runner. Hoshi was short, muscular, compact, like a bodybuilder. Matthew wanted to be loved. Hoshi knew he was loved because, after all, he was The Hosh. What Hoshi wanted was to protect Bobby and Sheila and Sol, because he knew they would always need it, some unseen will above their own that would keep them safe in spite of themselves.

"Come on, Matty, time to go back."

Matthew followed him back to the apartment where Sheila was waiting for them in the living room. "Did you have fun?" she said.

"Yeah. We both pissed on a tree."

Matthew went over to Sheila and stood on his hind legs and wrapped his front paws around her waist. Sheila hugged him and kissed him.

"I was jealous, baby," Bobby said, "I'd think Matty here was beatin' my time."

Sheila looked at Bobby. "He's devoted to me, Bobby. He was all I had up in the mountains. He saved me, and I guess he thinks I saved him, too."

Bobby went over to the sofa to get his glass off the arm of the sofa and put it in the sink. Sheila said, "Well, how do I look?"

Bobby looked at her. Samson had bleached her hair ash-blond like Bobby's, and cut it so short it stood up like spring grass. She stared at Bobby with her vivid blue eyes that could grow cold at times, scary cold. Her face was more lined than it had been, but still, she looked ten years younger than she was, forty-eight. She was tan again, and her lean body was as muscular as it always had been. Except for her tits. They were big, billowy, the tits of a fatter woman. They spilled out of her low-cut white spandex minidress that barely covered her small, high tight ass. Her thighs and calves were defined by her six-inch-high stripper's pumps.

"Not bad for an old broad," Bobby said. She smiled at him. "You wearing panties?"

Sheila hiked up her skirt to her waist to show him her trim, ash-blond bush that was nothing more than a long one-inch-wide line going down to her cunt. "Samson offered to do it," she said, "but I told him I think I'd better do it myself. He's a good kid, Bobby. He said, 'I knows what you mean, baby, only certain peoples should see your privates.'"

"He oughtta know, halfa South Florida seen his."

"Because he had to, Bobby, not because he wanted to. That's the difference."

"Maybe."

"He *is* a good kid, Bobby. Even Sol sees it." Bobby laughed. "You do, too."

"We'll see. It's a definite 'we'll see.'"

Sheila was staring at him now, hard, with her cold blue eyes narrowed like she was looking for something she couldn't put her finger on.

"Oh, baby," Bobby said. "I seen that look before."

"I was just noticing, Bobby, you don't look so bad yourself." He wore a black Hawaiian shirt splattered with pink orchids and green leaves, tight jeans, and. his ostrich cowboy boots.

"Baby, we gotta go," Bobby said.

Sheila came close to him and pressed the flat of her hands against his massive chest. "Don't we have time?" she said in a husky voice.

"We're late already."

"We have time," she insisted. She pushed hard against his chest until he fell back onto the sofa.

"Baby," he said, but she was already on her knees, unzipping his fly, pulling out his cock, staring at it for a long moment, and then she was sucking it and Bobby leaned his head on the back of the sofa and closed his eyes. He heard Matthew growl low in his throat.

Bobby sat up. "Jesus! it's like he's your fuckin' lover!"

Sheila pulled her head up and glared at Matthew. "No, Matthew! Go lay down in the bedroom." The dog hung his head, his tail between his legs, and slunk off. Bobby heard his gangly body hit the floor with a clatter of bones, and a disgusted whoomph of breath, and then Sheila was sucking his cock again.

Finally, she stood up, her eyes glassy, her lips moist. She squatted over him until her pussy was in his face and he was eating her while she moaned. She grabbed his hair in her hands and pressed his face hard against her pussy, and then she pulled it away and moved back a bit until she was squatting over his cock. She lowered her pussy down to his cock until he was inside her. She closed her eyes, a dreamy smile on her lips, and then, with her legs spread and her high heels planted on the tile floor, she began to squat up and down on his cock until she felt him spurt inside her and then she came, too, with a soft cry and fell forward against him, her face buried in his neck. She gasped for breath, whispering in his ear, "God, I'll never take that for granted. Bobby, I'll never take you for granted again."

He wrapped his arms around her and held her tight against him. "I know, baby. Me, too." Then she pulled away from him and stood up. As she wiggled her ass and pulled down her tight skirt, he said, grinning, "You been squatting heavier weight than before, haven't you?"

"Jesus, man, she was fuckin' scary, scarier even than Barry, I had to suck his teeny cock like I loved it."

"I don't wanna hear it," Sol said. "It's fuckin' disgustin'."

"It ain't disgustin' I got us inside the salon, Sol-O-Man."

"You did good, Reggie," Bobby said.

"Got me a job from that dyke broad," Reggie said. He shuddered. "Scarier than Barry, I tell ya. Uglier, too." He looked down at himself in his white dress shirt with the button-down collar and khaki pants. "Make me wear this fuckin' white-boy costume like I be a nigger come back from college."

"Sistrunk U," Sol said.

"I think you look cute, Reggie," Sheila said. "It's a nice look. Boyish, but a little masculine, too."

"She means not too faggy, Reg," Bobby said.

Reggie tossed a head fake at Bobby. "Fuckin' white-boy muscle dude be wearin' a flower shirt callin' me faggy got some nerve—ain't that right, Sheila?"

Sheila smiled at the slim black man with the tight orange Afro and threw her arm over his shoulder. "If you say so, Reggie."

Reggie glanced at her big tits pressing against his arm. "You keep rubbing those titties against me, baby, I switch teams and steal you from your faggot boyfriend." They all laughed.

Sheila and Reggie were sitting side by side, with their backs to the wall, at a table in Napoli's Ristorante Italiano in a strip mall in Pompano Beach, Florida. Bobby and Sol were sitting across from them, their backs to the rest of the small dining room. It was a mom-and-pop trattoria with red-and-white checked tablecloths, mismatched silverware, and bad paintings of Mount Vesuvius, the Amalfi coast, and the Isle of Capri on the walls. The other tables were filled with groups of older men, fleshy, pale, with silvery pompadours. They wore gaudy Hawaiian shirts and baggy shorts and black kneesocks over their skinny legs and white patent-leather loafers on their slim feet. They looked like tourists from Montreal, except they smoked cigars and hunched over their tables speaking with a crude Brooklyn accent. Every so often, one of the men would glance sideways at the blonde with the big tits and the black man sitting beside her. His eyes would narrow and he'd shake his head and say something to his friends.

"What that mean?" Reggie said. *"Mool-en-yam?"*

Sol looked behind him at the men, then back to Reggie. "It means nigger, Reggie, in Italian. The wiseguys don't think it's so cute a nigger rubbing his arm against a white broad's tits."

"Fuck them Eye-talians. Their time be gone, the brothers takin' over."

"That's what I hear," Sol said.

A waitress appeared at their table. "Can I take your order?" she said, smiling through bad teeth. She was pillowy, fat, with a heart tattoo on her shoulder with the names Chuck and Misty inside the heart.

"Yeah, honey," Sol said. "Bring us a big bottle a dago red, some hot antipasto for four, and lotsa garlic bread."

When the waitress left, Reggie said, "Bad enough I gotta hear the goombahs puttin' me down I gotta eat their food, too."

"It'll be good for you," Bobby said. "All that garlic and hot sauce make a man a you."

"I already a man, Bobby, you ain't noticed."

Sol said, "So tell us, Reggie, how do you like your job?"

Reggie shook his head. "Fuckin' dyke don't let me cut, jes' make me work my ass off in the back room doin' laundry like a Chinaman."

"That's not what Sol meant," Bobby said. "You been workin' there three weeks now, you got nuthin' for us?"

"I know what Sol-O-Man meant," Reggie said.

"Well?" Bobby said.

Reggie leaned over the table closer to Bobby and Sol. "It work out better than I cut hair. I always in the back room near the dyke's office. She got this Eye-talian chick sits at a desk by Miss Angel's door, don't let nobody in 'cept Barry and her hos, they bring her money from the night before. She got a button under her desk, she push and it open the door. A big ole metal door fuckin' dyn-o-mite wouldn't dent."

"What about a back door to the office?" Sheila said.

"Ain't none, honey. No windows neither. The onliest way in is through the metal door the chick watches like a hawk, she got one a them funny Eye-talian names."

"Moisha?" Sol said.

Reggie flashed his gold teeth at Sol. "Moisha chillin' ain't she Sol-O-Man you be watchin' the sister on the tube not be tellin' no one."

"What's her name?" Sheila said.

"Everybody jes' call her Lou 'cept Miss Angel, she call her by her Christian name . . . Lou . . . Cree . . . Sha."

Sheila took her arm from around Reggie's shoulder and looked at him. "Lucrezia?"

"Thass it, baby. Lou-Cray-Sia."

Sheila looked at Bobby and Sol.

"What?" Reggie said. "You know the chick?"

Sheila said, "Bobby and Sol go way back with Lucrezia if it's the same one."

Sol said, "How many Lucrezias can there be?"

"Could be thousands," said Bobby, "like Samson de la Plaine."

"Is she small and dark with a lot of makeup?" said Sheila.

"Thass her."

"She wear clothes like a squaw?" Bobby said.

"Yeah, man, all that leather and suede shit with the little fringe."

"She cut and bleached my hair two years ago," Sheila said. "She gave me some good vocational advice, too."

"What that be, Sheila?"

"Always keep a gun in my purse."

"She follow her own advice, I hear," Reggie said. "Keeps a little nine-millimeter in her purse on her desk, I think she know how to use it, too."

"That's no problem," Sol said. "Lucrezia's a good chick, stand-up, we can use her when we hafta."

"She ain't jes' gonna let you in that office, Sol," Reggie said. "Her dyke boss know she done it, she be pissed."

"We can work around that," Bobby said. "But we gotta get someone in that office first, get the dyke to open the safe, I gotta feeling she won't open it even with a gun to her head."

"I got that same feelin', Bobby," Reggie said. "But who?"

Sheila flashed her glossy actress smile. "Well, Sol," she said. "I guess you were right after all."

"Right about what?" Sol said.

"You and Bobby *do* need a broad."

The waitress appeared at their table with their wine and food. She put the big carafe of red wine on the table and then the steaming tray of hot calamari, scungilli, clams swimming in red sauce, and then the buttery garlic bread.

"Enjoy," the waitress said.

Reggie looked up at her. "You ain't got no fried chicken, do ya, honey?"

8

THE BLACK CADILLAC SEDAN DE VILLE PULLED UP IN FRONT OF La Donna Bellicósa and stopped at the curb. The receptionist inside at her desk looked up and out the window as the passenger-side door opened. A long tan leg appeared, and then another, and a woman stepped out of the Cadillac. She tugged down her short black leather skirt, adjusted her wide belt, and walked toward the door in her Manolo Blahniks. She wore a tight, filmy, low-cut, black T-shirt with spaghetti straps, and no bra. She entered the salon and stood in front of the receptionist, a big-boned girl with a wild mass of luxuriant, curly black hair and thick black eyebrows. The receptionist had a broad, big-featured face, very pretty, but odd—like one of the Hemingway sisters, the woman thought, Margaux or Mariel. But she didn't have the Hemingway sisters' hint of athleticism. She looked sedentary, ponderous, in her baggy black sweater and men's pleated pants, as if she was rooted to her chair behind her desk.

"Mrs. Weinstein," the woman said. "I have an appointment with Angel for a trim."

The receptionist stared at the woman's blond hair that was already cut so short it stood up like grass.

"Mrs. Weinstein?" the woman said. "If you'd check your book?"

"Oh, yeah, sure," the receptionist said and looked down at her appointment book. The woman looked around the salon. There were four chairs on either side of the room and a door at the back. Most of the cutters were women, except for a slim boy with bleached blond hair that fit his head like a stocking cap and, at the far right-hand chair, a slim black man with a tight orange Afro. A blond woman dressed in black men's clothes, was cutting hair at a chair in the middle of the room. She had a punk, boys'-rock-band haircut, her hair bleached a metallic silver-gold. Her small-featured face was heavily made-up to hide her bad skin, like the rough skin of an orange. She glanced over at the woman by the receptionist's desk, her small black eyes roaming down from the woman's face to her breasts half-spilling out of her flimsy T-shirt to her tight leather skirt and then her long, faintly muscular tanned legs. She leaned over and said something to the woman she was working on. Then she walked across the room to the woman at the receptionist's desk.

"Can I help you?" Angel said.

"I have an appointment," the woman said. "Mrs. Weinstein. Your receptionist can't seem——"

Angel smiled down at the receptionist tracing down her appointments with her finger and a furrowed brow. "That's all right, Maya, I'll take care of it." Then to the woman. "And who is your appointment with?"

"Angel," the woman said.

Angel smiled and reached out her hand, "I'm Angel."

"Oh, wonderful!" the woman said. She shook Angel's hand. Angel held it for a moment with a gentle pressure and then let it slip from her fingers. "I've heard so much about your salon," said the woman. "My friends said, 'Sheila, you just have to go to Angel. She's the best.'" The woman smiled. "So here I am."

"Well, I hope I don't disappoint you, Mrs. Weinstein."

"Actually, I don't know whether I'll keep it. Weinstein, I mean, after the divorce and all. I may go back to my maiden name. Ryan." She shrugged. "I don't know."

Angel smiled at her, this silly woman who didn't know herself and said, "Well, I'll be with you in just a few minutes." She gestured toward a black leather sofa in front of the receptionist's desk. "Why don't you make yourself comfortable? Maya will get you an espresso or juice, whatever you want."

"That's not necessary," Sheila said. "I'll just read." She sat down at the far end of the sofa to the right of the receptionist's desk so she had a view of the room, and everyone in the room had a view of her. She picked up a copy of *Vogue* and began flipping through it. Every so often she glanced over the top of the magazine toward Angel, cutting a woman's hair. When Angel glanced back at her, they both smiled and Sheila crossed her legs.

A girl came through the back door and walked over to Angel. She said something to Angel, who motioned toward the receptionist. The girl, dressed in a suede fringed vest and fringed miniskirt, walked over to the receptionist, leaned over her desk, and said, "Maya, I wanted to know—" She caught sight of Sheila out of the corner of her eye. She stood up and stared at Sheila, trying to place her, and when she did, and a smile spread across her face, Sheila gave her a little shake of her head and went back to reading *Vogue*. Lucrezia said nothing and leaned back over Maya's desk. "So, anyway," Lucrezia said, "I wanted to know—"

Ten minutes later, Angel walked back to Sheila and said, "I'm ready for you now, Mrs. Weinstein."

Sheila stood up, "It's Sheila, please," and followed Angel to her chair, Sheila sat in the chair, crossing her long tanned legs as Angel draped a smock around her and snapped it at Sheila's throat, her hand brushing Sheila's neck for an instant.

"And what will it be today, Sheila?" staring at Sheila's and her reflections in the mirror.

Sheila smiled at Angel's reflection. "Just a trim."

"It's already quite short," Angel said. "Very butch. It looks good on you."

Sheila laughed and fluttered her fingers. "After the divorce," she said, "I'm feeling a little butch, you know what I mean?"

"Absolutely." Angel ran her fingers through Sheila's short hair at the nape of her neck. "You can never be too butch, Sheila.."

"I've heard."

Angel began to trim Sheila's hair, taking her time, resting her free hand lightly on the base of Sheila's neck, her hand just resting there for a moment, and then massaging Sheila's neck gently.

Sheila's eyes fluttered shut for a moment than opened, half-lidded.

"So, you're divorced," Angel said. "How long?"

"Months. It was very ugly. He left me with barely anything, just the condo, the car, some furniture, oh, and the jewelry, too." She laughed. "I would have fought to the death for the jewelry."

"I hear you, honey."

"It wasn't that I wanted it that badly. I was just determined he wasn't going to get it so he could pass it on to the next bimbo."

Angel shook her head in despair. "It makes you want to swear off men forever, doesn't it?"

Sheila turned her head to look at Angel. "Tell me about it, Angel. Makes me furious." She turned back toward the mirror as Angel trimmed her hair. "I suppose I'll have to get a job now," Sheila said. "At my age."

Angel leaned over Sheila's shoulder, pressing her cheek against

Sheila's cheek, both of them staring at their joined reflections in the mirror. "Honey, you look fabulous for your age." Her eyes glanced down at Sheila's huge breasts outlined by the smock. "Absolutely fabulous." When Angel looked up, she saw Sheila's eyes on her in the mirror.

"They're real, you know," she said with a thin smile. "Just lucky, I guess, one of those thin women who were born with big breasts."

Angel turned sideways to the mirror and smiled at her own small breasts. "I wouldn't know," she said.

"Oh, they're adorable," Sheila said, flapping a limp hand at the mirror. "I'll bet they're so perky. Mine, well, they're starting to droop. I can't do anything about it. I suppose I could have some work done, but now, without his money. . . ." She shrugged. "The best I can do is work out to keep the rest of me in shape."

Angel went back to cutting her hair. "It certainly shows, Sheila." She reached out her free hand and squeezed Sheila's biceps gently. "Very firm," Angel said.

Sheila extended one of her long tanned legs and tensed it so that the muscles in her calf and thigh flared out. "It does show, doesn't it?" She recrossed her legs. "The son of a bitch didn't know what he had."

"I'm sure he knows what he'd lost now."

"I hope so."

"So," Angel said, "what do you think you'll do—for work, I mean?"

"I haven't a clue. I haven't worked in ages." She smiled at Angel's reflection. "I haven't had to. Oh, I suppose I have in a way. I found out very early in life what I was good at, and I stuck to it."

"I know what you mean. So many women don't accept what they are. They're always trying to be something else to please a man. It's such a waste."

"That's what I was good at, Angel," Sheila said. "Pleasing men." She sighed. "Now, I guess I'm going to have to find out if I have any other talents."

Angel stopped cutting and rested both her hands on Sheila's shoulders. She stared at Sheila's reflection until their eyes met, then said, "Maybe not, Sheila. As long as you have a talent, why give it up for something you're not good at?"

Sheila laughed. "You mean, like cooking? Wouldn't that be a gas? Maybe I can get a job at The Floridian making omelets and pancakes for the gay boys on Sunday morning?"

"But that would be such a waste of your talent, wouldn't it?"

"I suppose so. But until something comes along—some*one* comes along, I mean . . . well, I'll just have to . . ."

"It doesn't always have to be some *one*, Sheila. There are a lot of men out there."

"Oh, I never had any trouble meeting men," Sheila said. She laughed. "Sometimes I think I've met them all. But . . . it's weeding them out to find the right one that takes time. And an awful lot of energy, too, all those boring dates with a fixed smile on your face while you listen to some guy drone on and on." She pursed her lips and shook her head. "I tell you, Angel, you have to kiss an awful lot of frogs."

"I'm sure. But that's not exactly what I meant."

Sheila stared at Angel's reflection. "But . . . you said—"

"I said there are a lot of men out there. What I meant was, there are a lot of men who would love to have your company." She stopped cutting Sheila's hair and stared at Sheila's reflection with her small black eyes. "Who would probably pay for it— your company, that is." Angel smiled. "As long as you have to kiss a frog, Sheila, it might as well be worth your while."

Sheila stared at Angel's reflection as if a thought was slowly, painstakingly making its way across her brow. And then her eyes opened wide, and she gasped, "You mean—Angel, that's outrageous! I could never . . . I mean, I've fantasized about it, sure, I'll bet most women have, but . . . at my age . . . and besides, I wouldn't even know how to go about it . . . I mean, do you just *ask* for the money? I never had to ask for it before. Men just liked giving it to me, you know, to buy things." She shook her head, and flapped a limp hand at the mirror. "It's ridiculous! I don' t even know if I could actually *do* it—for money, I mean. A fantasy is one thing, but when it becomes a reality it kinda ruins it, don't you think?"

Angel shrugged, and went back to cutting Sheila's hair. "I don't know. Maybe when your fantasies are fulfilled, they become even more fun than you could ever have imagined. Didn't that ever happen to you?"

Sheila laughed. "Oh, boy, did it! I was eighteen, a convent-school girl in Connecticut. The nuns taught us to be terrified of sex, which only made us girls fantasize even more about it. And then when it happened to me for the first time, he was a Harvard senior and I was a Boston University freshman, it hurt so much at first I was just about to push him off me, when, Bam! it happened. It was like a thousand firecrackers going off in my body, one after another, never stopping. I thought I'd faint. Then it finally stopped. I thought, Wow! this is better than anything I could ever have fantasized about."

Angel laughed. "See what I mean?"

Sheila looked in the mirror as if the reflection she now saw was that of herself as an eighteen-year-old freshman. She said, "Actually, once I fulfilled that fantasy, it became addictive. I couldn't get enough." She laughed. "I wore that poor Harvard senior out and then I wore out his friends, too. I figured, what the hell, Madame de Volanges was right. You know, in *Dangerous Liaisons*. As long as it was so much fun why not do it as often as I could in as many different ways as I could." Then, as she stared at the mirror, the eighteen-year-old girl began to fade, recede and she saw, instead, the woman she was now, staring back at her. "But I was a girl then, and they were always boys I knew, handsome boys, and it was just for fun. None of us had any money. The money—that would make it so . . . so . . . tawdry. . . ."

"That's what would make it so exciting, don't you think? The money. The power."

"The power?"

"Of course. That's the only thing men understand. When they turn over money to you, it's acknowledging you have the power."

Sheila thought a moment, then said, "Yes. I never thought of it that way."

"And the excitement, too. Always a different man. The thrill of the unknown. I don't know, Sheila, but I think it might be a real turn-on . . . for some women, anyway."

"I don't know if I'm that kind of woman, though." She shook her head emphatically. "Some fat, hairy, smelly man all over me. I think I'd throw up."

"It doesn't have to be that way. You'd be surprised at the kind of men you'd meet. Rich, successful, handsome. They just don't want the bother of dating, all those phony rituals."

Sheila smiled at Angel's reflection in the mirror. "You mean, like Richard Gere? Now, if they were all like him. . . ." She sighed again. "But I'm no Julia Roberts, Angel. I'm a divorcée in my forties. I know I look pretty good for my age, but most men want young girls."

"Not always," Angel said. She stepped back from Sheila and studied her face in the mirror. "Did anyone ever tell you you look just like Jane Fonda, only younger?"

"As a matter of fact—"

"Wait just a minute," Angel said. Sheila watched Angel walk over to the coffee table by the receptionist's desk. She searched through a stack of magazines, picked one, and brought it back to Sheila. She flipped through the pages until she came to a full-page ad and showed it to Sheila.

"Celebrity Dream Dates Escort Service?" Sheila said.

"A little business of mine," Angel said.

Sheila turned in her chair and looked up at Angel. "You're kidding. You're a—a—"

Angel smiled. "Businesswoman, Sheila. It's just a business. I supply a service to people who have a need. My girls are very beautiful, very classy, and *very* expensive. And of course, I screen all my clients."

"Oh, Angel! I could never! I mean, these girls they must be—"

"They *are* very young. I have girls who look like Julia Roberts, Claudia Schiffer, even Meg Ryan, although she doesn't get many calls these days."

"See! They *are* all young, except for Meg Ryan—what is she, in her forties, but she's still cute."

"Yes. But that's not only what my clients are looking for. I sell fantasy, Sheila. Occasionally I get calls for more mature women, women who look like Susan Sarandon and Ann-Margaret and"— she smiled at Sheila's reflection—"Jane Fonda. It might just be occasional work, Sheila, pin money until something better . . . some*one* better, comes along."

Sheila's brows furrowed. "I don't know, Angel. I—" Then her face brightened. "Oh, fuck it! Maybe I could. What the hell! I've been doing it for years in a way, getting paid for it. Why should this be any different?" Then, suddenly, Sheila looked worried. She turned in her chair to face Angel and put her hand on Angel's arm. She said, "Do you really think I can do it?"

Angel smiled at her and put her hand on top of Sheila's. "Without a doubt, baby."

• • •

That night in bed, Sheila turned to Bobby and said, "She wants to meet me tomorrow night at her penthouse condo on the Galt Ocean Mile. To discuss the details, she said. Jesus! She couldn't keep her hands off me, the dyke."

"I don't like it," Bobby said.

Sheila turned her whole body toward Bobby. "Why, Robert! You're jealous!"

"Yeah, I'm jealous. But I still don't like it."

"Oh, Bobby, what could go wrong? She's going to come on to me, I'll flirt with her a little, then coyly push her away, tell her 'I'm really interested, Angel, but . . . I don't know . . . I don't think I'm ready yet . . . so soon after the divorce . . . I've never done it before . . . with a woman . . . but I've fantasized about it—being with a woman, I mean.'" Sheila looked into Bobby's eyes. "'A woman like you, Angel.'"

"Jesus! Cut it out! You're so fuckin' believable."

"I'm an actress, Bobby, remember? I'm *supposed* to be believable."

"I still don't like it."

"Oh, for Christ's sake, she's a skinny homely dyke!"

"I'll drive you, wait downstairs, something goes wrong . . . ."

"What could go wrong? We have a few drinks, get the seduction bit out of the way so it doesn't piss her off, then we talk some business and we're in." He didn't say anything. "Bobby, what if she sees you? I told her there's no man in my life. That's the fucking point. I've got to do this on my own. Don't worry, I can handle it."

"That's how we got fucked up last time, baby, you don't remember."

"I remember. But this is different. I learned my lesson. No cowboy shit this time. Besides, she's no spic gangster. She's a fucking dyke hairdresser who's got the hots for me. She doesn't want to kill me, Bobby. She wants to fuck me."

"What about Lucrezia? She recognized you, she could tell the dyke...."

"You tell me, Bobby. You know Lucrezia better than I do."

Bobby was quiet for a moment. "She'll keep her mouth shut. She's a good broad."

"See? There's nothing to worry about. Don't even wait up for me. If I'm late, it's because I'm taking care of business." Sheila smiled at him and added in a husky voice, "Or because Angel's turned me on."

At nine o'clock the next evening, Sheila parked the black '89 Ford Taurus SHO Sol had bought for Bobby in a guest parking space in front of the Embassy Towers condominiums on the Galt Ocean Mile. Sol had insisted Bobby get a decent car, "a fuckin' Cadillac, at least, show a little class. The money'll come outta your end anyway."

Bobby said, "An '89 SHO, Sol. Black. I find something I like, I stick with it."

"At least thinka Sheila," Sol said. "Shiftin' that five-speed alla time will wear her out."

"Actually, Sol," Sheila said. "It's good exercise for my arms and legs now that I'm an old broad."

So Sol had found him one, mint, with only 69,000 miles on the odometer and four 18-inch, BBS mag wheels, and a Fiberglas bubble hood.

Sheila checked her makeup in the rearview mirror, then got out of the car. Sol was right, she thought, as she walked toward the lighted entrance on a warm, windy night, the wind blowing hard off the ocean only a few yards away, bending the palm trees almost half over. It was a pain in the ass to shift, especially in six-inch-high Manolo Blahniks. It was a ridiculous car for Mrs. Sheila Weinstein to be driving. A hot rod that could do 150 on Alligator Alley. Which was the point. It was the perfect car for Bobby Squared and Sheila Ryan, a.k.a. Sheila Doyle, a.k.a. Mrs. Sheila Weinstein.

She went to the guard at his desk in the lobby and waited until he looked up at her. He was a short, fat, bald man in his sixties, with a drinker's splotchy-red face.

"Can I help you, ma'am?" he finally said, his eyes fixed on her breasts bubbling out of her black latex wet-look minidress that was so tight she had to wiggle into it. It was the dress she wore the night she shot Medina in a darkened restaurant in Miami Beach. My seduction dress, she thought.

"Yes. Tell Angel Scott that Mrs. Weinstein is here."

9

Angela Scarpetti, a.k.a. Angel Scott, a.k.a. The White Witch, sat on the black leather sofa in her penthouse condominium living room on the twentieth floor, smoking a cigarette, and sipped champagne from a fluted glass. A bottle of Cristal was chilling in a silver ice bucket on her black lacquered oriental coffee table alongside a cut-glass crystal platter filled with beluga caviar, bits of onion and hard-boiled eggs, and, alongside that, a platter of toast slivers. The room was vast and sparsely furnished. A black leather love seat across from her. A black lacquered Yamaha piano against one wall. A glass and chrome bookshelf against the opposite wall. There were a few photos in black frames on the bookshelf. Angel posing cheek-to-cheek with various women and girls, the women and girls smiling, oblivious, at the camera; Angel smiling, too, a thin, hard smile, her eyes shifted slightly toward the beautiful face up against her face.

The walls and the tile floor were white. The brightly lighted kitchen at the far end of the room, behind Angel, was all gleaming white cabinets and walls, with a black marble countertop and a black porcelain sink and a huge black Vulcan stove.

Angel took a drag of her cigarette, exhaled smoke, and crossed her legs. She was wearing a man's black silk shirt tied under her small breasts so that it exposed the gold hoop ring in her navel and her slim, hipless waist in black flared hip-hugger pants. She wore black silk ankle stockings and a pair of black low-heeled pumps with a little flap in front like the shoes women wore during the Salem witch trials.

Angel sipped her champagne and waited for Sheila, who was rising slowly up to her now in the elevator, being delivered to her like a pretty basket of ripe fruit. Angel liked these quiet moments before a seduction. She liked to envision it all happening, the little stratagems, the right words, the husky inflection of her voice, the light touch of her hand on an arm, the brush of her lips across the back of a neck. Sheila was like most of the women she had seduced. Beautiful and clueless and most importantly, straight. It was the corruption even more than the sex that gave Angel the most pleasure. It always had, from the very first, when she was Angela Scarpetti back in Levittown, Long Island.

She was a skinny, bony, homely, dark-haired guinea then, with dark hair above her lip and under her arms. The other girls all seemed so impossibly pale and beautiful to Angela then, and she seemed so grotesque to them. They laughed at her. She was so flat-chested at sixteen that she wore a camisole, while the other girls had been wearing bras since they were thirteen. They got their period, too, at thirteen, and chattered so excitedly about it, while she didn't get her period until she was sixteen, and hated every minute of it: the bloody mess, the sickeningly, sweet, putrid smell that reminded her of her sex.

She remembered the morning she got off the school bus for class. She was sixteen, a sophomore in high school. A clique of pretty girls, the ones who wore lipstick and makeup and tight sweaters, came up to her excitedly. They were the same girls who never spoke to her except to make some nasty comment when she passed by in the hall. She felt her heart skip a beat, her breath catch, and she was suffused with anticipation and happiness at the thought that maybe now it was her time. The girls fluttered around her, giggling, and one of them said, "Angela! Angela! Do you know the facts of life?"

She was so excited by their attention that she didn't think straight. She said, "Oh, no! Do we have to know them for class?" The girls laughed at her, and left her standing there, red-faced.

She knew the facts of life now. She had learned them quickly after that humiliation, and by the middle of her junior year she was ready to put those facts to use in a way she would do for the rest of her life. She picked a girl—a sweet, beautiful, clueless girl who had felt sorry for Angela because of the way the other girls treated her. "Don't mind them, Angela," the girl told her once. "They're jealous because you're smart and they're dumb." Angela accepted the girl's pity, even as she hated it.

Her name was Honey. She had creamy pink skin and a soft voluptuous body that would turn to fat when she got married and had children, but then, at seventeen, was still all lush curves. Her long blond hair was like silk and her eyes pale green and innocent. Honey and her football-star boyfriend had been elected Homecoming King and Queen in late fall. But her grades were poor, and she wouldn't be allowed to assume her crown unless she improved them. Angela offered to help her. She invited her to her home for a sleepover to study for Honey's tests.

They sprawled on Angela's bed in their nighties with Honey's books spread out on the covers, their heads close together, Honey's pale green eyes so naïvely intent on those books while Angela's eyes roamed over Honey's voluptuous body and she smelled her deliriously sweet smell and felt Honey's silken hair against her cheek.

Angela brushed her lips against Honey's neck. She felt Honey stiffen, and then the stiffening dissolved as Angela continued to caress Honey's neck with her thin lips and Honey turned her face toward Angela's face, her eyes opened wide, trusting, and then they closed and she offered her lush lips to Angela, who seduced her that night, so easily, so completely, so passionately, that Honey would drop her boyfriend and her Homecoming Queen crown and became obsessed with Angela. Angela fed that obsession, at first, pressing close against Honey at her locker in the hallway when the other girls walked by and stared in shock.

Finally, the other girls dropped Honey from their clique. "I don't care," Honey told her, "as long as I have you."

And now Angela began to torture her, to play her off. "I can't see you tonight, Honey, I have to study," and to ignore her in school until Honey became crazed with desire. That's when Angela dropped her, even though she still wanted her. It was a good discipline, begun then, when she was seventeen, to learn to cut out of your life the things you wanted most.

Shortly after that, Angela dyed her hair a silvery gold and the other girls began to call her "The White Witch." They no longer laughed at her now. They turned away from her gaze when she walked by them in the hall. They were afraid. That was even better than having the thing you wanted most in this world, Angel thought, as she heard the buzzer to her condominium door ring. She stubbed out her cigarette, put down her fluted glass, and walked across the white-and-black living room to the door.

Sheila sat on the black love seat. Angel sat on the black sofa across from her. Sheila fidgeted with her hands while Angel poured champagne into a fluted glass. She handed it across the coffee table to Sheila. Angel raised her own glass.

"To your new business venture," Angel said. They touched glasses over the coffee table and sipped their champagne.

"Actually, I'm a bit nervous about it," Sheila said.

"Don't be. You'll be fine." Angel's eyes moved down over Sheila's body in her tight wet-look minidress. She grinned. "They'll just love you in that dress."

Sheila looked down at herself, and then up at Angel. "I hope so. I thought you might like to see how I look . . . dressed for action, so to speak."

"I was hoping to."

Angel spread some caviar, bits of onion, and hard-boiled egg on toast and handed it to Sheila. Sheila peeled back her lips, painted a dark red, exposing her white teeth, and took a bite.

"Mmmm! Delicious!" Sheila said. "I love caviar."

"You better get used to it."

"I'll bet I could." Sheila put the rest of the caviar into her mouth and settled back in the love seat. She crossed her legs and looked around the apartment. "It's soooo beautiful," Sheila said. "I love the stark contrast between black and white, and the way you've decorated it—so minimalist."

"I like to keep things simple," Angel said. "Black-and-white. You can't go wrong." Sheila sipped the rest of her champagne and Angel reached across with the bottle and poured her another glass.

Sheila giggled. "I better not drink too much. Champagne makes me giddy. I want to be clear about my new . . . job—the details, I mean."

"We have plenty of time for that. Let me show you around first."

Sheila put her glass down on the coffee table and stood up. Angel poured more champagne into Sheila's glass and her own, then stood up with her glass. "Take your glass," she said. "We'll just sip our way through the grand tour."

"You're the boss." Sheila picked up her glass. "You know, I never worked for a woman before."

"Well then, it'll be a new experience, won't it?"

They walked over to the piano. Sheila ran her fingers along the smooth, cold sides of the piano. "It's beautiful," she said. "Do you play?"

"Not really. I never had time to learn. When I have parties, I usually hire someone to play. You'll have to come one night. I have some wonderful parties."

"I'd like that."

Angel walked across the room to the bookshelf. Sheila followed her. "These are some of my regular guests at those parties," Angel said. Sheila stared at the photographs in chrome frames.

"They're all so beautiful," Sheila said.

"I like beautiful things."

"I can see that." Sheila sipped her champagne. "Don't you have any men, though? I mean, at your parties."

"We try not to mix business with pleasure. These girls all work for me, and on their night off they really don't want to deal with any men."

"I guess I can understand that."

"You will after a while. It's liberating being with your own sex. You can let your hair down, speak the same language."

Sheila sipped more champagne and shook her head. "I wouldn't know, Angel. I spent most of my life with men. But you're right. It's starting to be boring."

Angel put her hand under Sheila's elbow and guided her toward the kitchen. Sheila stopped at the edge of the kitchen and took it all in.

"God!" Sheila said. "I don't even know where to begin with all these appliances. Meyer, my last husband, Meyer Weinstein, he used to—"

"How many have you had?"

"Husbands? Three. All lawyers, whatever that means." She laughed.

"None of them married me for my cooking. Look at that stove! It's like a work of art! A big, sinister, work of art. I'll bet you could cook a whole cow in it."

Angel laughed. "I could, I guess, but I never tried."

Sheila turned to look at her. "Do you really use all this stuff?"

"Yes. I'm a gourmet cook. A habit from eating alone all these years."

"I'll bet you don't have to eat alone that much, Angel."

"More than I like to."

"Haven't you ever found someone . . . that you wanted to live with?"

"Not yet. But I haven't given up the search."

"God, I hate living alone. As bad as my marriages were, the worst part of them was, those first few weeks living alone after the divorce." She shook her head. "I guess I'm the kind of woman who always has to be taken care of by someone." She looked at Angel. "That's pitiful, isn't it?"

"It depends on who's taking care of you."

"Yes. I guess it does."

Angel started walking down a long hallway. Sheila, sipping her champagne, followed her. Angel stopped at an open door and stepped back to let Sheila look inside.

"Oh, it's gorgeous!" Sheila said. She stared at the black walls and the ornate, black wrought-iron bed with white satin sheets and black pillows, and on the wall behind the headboard, a large oil painting of a nude woman lying on that bed. It took Sheila a moment to realize the nude was Angel—only an idealized Angel, with more delicate features, a more voluptuous body, smoother skin, but still Angel, with that hard, thin, lascivious smile.

"You look fabulous," Sheila said. "What a body!"

Angel moved close behind her and slipped her arm around Sheila's waist and pressed her face close to Sheila's. "Not like yours, though," Angel said.

Sheila sighed. "Yes, my body. Sometimes I think it's all I've got going for me." She turned around to face Angel, their faces close together. Sheila raised her glass between them and sipped. Finally, Angel stepped back and let her by. Sheila walked back down the hallway to the living room. She put her empty glass on the coffee table.

"Now for the pièce de résistance," Angel said.

"The what?"

Angel smiled at her. "The reason I bought this apartment." She walked to the far end of the living room and opened a pair of sliding glass doors. A warm breeze blew into the room. "Come and see," she said.

Sheila walked over to the glass doors and stepped outside onto the twentieth-floor deck that looked out over the ocean and the sky on a windy, gray-blue night. She saw the lights from passing ships far off in the distance on the ocean and, above, a handful of stars tossed into the night.

"I see what you mean," Sheila said. "It's breathtaking." A strong wind blew her back slightly and she felt her body pressed against Angel's body behind her. Angel slipped both arms around Sheila's waist and put her face in the curve of Sheila's neck. They both stared out at the ocean and the sky for a long moment. Sheila felt Angel's lips brushing against her neck and she closed her eyes. Angel moved her hands up Sheila's dress and cupped them over her huge breasts. She waited for a moment and then she began to rub the flat of her palms in circular motions over Sheila's breasts until she felt her nipples harden. Sheila moaned, "Ohhhh!" Angel hooked her thumbs over the top of Sheila's low-cut dress and pulled it down so that Sheila's huge, slightly pendulous breasts were exposed. Then she continued massaging her nipples.

"Oh, God!" Sheila moaned again. "That feels so good." Angel buried her face in Sheila's neck, smelling her smell, and kissed her neck. She reached up with one hand and turned Sheila's face sideways and kissed her lips. Sheila turned her face away and felt Angel's hands now firmly on her hips, turning Sheila's body around until they faced each other. Angel's hands slipped down to Sheila's ass, her fingers spread, and she pulled Sheila's ass toward her until their crotches were pressing against each other. Then she pressed her mouth hard against Sheila's until Sheila opened her mouth and their tongues touched for just an instant before Sheila pulled her head back.

"Jesus!" Sheila said, breathlessly. "You're making me so hot!"

"That's the point, isn't it?" Angel said.

"I never thought—I mean—a woman . . . I'd always assumed it would always be a man." She looked into Angel's eyes. "You make me hotter than any man I ever . . ."

Angel moved her face toward Sheila's to kiss her again, but Sheila pulled her head away. "I can't," Sheila said. "I mean, I want to . . . God, do I—" She threw her arms around Angel and hugged her tightly. Then she pulled back, her hands on Angel's shoulders. "Please don't be upset," Sheila said. "I just need some time. . . ."

"Are you sure?"

"Yes. No. Oh, Christ, I don't know. If you could just wait until I get used to it, the idea of it. I never felt this way before, Angel. It's so new to me. Please."

Angel stepped back from her. "If that's the way you want it."

"It is and it isn't. I wish I could just let myself go. I spent so many years holding back, you know, doing it with my body and not my mind. But this . . ."

"I'll wait, then. But don't take too long."

Sheila smiled at her. "I know I won't." Then she leaned toward her and kissed her on the cheek. "Oh, Angel, you're so understanding," Sheila said, and as she did she pulled her dress back up over her breasts.

Angel turned and went back into the living room. Sheila followed her. Angel picked up the bottle of champagne and shook it. "Empty," she said. "Let me get another." Sheila sat down on the love seat while Angel took the empty bottle and the two glasses into the kitchen. She was in there for a moment when Sheila heard the pop of a cork. A few moments later, Angel returned with two glasses of champagne. She handed one to Sheila and sat down on the sofa.

Angel held her glass over the coffee table. "Back to business, then." They touched glasses and sipped their champagne.

Sheila tilted her head slightly. "This tastes different," she said.

"It's a different year," Angel said. "It's a more complex vintage. I think you'll like it even better." She tipped her head back and drained her glass. "Try it."

Sheila tipped her head back and drained her glass. "Mmmm, you're right," she said.

"Now," Angel said, "I'll bet you have a million questions."

"I do. But I don't know where to begin. Why don't you just tell me what you expect?"

Angel began to talk, telling her how she screened her clients, how Barry, the limo driver, would always be there for her in case of an emergency. "You don't have to do anything you don't want to do," Angel's voice said. "Barry will see to that. He's quite effective in his way." Sheila was having trouble concentrating on Angel's voice, which seemed to be moving away from her. "The minimum price for a date is $3500," Angel's voice was saying. "You can negotiate more if you can, depending on what the client wants and what you want to do."

The room began to spin before Sheila's eyes, the black piano whirling around and around, and Sheila concentrated hard to make the room stop spinning and to hear Angel's voice which had a slight echo now. "The day after your date, you bring the cash to my office at the back of the salon at closing time. And Sheila, you must come alone. No one gets into my back office except my girls, Lucrezia, my associate, and Barry. Do you understand?" Sheila nodded her head that felt filled with lead. She felt a tingling sensation, a slight numbness in her arms and legs.

"Good," said Angel's voice. "Then I'll give you your cut and take mine. I usually get forty percent." Sheila saw Angel's face smiling at her, and then another face smiling at her, and still another, the faces weaving before her eyes. "But in your case, I'll reduce that to thirty percent. Oh, and one other thing. You should call me at least every other day to see if I have a date for you. I will never call you—do you understand?"

Sheila heard her slurred voice say, "I undershtand, Angel." She reached out her hand in slow motion to put her glass on the table but the glass slipped out of her numb fingers and shattered, on the tile floor. "Oh, I'm sho shorry," Sheila heard her voice say. She tried to stand up, tottering on her high heels, and had to put her hand on the arm of the love seat to keep from falling. Her arms and legs felt filled with lead. She heard her slurred voice say, "I should be going. . . ."

And then she heard Angel's voice echoing from down a long corridor, "I don't think you're in any condition to drive, baby." She felt Angel's arm around her waist, holding her up, leading her down a long corridor, Sheila's legs buckling, Angel's arms pulling her up until she got her into the bedroom. Sheila tried to say something, but she couldn't move her lips. And then Angel was laying her down on her back on the white satin sheets. Sheila tried to push herself up, but her whole body was numb now and she couldn't move. Still, she was conscious of what was now happening to her but she was powerless to stop it. It was as if she was outside herself, floating above herself, watching Angel unbutton her shirt and take it off, revealing her tiny breasts the size of lemons, and then slipping out of her pants and her panties. Angel was sitting on the edge of the bed now, kicking off her shoes and then peeling off her stockings. Sheila heard Angel's voice saying, "This is the way you wanted it, baby. It makes no difference to me."

Angel kneeled on the bed, over Sheila and began peeling off Sheila's tight dress, and, then her thong panties. "I think I'll leave the spike heels," Angel's voice said. She was smiling. She bent down over Sheila and began sucking Sheila's nipples, Sheila feeling it, the pleasurable sensation, and then the pain as Angel bit her nipple so hard Sheila tried to cry out but no sound came out of her.

Finally, the pain stopped and Angel got off the bed. She went over to a closet, reached in and pulled something out. She came back to the bed and spread her legs as if putting on panties, but it wasn't underwear, it was something attached to leather straps. Angel pulled the leather straps, tightening them at her waist so that the gigantic dildo between her legs stuck straight out from her thick black pussy hair.

"I'm sure you're used to this," Angel said. "Maybe not one so big. Let's see if you can take it, baby."

Angel got back on the bed, kneeling, and with her knees she roughly spread Sheila's legs apart. Then holding the gigantic dildo with one hand she inserted it slowly into Sheila's cunt until it was half in. Sheila felt the pain of the dildo splitting her apart, and then Angel rammed it hard all the way into her and the searing white-hot pain shot up to Sheila's stomach and her eyes began to water. But still she could not move. Angel began thrusting with her hips now, the dildo tearing into and out of Sheila, Angel's face grimacing as she worked, thrusting harder and harder, faster and faster until Sheila's eyes rolled back and she saw above her head the nude painting of Angel grinning down on her before she passed out.

Hours later, Sheila woke alone on the bed with the sunlight slanting in through the windows blinding her. Her head throbbed and there was a terrible pain between her legs. She tried to sit up. The room spun around her and she fell back on the bed. She lay there for a moment, forcing herself back to consciousness, and then, by a sheer act of will, she pushed herself up and sat on the edge of the bed. There was blood caked to the inside of her thighs and behind her on the white sheets. She forced herself to breathe evenly and then she got up, wobbly at first, picked up her clothes, struggled into her dress, and tried to walk out of the bedroom. She almost fell on her spiked heels. She leaned against the wall with one hand and took off each shoe with the other hand. Then she left the room, walked unsteadily down the hallway, listing first against one wall, then the other until she was in the living room, steadier now. She went to the front door. There was a note taped to the door. "Sheila, baby, you were great. Your dates won't be disappointed. Love, A." Sheila ripped the note off the door and crumpled it in her fist.

Bobby stood in the bedroom doorway of their apartment and looked down at Sheila. She was lying under the covers on her side, her knees pulled up to her chest, her blue eyes staring.

"You all right, baby?" he said.

"No," she said, in a weak voice he'd never heard from her before. "I'm not all, right, Bobby. That cunt hurt me."

"I told ya, baby, not to be so sure of yourself."

She turned her face away from Bobby. "She raped me, Bobby. She slipped me a Roofie and when I was paralyzed, she fucked me with . . ." She closed her eyes to blot out the image before them.

"Do you want me to take you to a doctor?"

"No, I won't give her the satisfaction."

Bobby shook his head. "Jesus, Sheila!"

"I said, no."

"Maybe we should call it off. . . ."

Sheila opened her eyes and turned her face toward Bobby. "Not this one, Bobby. That fucking cunt has no idea—" She turned over in bed, wincing with pain, until she was lying on her back. Then she said, "Did Sol make the call?"

"He made it."

"Did you tell him what to ask for?"

"I told him."

"Then I'd better call her." She tried to push herself up to a sitting position, but the pain stopped her. Bobby came over to her and tried to help her up. She flung her arm at his hand. "I don't need any help!"

Bobby stood over her. "You don't have to do this, baby. So soon after . . ." He bit his lip, then said, "You can wait a few days until you're healed."

She looked at him with her cold blue eyes and said, "This is going down as soon as possible so I never have to see that cunt again." She reached for the telephone beside the bed and dialed a number.

"Hello. This is Sheila for Angel." After a moment, Sheila's face assumed a dreamy smile. "It's me," she said in a husky voice. She listened for a moment, then said, "No, I'm fine. It was just so . . . so . . . intense! I'll never forget it, Angel. I just wish I hadn't drunk all that champagne so I could have"— Sheila giggled and Bobby stared at her—"you know, contributed more." She listened. "I know. Me, too. I can't wait for the next time." She listened again and her face brightened. "So soon? My first date." She nodded. "I understand . . . uh-huh . . . Mr. Rogers? Like on TV?" She nodded again. "Of course they don't use their real names. I shouldn't either?" She was quiet a moment, as if thinking. Then she said, "How about Doyle? Sheila Doyle?" She smiled. "I'm glad you like it." She listened a moment longer, her face assuming a dreamy smile again, and then she said softly into the phone, "Me, too, baby," and hung up.

Sheila sat there in bed, staring in front of her through glazed eyes. Then she gave her head a little shake to clear it, and looked up at Bobby. "Tomorrow night," she said.

Part Four

10

BARRY THE BEAR PULLED THE HUMMER LIMO UP ALONGSIDE THE APARTMENT complex on Bayview and parked. He beeped. the horn and waited. It was early, 9:00 P.M. He lighted a cigarette and tried to remember what Angel had told him.

"This is a new chick," Angel said. "Older, but she could be a good earner. Make sure you take good care of her, Barry."

Barry knew what that meant. She was one of Angel's girls, a shiksa dyke liked to eat pussy more than suck cock. Jesus, Barry thought, broads were disgusting, the things they could convince themselves to do they didn't even like. And you could never tell, the way broads were, whether they were fakin' it or not. He seen enougha that in the backseat of the limo, broads fakin' how much they loved kneelin' on the floor with some asshole's dick in their mouth like they couldn't get enough. Barry smiled to himself. Now, that little nigger, he liked it. Barry reminded himself to see him again. Angel said he worked out good, kept his mouth shut, cleaned up, until she found a chair for him. "He's a very talented cutter," Angel told Barry. "You did good, Barry." It made up a little bit for that mess in the swamp, the bullet holes in the upholstery Barry was afraid Angel was gonna make him pay for. "Next time, I *will* make you pay," Angel said. Which is why he'd better be careful with this new broad, Angel's new squeeze, not piss her off so she goes and tells Angel.

Barry saw the broad coming toward him in the darkness, walking down a narrow path between overhanging areca palms. When she passed the spotlight over the swimming pool, he could make her out, her short blond hair like a dyke, her dress looked like spray paint, her high heels. She didn't look so old, Barry thought as he got out of the limo, tossed his cigarette, and went around to the back door. When she got closer Barry could see she was older but he couldn't tell how old; she took care of herself.

She stopped in front of him and smiled. "You must be Barry," she said, and held out her hand. "I'm Sheila." Barry looked at her, smiling at him, and then her hand, and he shook it. He opened the door for her. "Why, thank you, Barry," she said, and slid into the backseat. Barry shut the door and went around to the driver's side, thinkin' she wasn't like the others, and then thinkin' what an asshole he was, she was a fuckin' dyke hooker, what made her any different?

Barry drove south on Bayview and stopped at the light at Sunrise. The broad said, "So, where are we picking up Mr . . . Rogers, Barry?"

He looked in the rearview mirror at her. Jesus, she was still smilin' at him. "The Harbor Beach, ma'am."

She faked a frown. "I told you it's Sheila, Barry. All right?"

"Whatever you say . . . Sheila."

"The Harbor Beach," she said. "That's nice."

When the light changed, Barry turned left toward the Sunrise Bridge, passed over it, came to A1A, turned south and drove along the beach. The broad was looking out the window at the ocean, the surf a little rough tonight, and then she turned her head and looked out the other window at the people across the street from the beach, eating at outdoor tables on the sidewalk.

"It's a lovely night, isn't it, Barry?"

What the fuck'd she expect him to say? Broads use words like "lovely" to throw you off. "Yes, ma'am."

"Barry," she said like she was a schoolteacher. "What did I tell you?"

"Yes, Sheila."

"Good boy."

Barry parked in front of the brightly lighted entrance to the Harbor Beach Hotel with the assholes in the red military coats standin' out front opening car doors, bowin', helpin' the broads outta the cars, holdin' their hands. Barry got out and went around to her door and opened it.

"I should only be a minute," she said.

She disappeared into the hotel. Barry stood by the limo and lighted another cigarette. After only a few puffs he saw the broad coming back toward him arm-in-arm with a short, fat, bald guy with a goatee wearin' one a them fancy suits with the stripes. Barry tossed his cigarette and opened the back door. He took the broad's hand like he seen the assholes do and helped her into the limo.

"Thank you, Barry," she said, and slid over.

The fat guy didn't get in right away. He just stood there, lookin' at Barry like he was tryin' to memorize his face. The broad wasn't who she was, Barry woulda said something, but he didn't.

"Hey, Slick," the fat guy said. Barry could tell he was a Jew, too, but not Orthodox. "This the best you could do, a fuckin' tank? You think I'm plannin' to take over Iraq tonight?"

"It was the only limo available," Barry said.

"The gelt I'm payin' the least I coulda had was a Caddy or a Lincoln."

Barry wanted to punch the little bastard but he didn't. Finally the fat guy got in beside the broad, the kinda broad he could never have if he didn't pay for it. She was just like all the others after all, sellin' herself to this little *pisher*.

Barry drove them back along the beach. He looked in the rearview mirror to see what they were doin'. Nuthin'?

"Hey, Slick," the fat guy said. "Keep your eyes on the fuckin' road and buzz up that window." Barry buzzed up the window that separated the front seat from the back.

Sol leaned toward Sheila and said, "You all right, baby? Bobby told me the dyke hurt ya."

"Yeah, she hurt me, Sol. Put me out of action for a few days." She smiled at Sol and stroked his cheek with her hand. "Poor baby. Four grand and you aren't getting a thing for it."

"Like I expected to, huh?" Sol leaned forward and tapped on the window. Barry lowered it. "Just drive around, Slick. I'll tell ya where ta go later." Sol sat back. "And raise the fuckin' window. How many times I gotta tell ya?"

When the window went up, Sol leaned close to Sheila and nuzzled her neck. Sheila pulled away from him. "Sol, what the fuck you doing?"

"Baby, it's two-way glass. He can see everything we're doin' back here, or not doin'. You're suppos'ta be a hooker. Show me a good time."

Sheila sighed. "Oh, for Christ's sake!" She threw her arms around Sol and they hugged, their faces touching, Sheila kissing Sol near his lips but not on his lips, on his chin. She whispered, "A stage kiss, Solly, that's all you're getting." She felt his hand on her breast, squeezing it. "Jesus, Sol, what the fuck you doing?"

"I ain't squeezed real ones in so long, I forgot how they felt." He squeezed again and grinned. "They feel different, spongey, ya know."

"They're not grapefruit, Sol. Could you please stop or I'm going to slap that stupid grin off your face."

"What? I'm payin'. I gotta right."

Barry watched them through the two-way glass, tusslin' in the backseat, but not gettin' down to it yet. The broad was a cool one, playin' the asshole off until she was ready. He saw her pull away from the fat guy, smooth her skirt, and then lean forward and tap on the window. Barry buzzed it halfway down.

"Yes . . . Sheila?"

"We're going to try Mango's tonight, Barry. Mr. Rogers is hungry." She smiled at the guy beside her.

"Yes . . . Sheila." Barry buzzed the window back up and turned west onto Sunrise toward Federal.

"Sheila?" Sol said. "The fuckin' Jew cocksucker calls you Sheila?"

Barry parked the limo on Las Olas across the street from Mango's. It was a Friday night, a lotta traffic, people sittin' at Mango's outside tables, eatin', drinkin', laughin' like they was havin' a good time whether they were or not. He got out and opened the back door. The broad got out and then the guy.

"We'll be a couple of hours, Barry, if you want to go get something to eat yourself."

"Nah, I'll just wait in the limo . . . Sheila."

"Suit yourself." She put her arm inside the little guy's arm and they walked across the street, all the people eatin' outside starin' at the tall blonde in the painted-on dress towering over the short, fat, bald guy in the too-tight suit. Barry waited until they went inside, then he went back and sat in the driver's seat in the limo. He lighted another cigarette, slunk down in his seat, and waited.

They came out after midnight, the broad laughin', hangin' on the fat guy, leanin' her head up against his like she had too much to drink, lettin' the guy know what he was in for tonight.

Barry got out of the limo and opened the door for them. The broad got in, and then the bald guy.

Barry drove them back to the Harbor Beach, watchin' them in the rearview mirror through the two-way glass that was Angel's idea, the broad all over the guy kissin' him on the cheek runnin' her hands through his hair like he had any. When he parked in front of the hotel, the broad tapped on the window. Barry buzzed it down.

"That's all for tonight, Barry," she said. "I won't need you anymore." She smiled at the fat guy. "Mr. Rogers has been kind enough to offer me a nightcap. I'll take a taxi home."

"But Angel said—"

"I *said,* I won't need you anymore." Her voice was different than before, hard like Angel's.

"Whatever," Barry said. Fuck her. He didn't bother to get out and open the door. He watched them walkin' arm in arm half in the bag toward the entrance and disappear inside. He put the limo in drive and headed toward Dunkin' Donuts.

A few minutes after the limo left the Harbor Beach, a black '89 SHO pulled up to the entrance with two men in the front seat, a muscular man with a blond ponytail, and a slim black man with a tight orange Afro. Sheila and Sol hurried out of the hotel, looking left and right, and got into the backseat of the SHO.

Bobby turned around in his seat and said, "So, how'd it go?"

Sheila held up a fistful of hundred-dollar bills. "Sol gave me a tip," she said, grinning. "A C-note to go with the $4000."

Bobby turned around and put the SHO in gear. "Wonderful," he said and drove off.

"Why don'tcha be throwin' them C-notes at me, Sol-O-Man?" Reggie said. "I show you a better time even than Sheila."

"Fuck you," Sol said.

"I worked for it," Sheila said. "I had to let Sol feel me up. I thought I was back in fucking high school."

When they got back to Bobby's and Sheila's apartment at 2:00 A.M.,

Sheila fixed them all drinks and led them outside to the deck on the canal. They sat around a picnic table with only a small battery-powered hurricane lamp for light. Matthew trotted out with them and sat down beside Sheila.

"I had all I could do not to cap the cocksucker right in the limo," Sol said. "What he done to Candy."

"Patience, Sol-O-Man, ain't that what you told me?" Reggie said.

"We're not in the revenge business, Sol," Sheila said. "We're in this for the cash."

"You should talk, what that dyke done to you," Sol said.

"Yeah, well, I won't take it personal. It's just business."

Sol looked at her. "That don't sound like you, Sheila. You sure that dyke didn't get to you, hurt you someplace else than your moneymaker."

Sheila smiled at him. "No, Sol, she didn't scare me, if that's what you mean. It's just there's no percentage in revenge; I already learned that once." She glanced at Bobby, then back to Sol. "I'm smarter now, Sol. I only want what can help us."

"Yeah, well, she done to me what she done to you, cappin' that fuckin' dyke, help me a lot." Sol reached down the front of his shirt and pulled out his gold Star of David. He held it up for them to see.

Reggie said, "Man, that be some piece a gold, Sol."

Sol ignored him. Still holding up his Star of David in the faint light of the hurricane lamp, he leaned over the table toward Sheila, the faint light giving his face an eerie greenish cast. "Maybe you forget, Sheila, this'll remind you."

"I haven't forgotten, Sol," she said. "Maybe you shouldn't forget how much an eye for an eye helped you Jews be so loved through the centuries."

"That's the fuckin' point, Sheila. You were a Jew, you wouldn't wanna be loved by cocksuckers don't understand you long as you loved yourself."

"'Man, you be talkin' some heavy shit," Reggie said, "the way white peoples think they pissin' on each other, it don't mean nuthin'."

"Reggie's right," Bobby said. "It's all bullshit. You do what you have to do. When you start plannin' it is when you get in trouble."

Sol put the Star of David back in his shirt. They all sipped their drinks, quiet for a moment, the only sound coming from the boats rocking in their moorings on the dock. Absentmindedly, Sol reached down his hand to pet Matthew. Matthew growled at him. Sol pulled his hand back.

"Jesus, Sheila, the fuckin' mutt don't like me," Sol said.

Bobby laughed. "He doesn't like me, either, Sol."

"He's just protective of me," Sheila said. "When Bobby and I have sex, he thinks Bobby's hurting me."

"You shoulda had the mutt with you with the dyke," Sol said.

"Dogs hate brothers," Reggie said.

"He ain't growled at you yet," Sol said.

"Cause I ain't try to pet him," Reggie said.

"Go ahead," Sol said. "See what happens."

"Bite my fuckin' hand off," Reggie said.

Sheila pointed at Reggie and said, "Go ahead, Matty, go over to Reggie."

The dog got up and walked around the table to Reggie. He sat down, wagging his tail, and looked up at Reggie. "Aw, Sheila, call him off, he bite me."

"No, he won't," Sheila said. "Go ahead, pet him."

Reggie reached down a tentative hand and patted Matthew on the head. Matthew licked his hand.

"I told you," Sheila said.

"A hamster faggot-lovin' dog!" Sol said.

"Matthew knows Reggie's no threat to me," Sheila said.

"Yeah," Bobby said. "He don't wanna get in your pants."

"Nice doggie," Reggie said, smiling. "He do like the brother." Reggie looked around at the boats, the canal, the condos, and then through the sliding glass doors of the apartment at the white leather sofa. "Bobby, man, you got a chillin' crib here," he said. "A doggie, man, an old lady, what you wanna be messin' with Barry the Bear and the dyke for?"

"Just the cash, Reg," Bobby said. "And the action."

Reggie looked at Sol. "What else?" Sol said. "The cash. And that Jew cocksucker."

Reggie looked at Sheila. "I do what Bobby does, Reggie. It's that simple." Then she said, "And to hurt that cunt the only way she'll understand."

"What about you, Reggie?" Bobby said.

Reggie didn't say anything for a moment. Then he said, "Sheila be a actress, right, Bobby? She be someone else and then she be Sheila when she want."

"You makin' a point, or what?" Sol said.

Reggie looked at him. "I'm tired be that faggot Samson. The nigger bother me."

"After the score," Bobby said, "you can be anyone you want, Reggie, get you a BMW M5 and a 'chillin crib' of your own."

Reggie laughed. "Right, Bobby, like the neighbors here bring me a fruit basket the nigger move next door."

"You got the cash, Reggie," Sol said, "you won't be a nigger no more. Look at that nigger singer calls himself Snoop-Puffy-Dog, designs his own suits, fucks that spic broad with the nigger ass, all the white people in New York take him serious like he was a white man because he got the cash."

"Speaking of cash," Sheila said, "You think maybe we could get down to it so we don't fuck up."

"Aw, Sheila, we be over it a hundred times," Reggie said. "I ain't back in school you be my teacher."

"Maybe if you listened to your teacher, Samson, you might be Vidal Sassoon today and not have to suck Barry the Bear's dick."

"Yeah, and you be on Broadway, Sheila," Reggie said, "instead a let some dyke hurt ya."

Bobby and Sol looked at each other.

Sheila smiled at Reggie. "Touché, Reggie."

"See what I mean?" Reggie said. "The nigger make a point, white peoples change the subject."

Sol said, "How much cash you think she got in that safe, Sheila?"

"I don't know. She's got maybe twenty girls working for her, $3500 a pop, each girl working maybe two-three nights a week. She gets forty percent. Add it up."

"I figure 150 Gs a week," Sol said. "How many weeks she keep the cash before she dumps it?"

"That's a good question, Sol," Sheila said. "How does she move the money out of the salon?"

"Barry the Bear," Bobby said. He looked at Reggie. "You ever see him come in the salon, Reggie?"

"Yeah, the fuckin' Bear don't even look at me like he never seen me before, I suck his cock."

Sol grinned. "He don't call, he don't write, he don't send flowers."

"How many times a week he come in?" Bobby said.

"He don't," Reggie said. "Maybe once, twice a month." Reggie smiled, flashing his gold teeth. "He come in once, twice a month and leave he be carrying a leather satchel."

"Jesus!" Sol said. "Two, three weeks must be half-a-mil in that bag."

"When was the last time Barry was in the salon?" Sheila said.

"Three weeks ago," Reggie said.

"We do it tomorrow then," Sheila said.

Reggie frowned, "Yeah, but what if Barry show while we doin' it?" Bobby got up from the table and went inside the apartment.

"He leavin' now?" Reggie said.

Bobby came back out carrying a canvas duffel bag. He dropped it on the table with a clatter. He zipped it open and then he began taking out guns and boxes of bullets, laying them on the table.

Reggie held his hands up, palms out. "Aw, man, guns, I don't like guns—they can go off."

"They're *supposed* to go off, Reggie," Sol said. "You point 'em and they go off. Problem solved."

Sheila said, "I don't like it either, Bobby. I thought we weren't going in on the muscle?"

"You don't wanna do it tomorrow, we can wait," Bobby said. "You have two, three more dates with the dyke. That what you want?"

Sheila turned her face away from Bobby and looked out at the canal. Sol picked up a snub-nosed .38 revolver, opened a box of shells, and began putting bullets in the cylinder. Bobby handed an East German Makarov automatic and a box of shells to Reggie. Reggie held the gun between his forefinger and thumb like it was something dead. Then he laid it gently down on the table.

"No, thanks, Bobby," Reggie said. "It ain't my style. I may be a brother from Sistrunk, but I no Jackboy."

"Suit yourself," Bobby said. He picked up his CZ85, 9mm from Czechoslovakia, dropped the clip and began thumbing hollow-point bullets into the clip.

Sol spun the cylinder of his .38 revolver and then slammed it shut.

Bobby put fifteen rounds into his clip and slammed it into the pistol grip with his palm. He racked the slide to chamber a round, then eased down the hammer.

Sheila turned back to them. She looked down at the table until she saw her chrome-plated, Seecamp .32 ACP. She picked it up. It was the gun Bobby had first given her when they went to meet Medina. She remembered what he'd told her. "It's better to have a gun and not need it than need a gun and not have it." She pulled out the clip, searched for the box of Silvertip shells and began thumbing them into the clip. When it was loaded, she slammed the clip into the grip, and racked the slide.

"One more thing," Bobby said. "The dyke close that safe, she ain't opening it with four guns to her head. We gotta make sure that safe don't close 'til we make our withdrawal."

Bobby looked at Sheila. Then Sol looked at her. Then Reggie.

Sheila looked around the table at the three men staring at her.

Then she said, "The safe will be open."

At 4:30 on the following afternoon, a tall, muscular man with a blond ponytail walked through the door of La Donna Bellicósa and stopped at the receptionist's desk. Maya looked up at him, his narrow black eyes and slanting cheekbones, and smiled. He was wearing a pale green Hawaiian shirt outside his tight jeans, and cowboy boots.

"Can I help you?" Maya said, still smiling. He smiled down at her.

"Yeah, honey. Mr. Roberts. I have an appointment with Samson."

Maya checked her book, then looked up. "Robert Roberts?"

"That's it. But you can call me Bobby Squared."

Maya looked at him, her smile fading, frowning. "But it says here—"

"Yeah, I know. Robert Roberts, that's me."

"But you said—"

"It's just a joke."

"Oh!" Maya laughed. Then, when she stopped laughing, she called out, "Samson! Your four-thirty is here!"

Samson de la Plaine, in his tight red-leather pants, walked over to her desk and put his hands on his hips. "Mr. Roberts?" he said. "I thought you were never gonna show."

"I said four-thirty. It's four-thirty."

"We close at five," Samson said. He narrowed his eyes and tilted his head left-then-right studying Bobby's hair. "It's gonna take me a hour to straighten out that mess. Who butchered it?"

"Some little asshole."

"I'm sure. Come with me." Samson led him across the room past a blond girl in a leopard-print T-shirt cutting a woman's hair and a slim, blond boy cutting a very plump woman's hair until he came to his cutting chair at the end of the room near a door. "Have a seat," Samson said.

Robert Roberts sat in the chair and Samson swept a smock over him as if it were a cape he was taunting a charging bull with. He snapped it at his throat and got his scissors. The man under the smock shifted in the chair, reached his hand into the back of his jeans, withdrew an object, and laid it on his lap.

Samson de Plaine leaned over and whispered in his ear, "That thing go off, Bobby, your johnson be all over the mirror." Then, with a little flourish, he slipped the elastic off Bobby's ponytail, spread his hair around his face, and began to snip. "Fuckin' Conan-lookin' dude I always say."

Lucrezia came through the back door and walked past them to Maya's desk. Bobby and Samson heard her say, "She'll be in any minute. Send her right back to Angel's office." Then she walked back across the room toward the door and as she passed Bobby in the chair, she glanced at his reflection in the mirror, stopped, was about to say something, until she noticed Bobby give her a little shake of his head. She went through the door.

The blond cutter in the leopard T-shirt finished with her client, who thanked her, slipped her a tip, and went to Maya's desk to pay her. The blonde swept up around her chair as the client left the salon. She held open the door for a woman in a flowered-print rayon summer dress with a short, flouncy skirt and a straw handbag slung over her shoulder. The woman went to Maya's desk.

"Hiya, Sheila. She's expecting you. Go on back."

Sheila walked across the room, past Bobby and Samson, and through the back door. She walked down a corridor past little cubicles until she came to Lucrezia sitting at her desk.

Lucrezia looked up and smiled. "Sheila, honey! It's been a long time."

"Yes it has, Lou."

"Angel said Sheila Weinstein, I figured it was you, I seen you the other day." She glanced down the corridor. "Then I seen Bobby today."

"You're lookin good, Lou."

"You, too, honey. Don't you ever get old?"

"I'm tryin not to."

"You come a long way since that scared, straight chick was in my chair . . . what . . . two years ago?"

"About that."

"A lotta water over the bridge since then. I heard about Medina, figured you done him."

"Water under the bridge, Lou."

"Yeah, I just said that." Lucrezia was quiet for a moment, then said, "I never figured a chick like you workin' for Angel, though."

"A girl's got to do what a girl's got to do."

"So they say." Lucrezia tossed a head fake toward the big metal door. "This ain't exactly what I thought'd be my career vacation, either."

Sheila smiled at her. "Vocation, Lou."

"Yeah, whatever."

"You want to buzz me in?"

"Sure. Angel's got another girl with her, but she's anxious to see you. You and Angel are close, I hear."

"You can't believe everything you hear, Lou."

"That's a fact." Lucrezia leaned over and said into the intercom, "Angel, Sheila's here."

Angel's voice said, "Send her in." Lucrezia reached under her desk and pressed a buzzer.

Sheila went to the door and looked back. "Good to see you again, Lou."

"You, too, honey." Sheila pushed open the heavy metal door and went inside.

Angel was sitting behind her desk, the print of Venus on a half shell looking down on her. A girl was sitting across from Angel. Angel stood up, smiling. "Sheila, baby, it's so good to see you." She came around her desk to Sheila, threw her arms around her, and kissed her on the lips. The girl turned in her chair and stared at Sheila. She had a cute small-featured face with a little lip-curling grin that reminded Sheila of Meg Ryan.

Angel stepped back from Sheila and looked at her. "You look great, baby. I love that dress."

"I thought you would." Sheila smiled at her.

"Sheila, this is Amber, another one of my girls."

Sheila reached out her hand to Amber, who flashed her a fake smile. Amber shook her hand, "Glad to meet ya," she said.

"Me, too, Amber."

"Have a seat, Sheila." Angel gestured to the chair beside Amber. Sheila sat down. Angel went back behind her desk and sat down, too.

"Sheila's one of my new girls, Amber. Last night was her first date."

Amber flashed her fake smile at Sheila. "She looks a little like that old-time actress who's related to Bridget Fonda," she said.

"You mean Jane Fonda, dear," Angel said. Then, to Sheila, she said, "Amber's one of my old girls. She's been with me for ages, ever since *Sleepless in Seattle.*"

"I was trying to place her," Sheila said. "She does, doesn't she?" She smiled at the girl in the tight black T-shirt with "Real!" written in gold across her massive breasts. "Much better body though than Meg Ryan."

Angel sighed. "Yes. Not that it's doing her much good these days."

Amber looked at Angel as if worried. "You think maybe I shouldn'ta had them done?"

"That's not the problem," Angel said.

"I can have them taken out," Amber said.

"Don't worry about it," Angel said. "Things will turn around for you, honey. I mean, the bitch has got to have another hit movie *sometime* in the next twenty years."

"Twenty years!" Amber said.

"I'm just kidding, Amber," Angel said. Sheila sat back and crossed her legs. Angel glanced at her short skirt sliding up to her thighs, then turned back to Amber. "Now, honey, if you'll excuse me. Sheila and I have some business."

Amber stood up, pouting. "Yeah, I got things to do."

"Lovely to meet you, Amber," Sheila said.

Amber glared at Sheila and then flashed her her fake Meg Ryan smile. "Me, too." Angel reached under her desk and buzzed open the door.

After Amber left, Angel leaned her elbows on her desk and said, "Let's get business out of the way first. How'd it go last night?"

"Fine, he was a bit of an asshole but . . ." Sheila smiled at her.

"Yes, that's what Barry said."

". . . but he was quick."

"That's the kind of date you want. Quick and generous."

"I don't know how generous he was, He gave me a hundred-dollar tip." Sheila reached into her straw bag and took out a wad of bills fastened with a rubber band. She reached across the desk and handed the bills to Angel. Angel snapped off the rubber band and counted the bills. "Excellent," she said. She peeled off one hundred-dollar bill and handed it to Sheila. Sheila looked at it.

"I thought—you said seventy percent. . . ."

"I did. But the first date, all the money goes to the house except for the tip. I must have mentioned that, Sheila." She smiled at Sheila. "You had so much champagne that night, maybe you forgot."

Sheila smiled back. "Yes, I must have." Then she said in a husky voice, "That was some night, Angel. So intense."

"It was for me, too," Angel said as she stood up and turned her back to Sheila. She pushed the print to one side, revealing a wall safe, and began turning the dial, first one way, then another.

Bobby yanked his head away from Samson's scissors and said loudly, "What the fuck you doin'? I told you a trim."

"I beg your pardon?" Samson said, his hands on his hips.

"You heard me. You're fuckin' up my hair."

"I'm doing no such thing, sir. I've never—"

Maya looked up from her desk at the two men arguing. The salon was deserted except for them, but she couldn't leave until Angel left. The blond guy got out of the chair, his back to the mirror, and began poking his finger in Samson's chest.

"A simple fuckin' trim and you—"

Samson called out, *"Maya, please, we've got a problem!"*

Maya shook her head, then pushed herself up from her desk and walked over to the two men. She faced. the blond guy whose huge body covered the mirror. He was holding something under his smock that she couldn't make out.

"What's the problem?" Maya said.

"I'll tell ya what the fuckin' problem is," the blond guy said, as a short, fat, bald man entered the salon and walked quickly across the room. He wore a nylon jacket zipped up to his neck that bagged out in front of him. He passed behind Maya and went through the back door.

"The problem is," said the blond guy, "this fuckin' coon—"

Once he was into the back room, Sol zipped open his jacket, pulled out a ski mask, and slipped it over his head. Then he took his .38 special out of his jacket pocket and walked down the corridor to Lucrezia's desk, holding the gun at his side.

Lucrezia looked up and then reached for her suede bag.

"I wouldn't do that, Lou," Sol said.

Lucrezia took her hand away from her bag and looked up at the man in the ski mask pointing a .38 at her. "You put on weight, Sol, or is it just the jacket?"

Sol patted his ample stomach. "Both," he said. "Keep your hands on the desk, Lou."

"I don't, you gonna shoot me, Sol?"

"No, I'm not gonna shoot ya. I'm gonna hit you over the fuckin' head, give you a headache for a month. Is that what you want?"

"You tryin' to turn me on, Sol? You know I love the rough stuff."

"For Crissakes, behave yourself. This'll be over quick. You know the drill."

"I seen Bobby and Sheila," Lucrezia said, "I shoulda known something's going down. Now you, Solly. You think I'm right?"

"You was always a smart chick, Lou. Don't get stupid now."

She smiled at the ski mask. "I'm not about to, Sol."

"You be a good girl, there's a piece a change in this for you."

Lucrezia glanced toward the metal door, then back to Sol. "Fuck her, anyway."

"Buzz me in, then stand up."

Lucrezia smiled at the ski mask. "I missed you, Sol."

"I was away."

"Now you're back." She reached her hand under the desk.

Angel opened the wall safe that was filled with stacks of hundred-dollar bills. She put in the bills Sheila had given her just as Sheila got up from her chair and went around her desk behind her. Angel felt Sheila's arms around her waist, her head in the crook of Angel's neck. Sheila kissed her neck. Angel inclined her head toward Sheila's lips and closed her eyes.

"Mmmmm, I've been waiting for that," Angel said.

"I told you it wouldn't take me long. I've been thinking about it from the moment I woke up that morning. If only you were still there in bed beside me."

Angel turned around and draped her arms over Sheila's shoulders, "I had to get to work."

Sheila said, "You're at work now."

"Yes. And no." Angel reached her hand behind Sheila's head and pulled her face to hers. She pressed her lips against Sheila's lips and felt her mouth open, their tongues touching, and this time Sheila did not pull away.

The office door buzzed and Lucrezia walked through it with Sol in his ski mask behind her, holding his gun to her head. The two of them stopped and stared.

Sheila was sitting on the edge of the desk facing them, the safe behind her still open. Sheila was leaning back, her hands planted on the desktop behind her, her legs spread wide, her skirt pulled up to her waist, Angel kneeling on the floor in front of Sheila, her face buried between Sheila's legs. Sheila's eyes were half-lidded and she was turning her head from side to side, moaning. When she saw Lucrezia and Sol standing in front of her, she smiled at them and winked, then screamed, "Oh, my God! He's got a gun!"

Angel pulled her head from between Sheila's legs and looked over her shoulder. When she saw the man in the ski mask with the gun, she jumped up and made a move toward the safe. Sheila throw her arms around Angel, holding her tight, screaming, "Angel! He's going to kill us. Oh, my God!"

Sol pushed Lucrezia to one side and grabbed Angel by her hair, pulling her away from Sheila. He stuck the barrel of the gun against the side of her head. "Relax, cunt, this'll be over soon." He gripped her hair tightly and held her head back so that she was facing the ceiling.

"You know who I am?" Angel said to the ceiling. "You're a fucking dead man."

"Yeah, I know who you are. A cunt-lapping pimp. I'm gonna lighten your load."

Sheila was standing against the desk, her eyes wide with fear. "Please! Don't hurt her! We'll do anything!"

"Sheila!" Angel said. "Shut the fuck up!"

Sol yanked her hair, snapping her head back. "You listen to your girlfriend. Be smart, or your muff-diving days are over." Then, with a toss of his head toward Sheila, he said, "You, Blondie, come over here."

Sheila hesitated. Sol pressed the barrel of his gun hard against the side of Angel's head.

"All right! I'm coming!" She walked closer to Sol.

"Reach into my jacket pocket, dyke, and take it out."

Sheila reached into his jacket pocket and took out a rolled-up garbage bag.

"Now go over to the safe and put all the cash in it," Sol said.

"Don't do it, Sheila!" Angel said. "He's bluffing. He doesn't have the balls."

Sheila began to cry. "Oh, Angel! What should I do? He'll kill us!"

"Fuckin' right I will," Sol said. "And sit down to a steak dinner afterward. Now, do it!"

Sheila went over to the safe and began putting the stacks of bills into the garbage bag. Sol leaned his face close to Angel's ear, and said, "I wasn't in a hurry, I woulda watched you and your girlfriend a little more. You was puttin' on a good show."

"Fuck you!"

When the garbage bag was filled and the safe was empty, Sheila turned around to face Sol. "What should I do now?" she said.

"Bring it here," Sol said. She brought the bag over to him. "Drop it at my feet." She dropped it. "Now reach into my other pocket." Sheila reached into his jacket pocket and took out a roll of duct tape. "Tape your girlfriend's mouth shut."

Sheila hesitated. "I can't do that!"

"You can't?" Sol thumbed back the hammer of his revolver until it clicked.

"All right! All right!" Sheila said. She peeled out a strip of silver tape, bit it off with her teeth, and taped it over Angel's lips.

Sol let go of Angel's hair and grabbed her two hands by the wrists and held them tight behind her back. Angel struggled to pull her hands free until Sol slapped the gun against the side of her head just hard enough to daze her.

"Don't hurt her!" Sheila screamed. "Please!"

"Tie her hands up with the tape," Sol said.

Sheila wrapped the tape around Angel's wrists and then bit off the end of the tape from the roll.

Sol gestured with his head toward Lucrezia standing against the wall. "Now her," he said. While Sheila was taping Lucrezia's mouth and then her hands behind her back, Sol dragged Angel behind her desk and forced her down into her chair. She wasn't struggling anymore. She was calm now, looking up at him with her small black eyes.

"There," said Sheila. "Now what?"

"Now, whaddaya think?" Sol said. "Come here." Sheila went over to him. He took the tape from her, put the gun in his jacket pocket, and taped her mouth shut and her hands behind her back. He pushed her toward the desk. "Sit on it." He looked toward Lucrezia. "You, too, honey."

Sheila and Lucrezia sat on the desk facing Sol. Sol picked up the bag of money, taped the open end, and stuffed the bag inside his jacket. He zipped up his jacket so that he looked like a grossly fat little man, then backed away from the women toward the door. He tried the doorknob, but the door wouldn't open. He turned back toward the women. Sheila's eyes shifted to her right. Sol went around the desk, searched under it until he found the button, than buzzed himself out. The door locked behind him. He ripped off his ski mask, dropped it, and walked quickly down the corridor into the salon. Bobby and Samson were still arguing by Samson's chair. The chunky broad with the wild hair was trying to calm them down. Sol walked quickly behind her toward the door.

Maya looked over her shoulder as Sol reached the door. "Excuse me!" she called out. "Excuse me, sir! Where— "

Sol pushed open the door, stepped outside, and was gone.

• • •

Angel sat behind her desk in her office, staring at Lucrezia and Maya sitting in chairs across from her. Maya glanced over her shoulder at Barry the Bear standing behind them, his hands folded at his crotch. Lucrezia glanced at the safe behind Angel, its door open, the safe empty, and then at Angel, a red bruise on the side of her forehead.

"You didn't recognize him, Lou?" Angel said.

"I seen what you seen, Angel. A short, fat guy in a ski mask standin' over me, scared the shit outta me. I went for my piece in my bag, but he put this .38 to my head, I didn't think it such a good idea get my brains splattered all over the wall."

Angel didn't say anything. She just stared at Lucrezia through her narrowed black eyes. Finally she said, "How'd he get there?"

Lucrezia said, "I dunno."

Angel's eyes shifted toward Maya. "Maya?" she said.

"I never saw him come in," Maya said. "Honest, Angel. I was tryin' to settle this argument between Samson and this blond guy he was givin' a trim to."

"What blond guy?" Angel said.

"A big guy in a Hawaiian shirt," Maya said. "His name was . . . Roberts, that's it. Mr. Squared."

Angel closed her eyes then opened them. "Which is it, Maya? Mr. Roberts or Mr. Squared?"

"I dunno. First he said 'Mr. Roberts,' then he said—"

"All right, Maya, relax. Now, he was arguing with Samson, you said?"

"Yeah. He didn't like the way Samson was cutting his hair, He started screaming so loud I had to go over to them, try to calm him down. I thought Samson would faint, he was so upset."

"How long were they arguing?" Angel said.

"Ten, fifteen minutes. The big guy wouldn't drop it. I must have had my back to the salon when the other guy came in. I never saw him until—"

"Until what?"

"He was leaving. He must have come out of the back room. I didn't see it, but then saw him in the mirror. I looked over my shoulder just as he was opening the door. I tried to stop him but—"

"What did he look like?"

"Like Lou said. He was short, fat, and bald, that's all."

"Anything else?"

Maya squinted as if thinking hard. Then she said, "Yeah, one other thing. He had a trim little beard."

"After the fat guy left," Angel said. "What did the blond guy do?"

"That was the strangest part. All of a sudden him and Samson stopped arguing. The blond guy threw a crumpled-up bill at Samson, called him a coon one more time, and then stormed out. Samson was so shook up I told him to take the money, go home, and have a stiff drink."

After Maya and Lucrezia left the office, Angel looked up at Barry. "Well, Barry, you recognize the blond guy your little boyfriend was arguing with?"

Barry shook his head. Then he said, "But the other guy, the fat one...."

11

The waitress at The Mark's Chickee Bar went inside to the bar and said to the bartender, "Bottle of Dom."

"Bottle of Dom?"

"What? Is there an echo? You heard me."

"Who's drinkin' Dom in the middle of the afternoon?"

The waitress turned and looked out onto the deck. The outdoor tables were all filled with locals on a hot, brilliantly sunny day. "See the table at the corner of the deck, close to the beach?"

The bartender leaned over the bar and stared. "The good-looking chick in the black bikini and the muscle-beach dude with the ponytail?"

"Yeah. And the fat Jew with the black dude must be his boyfriend."

"What a crew!"

"Yeah, well, they got the cash, so got me the Dom."

"She sees Sol's ski mask I thought she'd have a heart attack," said Sheila.

"Her?" Sol said. "I seen her muff-divin' you, I almost dropped my piece. Jesus, Sheila!"

"You didn't seem to mind, Sol," Sheila said. "I saw the look on your face. I thought you were maybe going to pull up a chair, take in the show if I didn't scream."

"The way you was moanin' your eyes all dreamy-like it didn't look like no show."

"Oh, Sol, it was just business."

"Yeah. She was givin' you the business, and you looked like you was lovin' it."

"I had to make it believable, Sol."

"Yeah," Bobby said. "She's an actress. Remember, Sol, she's supposta be believable." He glanced at Sheila. "Ain't that right, baby?"

Sheila looked at him for moment, but before she could say anything, the waitress appeared at their table with a bottle of Dom and four plastic cups.

Sheila looked at the plastic cups. "You don't have any glasses?" she said to the waitress.

"Sorry, honey," the waitress said. "You're lucky I found a bottle of Dom." The waitress put the tray on the table, opened the bottle of Dom, holding the bottle between her legs, and tugging on the cork until it popped and the champagne bubbled out. She poured the Dom into the plastic cups, put the bottle on the table, and left. Sheila picked up her cup and held it over the table.

"To a job well done," she said. "Only you should have hit her harder with your piece, Sol."

"Fuckin' A," Sol said. They all touched their plastic cups over the table and sipped their champagne.

Reggie looked at his plastic cup and frowned. "So this be what white peoples think so fine. Shit, taste like white Thunderbird with bubbles."

Bobby threw his big, muscular arm over Reggie's shoulders. "My man, here, was awesome."

Reggie shrugged. "Jes' hold my own, you white dudes don't think a nigger can."

Sol said, "Cut the nigger shit, Reggie. You're a white man now all that cash—what, a hundred large?"

"He was such a prissy fag," Bobby said. "The receptionist thought he was gonna cry. 'Please, Samson,' she kept sayin', 'Don't be upset. We can work this out.'"

"Jes' actin', Bobby," Reggie said. "Like Sheila." They all laughed.

Bobby touched his plastic cup to Reggie's. "To Samson de la Plaine, fuckin' hamster faggot."

"To Reggie," Sol said. "You done good."

"Actin' be easy," said Reggie. "Bobby screamin' at me, callin' me a coon, I jes' believe he don't like the brothers even I know it ain't true. Right, Bobby?"

Bobby's muscular arm crushed Reggie to his side. "Aw, Reggie, I was just actin' like everybody else."

"What about Angel?" Sheila said. "She think anyone was acting?"

They looked at Reggie.

"I dunno," he said. "She ax me who the dude be I cut his hair. I say some fuckin' redneck I never see before, don't ever wanna again."

"She believe you?" Sheila said.

Reggie shrugged. "You tell me, Sheila, you know the bitch better. She don't show nuthin' behind those eyes."

"What about you, baby?" Bobby said.

"Please, Bobby, don't insult me," Sheila said.

"Yeah, I forgot. You're always so fuckin' believable."

Sheila looked at him. "When it suits my purpose, Robert. *Your* purpose, actually. You *did* need a broad, didn't you?" Bobby didn't say anything. Sheila smiled at him, and said brightly, "Actually, I might have been too fucking believable, screaming and crying so hysterically, I think the cunt might want to rethink our relationship, I'm such a pussy."

"She wants to rethink it, fine," Bobby said. "She don't, you hang in with her."

Shelia looked at him. "You want to watch, too, Bobby?"

"No. I don't wanna fuckin' watch. I just think she'll get suspicious you disappear on her."

"I already thought of that, Bobby. I told her it was all too much for me, the date with that terrible Mr. Rogers." She smiled at Sol. He raised his plastic cup. " . . . our 'intense' relationship, that scary man in the ski mask. She said she understood. She told me to take a few days off." Sheila smiled at Bobby. "She's very understanding, Bobby."

"You can play her off, all right," Bobby said. "But sooner or later you gotta call her, ask about dates."

"And if she has one for me and his name isn't Mr. Rogers, what do I do then?"

"You'll think a sumthin', baby, you always do." Bobby turned to Reggie and said, "You, too, Reggie. You gotta keep goin' to work for a while."

"Aw, man, I swear to myself this thing go down so do Samson de la Plaine. I'm sicka that faggot cocksucker."

"It'll only be for a few weeks, Reg," Bobby said. "Then we can all disappear, spend our money."

"Man, I'm goin' to the islands," Reggie said. "Be with the real brothers, drink some Red Stripe, smoke me some ganja. Relax, man, being with white peoples be scary, they so fucked up."

"Speakin' of scary," Bobby said. "What about your boyfriend?"

Reggie scrunched up his features, as if feeling pain. "You mean Barry the fuckin' Bear? Man, he ain't my boyfriend. He be with Samson, Samson gone."

"He start sniffin' around you, you can't play him off, Reg," said Bobby.

"He already sniffin'. Come in the other day, tell me he miss me, his regular boy, give me that sick smile a his make my johnson fall off."

Bobby smiled. "Keep it on a little longer. You might need it."

"He already ax me out. Like a date, I said. Dinner and cocktails. Fuckin' Barry grab his johnson say, 'Yeah, nigger, I got your cocktail.'" Reggie shook his head. "Man, the thoughta havin' to suck that weeny cock again make me sick."

"It's not like it's the first time, Reggie," Bobby said.

Reggie looked at Bobby. "No, it ain't, Bobby. But it be the last time I do it I don't wanna."

"You gotta do what you gotta do, Reg," Bobby said. Then he looked at Sol. "That leaves Lucrezia. Sol?"

Sol didn't say anything for a moment. Then he said, "I don't like it?"

"What?" Bobby said.

"Reggie goin' off with that Jew cocksucker."

Reggie smiled at Sol. "You be worried about me, Sol, or you be jealous?"

"I'm worried about myself," Sol said.

"No," Reggie said. "You be worried about me, Sol, like before, I walkin' Sixth Street, think I don't notice you followin' the Bear's car into Holiday Park, keepin' an eye on me he don't hurt me. That's sweet, Sol." Reggie reached up a hand and touched Sol's cheek. Sol yanked his head away.

"Cut that shit out!"

Bobby and Sheila laughed. Reggie said, "Maybe you wanna go to the islands with me, Sol, like a honeymoon all the niggers do from Pittsburgh. You be the onliest white bride."

Sheila smiled. "I got a nice white dress for you Sol, off-white. Tan, actually, if I can be the bridesmaid."

"Fuck you, too!" Sol said. "But I still don't like it."

"Reggie can take care of himself, Sol," Bobby said. "It's Lou's the wild card."

"She'll keep her mouth shut," Sol said. "I told her I'd give her a piece outta my share. Besides, she hates the dyke bad as Sheila."

"That's it, then," Bobby said, and sipped his champagne. Sheila and Sol sipped theirs, too. Reggie didn't. He put his plastic cup down on the table and looked at Bobby.

"What, Reggie?" Bobby said.

"Maybe nuthin'," Reggie said.

"You gonna tell us?" Sol said.

Reggie leaned over the table closer to Sol, and said, "You be walkin' out, Sol, Bobby and me still fightin', Maya tryin' to calm us down—"

"Yeah?" Sol said.

"You at the door, Sol, she look over her shoulder at you."

"So?" Sol said. "She don't know me."

"Maya's not the brightest bulb in the chandelier, Reggie," Sheila said. "She's so fucking stupid, it never dawned on her to go down and check on Angel for two hours after Sol left. The three of us were strugglin' with that tape until we were raw." Sheila held up her hands to show the scraped red skin around her wrists. "She finally gets an idea in her head. She hasn't heard from Angel in hours, so she goes to the office finds us all tied up and screams, 'Oh, Angel, what happened!' Like we could tell her with the tape on our mouths. I thought Angel was going to kill her just to hurt someone."

"Maya may be stupid, yeah, but Barry the Bear seen Sol," said Reggie. "Maya tell him and Angie what Mr. Ski Mask look like without his mask, even Barry get an idea in his thick head."

"Barry don't know nuthin'," Sol said. "Just a phony name stayin' at the Harbor Beach."

Sheila didn't say anything for a moment. Then she said, "Reggie's right, Sol. Angel's a lot of things, but stupid isn't one of them. She figures out Mr. Rogers is Mr. Ski Mask, it won't take her long to connect the dots."

12

It was a lazy, South Florida Sunday afternoon. The hot sun, the cloudless blue sky, the wild parrots squawking in the gumbo-limbo tree, the geckos scampering through the lariope, Matthew paddling in the swimming pool, Sheila, in her G-string bikini, lying on her stomach on a chaise longue at the edge of the pool, a neatly folded Sunday *New York Times* on the tile deck beside her, Sol and Bobby off to her right standing at the redwood gazebo shaded by an areca palm, barbecuing steaks on the charcoal grill, drinks in their hands, a neatly folded *Miami Herald* on the wooden bench beside them.

"Did you tell him one o'clock?" Sol said. He was shirtless in the heat, his gold chains glistening in his chest hair, his big belly hanging over the waistband of his baggy shorts.

"I told him a week ago," Bobby said, tanned and muscular in his bathing suit.

"He must be on hamster time," Sol said.

"Maybe he went to the islands?"

"You told him not to disappear on us, the dyke get suspicious."

"What can I say, Sol? He's a big boy."

"Go call him."

"Watch the steaks." Sol poked at the sizzling steaks and wiped sweat from his brow.

Bobby walked down the little path, overgrown with areca palms and bougainvillea, to the door of their first-floor apartment and disappeared inside.

Sol called out, "How do you want your steak, baby?" Sheila mumbled something into the chaise longue. "I didn't hear you," Sol said.

"Whatever."

Bobby came back out of the apartment. "No answer."

"Fuckin' hamster gets nigger-rich can't wait to spend it."

"Reverting to type, I guess."

Sol cut into one of the steaks on the grill. He called over to Sheila, "Baby, ya think you can get off your ass get us some plates and shit and the salad?"

Sheila pushed herself up off the chaise longue and shook her head. "I must have dozed off," she said. "Wow, it's hot." She walked to the edge of the pool and dove in. When she came back up, Matthew swam over to her. They both swam to the shallow end and walked up the pool steps to the deck.

"You said something, Sol?" Sheila said.

"I said these steaks are done, maybe you can get the plates and salad."

"What about Reggie?"

"Fuck him he don't show," Sol said.

"He's probably on his way, baby," Bobby said.

Sheila went into the apartment and came back out a few minutes later with a big bowl of salad, plates, knives, forks, and napkins. She set them up around the picnic table shaded. by a green Cinzano umbrella. Sol brought over a platter of sizzling steaks and thumped them down on the table. Bobby put a pitcher of Bloody Marys on the table. They all sat down. Bobby poured the Bloody Marys into their glasses. Sol speared steaks and dropped them onto each of their plates. Sheila picked up tongs and passed out little wooden bowls of salad.

Matthew came over to them and sat down beside Sheila, wagging his tail.

"Not from the table, Matty," she said. "Go on. Go lie down." Matthew slunk off, his tail low, and flopped down in the grass beyond the pool. He put his big nose on his crossed paws and stared at them as they began to eat.

"You should call her, baby," Bobby said. Sheila made believe she didn't hear him. "It's been a week."

"Bobby, you have to ruin a pleasant Sunday afternoon?" Sheila said. Bobby didn't say anything. Sheila looked up from her steak. "I'll call her tomorrow, all right? Now can I enjoy my steak, please?"

"Over a week, Bobby," Sol said. "They knew something, they'd find us."

"Maybe," Bobby said.

"Oh, Bobby, for Crissakes!" Sheila said. "They know where we live—Barry picked me up, remember? If she suspected anything, he'd already have paid us a visit."

They ate their steaks in silence for a few moments. Finally Sol said, "I think I'll take a trip."

Bobby grinned. "Go to the islands with Reggie?"

"No, I'm not goin' to the fuckin' islands with Reggie. I'm thinkin' of going back to Florence."

Sheila smiled. "Touch base with Frenchie, Sol? Maybe you can let her scam *this* money, too."

"Jesus, Sol, how stupid *are* you?" Bobby said.

Sol shrugged, grinned. "I'll let ya know. What are you two gonna do? Go back to the mountains?"

"I don't think so," Sheila said. "Bobby's not crazy about the mountains." She was silent for a moment. "After Hoshi died up there, I don't know if I can go back, either. I think we'll just buy a little house down here, maybe in Victoria Park, settle down."

"Settle down?" Sol said. "You mean like have kids and shit?"

Sheila laughed. "That's not an option, Solly."

Bobby said, "Maybe get another dog."

"You already got a dog don't like you, Bobby. You want another?"

"Matty's Sheila's dog," Bobby said. "I might get a Shiba puppy."

"He misses Hoshi," Sheila said.

"There'll never be another Hosh," Sol said.

"No," Bobby said. "But all Shibas are a lot alike, Sol. Maybe he'll remind me of Hosh."

"I might get a job," Sheila said.

"A job!" Sol said. "What? Hostess at Denny's. Maybe dance at the Booby Trap. I hear they're looking for old broads, turn on geriatrics."

"I'm not just a body, Sol." Sheila fluttered her eyelashes at Sol. "I have a brain, too."

"Yeah, the way your brain works, Sheila, I don't think too many bank presidents wanna find out."

"Maybe you forgot, Sol, but I had a job when you came looking for me."

"With Charlie there, a poker up his ass, and that little bitch kid shoot you daggers. Some fuckin' job!"

"It doesn't have to be like that," Sheila said. "Besides, I kinda liked it, teaching kids about acting and the theater."

"Ain't you had enough actin' to last you a lifetime?"

"It's not that kind of acting," Sheila said. "It's not not for real, it's for fun."

"Then what's the point it's not for real?"

"The real kind takes a toll, Sol," Sheila said. "It wears you down. No matter bow big the score you always feel . . . you lost something."

"So what? It keeps you alive."

"We've been lucky," Bobby said. "We had a good run, Sol, but it can't last forever. It only takes one mistake."

"You're not getting any younger, either, Sol," Sheila said. "You should be thinking about something legit, maybe invest your money, no hassles."

"You mean, like T-bills?" Sol said. "You think Uncle would even sell them to me the things I done to him? Sometimes I don't know where your brain is, Sheila, for such a smart broad. I ain't filed an income tax in twenty years. I don't exist as far as Uncle's concerned, except the time I done in Jessup."

"There are ways," Bobby said. "Offshore accounts, get Meyer to set something up for you under a phony company, you be set for life."

"What kinda life?" Sol said. "The only thing I know is the action. Maybe you two done things ya didn't wanna do, but you did 'em to get what you wanted. I seen it. Sheila was always a straight broad even what she did. And you, Bobby, you always wanted to be straight just didn't know it."

"And you, Sol?" Sheila said. "What don't you know?"

"Nuthin'. That's the point. I am what I am. I knew ever since I was a kid in Brooklyn seen the Jews become orthodontists and the guineas Mob guys. So I made a choice. Like Yogi said, I come to a fork in the road and I took it. I didn't even hafta think about it like youse two. I didn't do it like Bobby because he was a fuckin' redskin hamster got pissed on alla time so he got even, or like you, Sheila, because you met a guy fucks your brains out you're grateful do anything for him. It ain't even the score for me, why I'm more guinea now than Jew. I just like the action."

"I have to admit the action is part of it," Sheila said. "It's just not the bottom line for me, Solly."

"What about you, Bobby?" Sol said.

Bobby shrugged. "I dunno. I been in the action so long, I never thought how it'd be without it."

"I have," Sheila said. "Ever since that dyke rammed a dildo the size of a tree trunk up my pussy."

"That is the action, Sheila," Sol said. "They do something to you, you do worse to them see how far you can go until one a youse quits." Sol shrugged. "Or the other can't go on."

"I don't think I've crossed that line yet, Sol," Sheila said.

Sol looked at her. "You crossed it, Sheila, a long time ago. You're just afraid to admit what it means. Your boyfriend there, he ain't never crossed it all these years 'cause it ain't in him like it's in you and me. You're fuckin' dreamin' you think he can go back to dancin' the broads grabbin' his dick maybe you teach at some snooty school you introduce Bobby at faculty parties as 'Robert Roberts,' but his buddies call him 'Bobby Squared.'" Sol grinned. "Least that's how it reads on his rap sheet at the Broward lockup."

Bobby laughed. "I got things I can do, Sol. I was thinkin' maybe brain surgeon or computer genius like that guy in Seattle buildin' that eighty-million-dollar house."

"What he isn't doing, Sol, is ever dance again," said Sheila. "Isn't that right, Robert?"

"You say so, baby."

"You think it's funny, Sol," Sheila said, "but the school I teach at will have a football team. They're always looking for conditioning coaches, guys like Bobby to teach the kids how to lift weights."

"They got cheerleaders at them schools, too, I hear, look like that chicklet singer Brittany Spaniel, they'd liketa get a shot at Mr. Squared there."

"I think I could handle them," Sheila said.

"They're different than when you was a kid, Sheila," Sol said. "An old broad like you, they think it's made a Brillo and theirs is made a mink."

"Bobby doesn't like mink," Sheila said.

"I don't?" Bobby said. Sheila looked at him. "Just kiddin', baby."

After they finished eating, Sheila picked up the plates and brought them inside. While she washed the dishes, Bobby lighted a cigar and Sol lighted a cigarette. Sol got the *Miami Herald* from the bench, dropped it on the picnic table, and sat down.

"You really think you can do it, Bobby?"

"I'm gonna try, Sol. Sheila deserves it, the things she's hadta do."

"I hope you can pull it off, Bobby." Sol picked up the paper and took off the front section.

"Gimme the sports," Bobby said.

Sol passed Bobby the sports section and began reading the front page. A few minutes later, Sheila came back out carrying a tray of espresso, cups, a bottle of Sambuca, and a key lime pie. She put the tray down on the table. Bobby and Sol looked over their newspapers at it.

"Where'd this come from?" Sol said.

"I made it myself," Sheila said. "I'm polishing my Betty Crocker skills."

She cut out three sections of the pie, put them on plates, and handed one each to Bobby and Sol. She stood over them, waiting. "Go on," she said.

"I'm takin' my life in my hands I don't like it," Sol said.

"Just eat the fuckin' pie," Sheila said.

Sol took a bite of the pie, looked up at Sheila, and smiled.

"I told you," Sheila said.

"My old lady's gotta lotta talents," Bobby said.

"I heard," Sol said.

Sheila passed out their espresso, poured a shot of Sambuca in each one. Then she sat down and took a bite of her pie.

"Mmmm!" she purred to herself.

After they finished their pie and espresso, Bobby and Sol sat back, smoking, and began to read their newspapers. Sheila got up and went over to the chaise longue. She lay down on her back, adjusted the chaise to a sitting position, and reached under it for her *New York Times*.

"The Marlins drew thirty-three hundred for last night's game," Bobby said.

"Fuckin' Arafat!" Sol said. "I was Sharon, I'd just go in there, pave the whole fuckin' thing put up a Wal-Mart."

"Pretty soon the Marlins are gonna be pullin' people off the street to go to a game," Bobby said. "They had five thousand bobble-head dolls left over. Jesus, they couldn't give them away."

Sol looked over his paper. "What the fuck's a bobble-head?"

"These little dolls look like the players," Bobby said. "You know, A. J. Burnett, Brad Penny."

"Who the fuck are they?" Sol said.

"Never mind," Bobby said.

Sheila said out loud, "Jesus, he's on Broadway now. The little prick couldn't act his way out of a paper bag when he was in summer stock."

Sol muttered, "Lettin' their own kids blow themselves up, fuckin' ragheads."

Sheila was shaking her head while reading the *Times*. "He must be fucking somebody or somebody's fucking him."

"Looks like Alonzo's career is over," Bobby said. "Poor nigger's got some kinda kidney disease nobody's ever heard of." He looked over his paper at Sol and grinned. "What do ya think about that, Solly? You feel sorry for him?"

Sol didn't say anything. He was hunched over the table reading the Broward section of the *Herald.*

"He sounds like a nice man," Sheila said.

"Alonzo Mourning?" Bobby said.

"Who?" Sheila said. "I'm talking about Jack Nicholson. There's a nice piece about him in the *Times."*

"Mutha-fucker!" Sol said.

"Jack Nicholson?" Bobby said.

Sol grabbed the paper he was reading in both fists and crumpled it up, his fists squeezing the paper so hard it drained the color out of his hands. Sol was breathing heavily, his glazed eyes staring at the crumpled paper.

"What, Sol?" Bobby said. Sol didn't answer. He just held the crumpled paper in his fists and stared at it. Then he gave his head a little shake as if bringing himself back from somewhere. He shoved the paper at Bobby. Bobby smoothed it out on the table and began to read. His face drained of color and his hard, sharp features seemed to melt like wax under a flame. "Oh, sweet Jesus!" Bobby said softly.

Sheila looked over at them. "Who's Alonzo Mourning?" She saw the devastated look on Bobby's face and the fury in Sol's. "Jesus, Sol, I didn't know you were such a sports fan. You either, Bobby." Neither of them answered her.

Finally Sol said, "The fuckin' hamster didn't deserve it."

"I pushed him into it," Bobby said. "I shoulda known."

"It's not your fault, Bobby. I tried to warn him."

"You warned Alonzo Mourning about what, Sol?" Sheila said.

Bobby stood up and brought the paper over to Sheila. She sat up in her chaise. He handed her the paper. She began to read aloud. There was a photograph of a body under a sheet with the headline: "Murder Victim Pulled Out of Swamp," and then the story:

"Broward County homicide detectives pulled a lifeless body out of the swamp off Alligator Alley on Saturday morning. The victim was apparently beaten to death so savagely that it took the detectives twelve hours to identify the remains. His face was smashed beyond recognition, but the police finally identified the victim through his dental charts."

"Reginald Johnson, twenty-four, a small-time grifter and sometime homosexual prostitute, was apparently the victim of a crime of passion. Police theorize his assailant might have been a sexual partner of Mr. Johnson's who beat him to death with a baseball bat either in a dispute over money, or jealousy. The police are looking—"

Bobby stood over Sheila, looking down at her. Tears were streaming down her cheeks, her breathing labored as if she was struggling for breath. She began to mutter to herself, "No ... no ... no ... ," turning her head slowly left and right as if by denying what she was reading, it would no longer be true. Suddenly she burst into hysterical, gasping sobs that convulsed her body. "No! No!" she screamed. Matthew jumped up and ran to her side, growling. Bobby crouched down beside her and tried to put his arms around her. She pulled away from him with a fury and screamed out again, "No! No!" Then she threw herself into Bobby's arms and he held her sobbing body tight. After a long moment, her sobs began to subside and she pushed herself back from Bobby. She looked into his eyes with her own swollen red eyes, the blue in them drained so that they looked almost white.

"He was a good kid," she said. "He was just trying to get his life—" She shook her head.

Sol turned his head slowly toward Sheila and stared at her without expression. "You still wanna be a schoolteacher, Sheila?" he said.

Sheila looked at him, her eyes wide now, glaring back at him in fury. "He was just a fucking hamster cocksucker. Right, Sol?"

"Yeah, that's all he was," Sol said.

Bobby said, "Do you think he ratted us out?"

Sol looked at Bobby. "You think Barry beat him like that because he told him what he wanted to know? He did, Barry'd be knockin' at our door three days ago." Sol shook his head, a thin smile on his lips. "No, Reggie went out like a man, kept his mouth shut."

"You mean he *wasn't* just a fucking hamster cocksucker, Sol?" Sheila said.

"That's what he did," Sol said. "Not what he was."

"We let it drop then, Sol?" Bobby said.

"Whadda *you* think?"

"I seem to remember you tellin' me you try to make things right is when you fuck up."

"I remember."

"You walk away with the cash clean, you said, you keep walkin'."

"That's what I said."

"So? We walk?"

"You and Sheila can walk." Sol said. "You got a life to live."

Sheila got off the chaise longue and went into the apartment. Sol and Bobby stared after her. Then Bobby turned to Sol and said, "What about you?" Before Sol could answer Sheila came back out of the apartment and walked over to Sol sitting at the picnic table. She looked down at him without expression.

"I made the call," she said. "Tomorrow you make one."

Sheila came out of the bedroom. "This is the last time, Bobby."

She was wearing a white bandeau top that exposed her navel, white spandex capri pants that fitted her like paint, and white stripper's pumps with six-inch stiletto heels.

"You look good, baby," Bobby said. He was sitting on the sofa, sipping from his glass of Jim Beam.

"I don't care if I look good, I just want this over with."

"You don't have to do it, baby."

"You think we should just forget about Reggie?"

"No. But you don't have to get involved. Me and Sol can take care of it."

"And I just watch?"

"Just because she hurt you doesn't mean—"

"This isn't about me, Bobby. Or her. Sure, she hurt me, but we hurt her right back. If that's all it was, I could forget it. We just take the money and run."

"We could still do that."

"And Reggie?" He didn't say anything. "We just forget him?"

"No."

"He trusted us, Bobby, and we hung him out there. He didn't know. He was just . . . he was just—"

"I know, baby."

"If it was you or me or Sol, would we just let it go?"

"No."

"Would you expect me to just sit back and watch?"

"No."

"Don't worry, Bobby. I'm not the same person I was when you left me. I don't want to do this. But I have to. Do you understand?" He nodded. "What time is it?"

"Quarter to nine."

"I've got a few minutes."

"Want me to fix you a drink?"

"No. I want to be sharp." She sat down beside him and put her hand on his thigh. "You know what to do, right?"

He nodded. "I'll be right behind you," he said as he sipped his drink. Matthew came over to her and stood up on his hind legs and wrapped his paws around her waist. She hugged the big dog and he wagged his tail.

"Did you call the Shiba breeder?" she said.

"Yeah. He's got a litter of four. Three males, one female. I said we'd be interested in a male."

"How do you think Matthew will react to a newcomer?"

"He'll adjust. He'll probably raise the little guy. That's the way it usually works."

"I hope so." They sat there silently for a while, in the darkness of their unlighted apartment, Sheila's hand resting on Bobby's thigh, Bobby's arm tossed lightly over her shoulders. When they heard a car horn, Sheila jumped forward with a start. "It's him," she said. She stood up and went over to the mirror. She checked herself in the mirror, her short blond hair that stood up like spring grass, the slashes of blush that made her cheekbones so sharp, the dark red lipstick that made her mouth look hard, lascivious. Satisfied, she said, "Wish me luck, Bobby."

"Leave everything to Sol, baby. He knows what to do."

"I plan to, Bobby. I'm just going along for the ride."

Bobby stood up and went over to her. He stood behind her and put his arms around her waist. He said into her ear, "I saw a house the other day. I think you'll like it."

She turned around and smiled at him. "I'm sure I will."

She kissed him on the cheek and walked toward the door. Just as she was about to open it, Bobby said, "What about your purse?"

She turned toward him. "Do you think I need it?"

"Maybe not, but it's better to have—"

"I remember," she said. Then she opened the door and was gone.

Sheila walked along the narrow path that led from their apartment past the swimming pool to the parking lot where a black Hummer limo was waiting for her. She felt a few drops of rain and looked up at the gray clouds in the night sky.

Barry got out of the limo on the driver's side and came around to open the back door for her.

She smiled at him. "Hello, Barry. How are you, tonight?"

"O.K . . . Sheila."

"You remembered! Good."

Barry opened the back door and Sheila, turning toward Barry, slid into the backseat. Barry closed the door.

"Hello, baby," said Angel. "You're looking ravashing as usual."

"Angel! What are you? . . . " Angel was sitting in the backseat beside Sheila, smiling at her. She wore a man's double-breasted black jacket over bare skin, a short black skirt, and her low-heeled pumps.

"I missed you," Angel said, putting her hand on Sheila's thigh. "I thought I'd keep you company." She leaned toward Barry in the driver's seat. "You can go now, Barry." Then she sat back and crossed her legs, her purse on her lap. "You must have made quite an impression on Mr. Rogers, baby. He insisted on . . . how did he put it?—oh, yes—'On the same broad as last time with the big tits and dyke haircut.' He'd even forgotten your name. Such a charming man."

"He's even more charming in person," Sheila said.

"I can't wait."

"Does he expect two of us?"

"Not at all. But I don't think he'll turn us down, do you? We'll double his pleasure." She smiled across at Sheila. "And our own." She leaned over and kissed Sheila on the lips. "Mmmmm! I missed that."

"Me, too," Sheila said. "I'm sorry it took me so long, Angel. But that scene in your office, that man with the gun, it just frightened me."

"I know, baby. I don't blame you."

"Do you have any idea who it was?"

"We're working on it. Now come over here, let me work on you." Sheila slid over close to Angel.

Barry drove along the beach as it began to drizzle. He put on the windshield wipers. The ocean surf to his left was churning white as it hit the beach. To his right, across from the beach, waiters were hustling patrons at the outdoor tables into the restaurants. The lights from the restaurants, red and blue and green, were blurring through the limo's windows, beginning to run like wet paint down the tinted glass.

In the backseat, Angel and Sheila were kissing, Angel's hand cupped between Sheila's legs, pressing against her pussy. Sheila moaned and arched her back, thrusting out her breasts. Angel slid her hand up to Sheila's breasts and pulled down her bandeau top so that her pendulous breasts were exposed. Angel pulled back her face from Sheila's face and stared at her breasts for a long moment. Then she leaned over and began to suck first one breast, then the other, while Sheila lay back in her seat, staring up at the underside of the roof through her cold blue eyes. Every so often, she moaned, as if with pleasure.

The limo began to move up the long driveway that led to the covered entranceway of the Harbor Beach. When it stopped in front of the brightly lighted entrance, Sheila pulled away from Angel and tugged up her bandeau top until it covered her breasts again. "God!" she said, "that was sooo good." She reached out a hand and lightly touched Angel's face, feeling the coarse, pitted skin under her heavy makeup. Angel didn't say anything. She just stared at Sheila with that thin, knowing, smile of hers. Barry got out of the limo and Sheila waited for him to open her door. When he didn't, when she saw him walking toward the hotel entrance, she put her hand on the door handle. Angel stopped her with a hand on her arm.

"Barry will get Mr. Rogers," Angel said.

"But he expects—"

"Yes, he does. But we're going to surprise him, baby." Angel hiked up her skirt to her waist, exposing her black bush.

"Angel, for goodness' sake!" Sheila gasped. "We're right under a light. Anyone can see."

"Actually, they can't, baby, not through these blacked-out windows." Angel lay back in her seat. She raised her left leg and planted her shoe against the back of the front seat behind the driver's seat. Then she spread her right leg and turned her face toward Sheila. "I've been waiting for this a long time, baby. I usually don't have so much patience." She put both hands on Sheila's face and pulled it toward her face. She kissed Sheila, hard on the lips, forcing her tongue into Sheila's mouth for a long moment. They separated, both women breathing heavily, Angel's hands still on Sheila's face, and then Angel tried to force Sheila's face down between her legs. Sheila pulled her face free of Angel's hands.

"Angel! Jesus! Not here!" Sheila saw the look in Angel's eyes that she had seen once before when Angel was kneeling over her on her bed in her apartment. "Oh, Angel," Sheila said, smiling, "I thought . . . when we came back from dinner." She fluttered her eyelashes as if already experiencing the pleasure. "At the hotel we can do it right, on a bed, all the things I've been wanting. . . ."

Angel looked at her, not smiling now. "I know what you've been wanting, Sheila. You've been telling me often enough. Now's as good a time as any." She smiled. "I'm sure Mr. Rogers will appreciate it, and I know I will. I've been waiting too long, Sheila, and I seem to always be doing all the work. I was beginning to wonder."

With both hands, Angel pulled down Sheila's bandeau top to her waist, exposing her breasts. "You don't want me to wonder anymore, do you?"

"No . . . it's just—"

"Good girl. Now get down on your knees on the floor, baby." Angel put her hands on Sheila's bare shoulders and pushed her down until Sheila was kneeling on the floor of the limo between Angel's legs.

Sheila looked up at Angel. "Angel," she said. "Not here."

Angel put her hands behind Sheila's head and forced her face down between her legs. Sheila's face was pressed against Angel's pussy for a long moment until she heard Angel's voice: "Well?" Sheila began to use her tongue.

Angel lay back again in her seat, her eyes looking down on the top of Sheila's head, watching, less with pleasure than curiosity. "Mmmm, that's good, baby. You *have* eaten pussy before."

Barry came out of the hotel with Mr. Rogers, dressed in a loose-fitting lime-green sports jacket, white pants, and white patent-leather loafers. Barry opened the back door and Mr. Rogers slid into the backseat. Barry looked over the roof of the limo and saw a black Taurus parked at the end of the entrance driveway. He couldn't see if anyone was inside.

"Jesus! What the fuck!" Sol shouted.

Sheila looked up from between Angel's legs, her eyes staring at Sol. "Did I tell you to stop, baby?" Angel said. She pulled Sheila's face back down to her pussy. Then she smiled at Sol. "I thought we'd double your pleasure, Mr. Rogers. Sheila's told me so much about you."

"Yeah," Sol said, looking down at Sheila. "But some things about her she didn't tell me."

"You can't blame her. Maybe she didn't even know herself."

"She learns quick, I see."

Angel looked down at Sheila and for the first time her eyes had that dreamy look of someone experiencing pleasure. "Yes, she does, doesn't she, Mr. Rogers?"

"Just call me Sol."

"Of course, Sol. I'm Angel. Sheila's . . . employer." Then Angel looked at him, her brows furrowed. "Sol, your voice, it sounds so familiar. Have we met before?"

"I don't think so. Maybe over the phone, I called you twice for the broad here."

"Of course, that's it." Angel leaned forward, tapped her fingers on the glass partition that separated the driver from the passengers in back. "Barry, just drive around for a while, please."

"I thought we was gonna have dinner first," Sol said. "I made reservations at 'Smoke.'"

Angel lay back in her seat, her legs spread, Sheila's face between her legs. "Oh, we will . . . Sol." She pressed her body close to his. "I just thought maybe you'd enjoy"—her eyes fluttered shut—"Jesus, baby, you *are* good."

Barry drove west on Sunrise in a heavy rain. He drove past the Gateway Theater and Paradise Auto Works and then turned south onto Federal toward the airport. He looked into the rearview mirror through the two-way glass and he saw Angel kissing the fat guy. Jesus, Barry thought, the asshole's actually paying to kiss a homely dyke. Barry couldn't see Sheila, but he had an idea where she was, crouched down on the floor, working, Barry cursing himself for being such a *putz,* thinking this one was different because she talked to him—"Call me Sheila, Barry"—and here she was just like all the other shiksa whores he drove, on her fucking knees eating a homely dyke's pussy because she was a piece a shit did anything she was told for money.

That was the thing about Angel. She never surprised Barry. She was a dyke, but she was still a cunt. They got off on cruelty more than they did sex. Barry never thought of what he did as being cruel. It was just work, a job, like digging a ditch or chopping down a tree, swinging the bat against the nigger's head over and over until he worked up a sweat smashing the nigger's head into a bloody pulp 'cause he wouldn't tell Barry what he wanted to know, how to find Mr. Sol Rogers. Barry shook his head and smiled to himself as he drove through the heavy rain, the bright lights of other cars coming toward him. Angel put it together quick, the nigger's phony fight with the ponytail guy, "a fucking diversion," Angel called it, and then the fat guy with the ski mask who looked too much like Mr. Sol fucking Rogers to be a coincidence.

Barry wouldn't have hit the nigger if he'd just talked. But the stupid nigger wouldn't talk, he just kept pleading, 'I don't know nuthin', Barry, honest, man,' until Barry decided either he didn't know or would never tell if he did, which surprised Barry, the little nigger having big balls. So he began to beat him with the bat because that was his job, and the nigger stopped pleading, began to moan, and then nothing as Barry worked up a nice sweat raising the bat over his head and bringing it down on the bloody pulp that used to be the nigger's head, hard as a fucking coconut, at first, until Barry got into his work, never thinking about the pain he was causing, just thinking how he was doing his job the best he could.

It was all for nothing, anyway, Barry thought. The asshole made it easy for them, calling Angel for another date with the shiksa whore, she must have been so fucking good he had to have another piece, except he didn't figure he'd have to get in line behind Angel until she got hers. Angel always got hers, whatever she wanted. The shiksa was finding that out right now.

Sheila pulled her head up from between Angel's legs. She was breathing heavily. She wiped the back of her hand across her lips. "Angel . . . I . . . can't."

Angel stopped kissing Sol and looked down at Sheila. Sheila put her hands on the floor to push herself up to the seat. Angel put her hands on Sheila's shoulders and pushed her back down. "You're just getting into it, baby," she said.

Sheila looked up at her. "Please, Angel . . . I can't . . ."

"Sure, you can, baby," Angel said. "You've got a taste for it now." Sheila gave her head a little shake. "Yes, you do. Don't fight it, baby." Sheila, breathing more heavily now, stared at Angel. Angel smiled at her and nodded. Sheila inhaled, held it a moment, then exhaled deeply, closing her eyes. When she opened her eyes again, her face looked strangely different. Her slightly parted lips looked softer, pliant, and the coldness in her blue eyes had been drained out of them. She stared at Angel's face and then her eyes moved down from Angel's face to her pussy. Sheila reached up her hands and put them on the soft inside of Angel's thighs. "That's it, baby," Angel said. Sheila's hands spread Angel's thighs farther apart. Then she lowered her face to Angel's pussy. Angel waited, then she said, "Go ahead, baby," and Sheila began to use her tongue again.

Sol looked down at Sheila's head, then looked at Angel with a grin. "The chick's gonna smother she don't get some air."

"Don't worry about her, Sol. She loves her work. Isn't that right, baby?" Sheila nodded her head between Angel's legs without stopping her tongue. She was breathing heavily as she worked. "See?" Angel said. "She can't get enough."

"I wasn't worryin'," Sol said. "She's being paid, ain't she?"

"Precisely," Angel said. "Now where were we?" She moved her homely face toward Sol's and pressed her lips against his.

Barry drove west now on Alligator Alley in the driving rain. He kept the limo at 60 in the right-hand lane. Other cars shot past him on the left, splashing water over the windshield, except for the headlight of a car far behind him in the right lane driving very slowly in the rain. He couldn't make out the car. Probably a fucking tourist heard horror tales about Alligator Alley, the ten-car pileups, the cars drove off into the canal drowning everyone in them. He looked back up ahead. The lights of the big semis traveling east in the opposite lane almost blinded him until they passed and it was dark again. His eyes hurt behind his tinted glasses. He put a finger under his glasses and massaged one eye and then the other. It won't be long now, he thought. He glanced to his right through the passenger side window and saw a canal and beyond it the tall grasses of the swamp.

Angel pulled her face back from Sol's. "Mmmm, nice," she said, and lay back against the seat. She looked down at Sheila, her face moving up and down quickly now over Angel's pussy. "I told you you had a taste for it, baby." Angel closed her eyes, the back of her head resting against the seat. She said softly, "Not so hungry, baby, a little slower, that's it, oh, Jesus. . . ." Suddenly Angel forced her eyes open and pulled her head off the seat. "All right, Sheila! That's enough!" Angel tried to sit up, but Sheila held her thighs tightly in her hands, her face buried in Angel's pussy, her tongue working feverishly now. Angel watched her, and then she smiled and shook her head. "You are something else, baby," Angel said. "But you can stop now. It's time for a champagne break." But Sheila didn't stop. Angel tried to sit up again, but Sheila only clamped her thighs tighter. Finally Angel reached down and grabbed a fistful of Sheila's short blond hair. "Jesus, Sheila! Enough, already!" Angel yanked Sheila's head back from her pussy and held Sheila's head up by her hair.

"What?" Sheila said, her eyes opened wide and glassy, her huge breasts rising and falling with her labored breathing. "What, Angel? What do you want me to do?"

Sol stared at Sheila. The dazed look on her face, her smeared lipstick, the skin around her mouth and cheeks a bright pink. But she didn't see him staring at her. She just knelt there on the floor of the limo, breathing heavily, staring up at Angel, Angel's fist still gripping her hair.

"I told you to stop," Angel said. She let go of Sheila's hair. "When I tell you to do something, you do it."

"I'm sorry," Sheila said. "I didn't hear you."

"No, you didn't, did you?" Angel said. "You lied to me, baby."

"Angel, I would never—"

"You told me you never ate pussy before."

"But I haven't, Angel. This is the first time."

Angel looked at her. "A sea change, huh, baby?"

Sheila didn't say anything. Her breathing was steady now, her eyes no longer glassy. She turned her face away from Angel and looked out the window. She stared at the falling rain, and the lights of passing cars, and her own reflection in the window. "Yes," she said. "I suppose it is."

"You look shocked," Angel said. "You're not the first straight chick to eat pussy."

"I know. That's not it."

"Then, what is it?"

Sheila turned her face back toward Angel. "I like it."

Angel laughed. "Of course you do, baby. I knew you would, even if you didn't. So don't be so shocked."

Angel turned toward Sol. He was staring at Sheila. Sheila looked at him, then looked away. "What about you, Sol?" Angel said. "Would you like a taste? See what Sheila likes so much?" Angel put her hand between Sol's legs and began to rub his cock under his pants. "What do you think, Sol?"

Sol looked down at her hand, then at Sheila. Her face was still turned away from him. "I think the chick there likes it too much for me to deprive her, ya know?" He smiled at Angel. "I think you both like it too much. I didn't know better, I'd swear you was dykes."

Angel laughed. "Don't be ridiculous, Sol. It's just a girl thing. Isn't that right, Sheila?" Sheila nodded. "Sheila," Angel said, "why don't you put Sol's mind at rest?" Angel unzipped Sol's fly and reached her hand into his pants. "Come on, baby," Angel said. "Remind Sol what he's paying for."

"Yeah," Sol said. "But I think I'd rather it be you, Angel. The chick there might not be into it what I seen."

"You might be right, Sol," Angel said. "Her tastes seem to have changed, haven't they?" Sheila was staring out the window again. "Have they, Sheila?" Sheila didn't say anything. "Well, have they?" Sheila was silent. Angel put her hand on Sheila's jaw and turned her face toward hers. Sheila tried to turn her face away, but Angel held her jaw tight. "I asked you a question," Angel said.

"Do I have to say it?" Sheila said.

"Yes. You have to say it."

Sheila looked into Angel's eyes. Then a small smile formed on her lips. She said, "My tastes have changed, Angel."

"Good girl," Angel said. "That wasn't so hard now, was it?" Angel sighed. "Well, Sol, I guess it is up to me, then, isn't it? But first, let's have our champagne."

Angel reached toward the little refrigerator embedded in the back of the front seat and opened it. She took out a bottle of Dom and three fluted glasses. Sol reached for the bottle. "Let me open it," he said.

Angel pulled the bottle back from him and handed it to Sheila. "Sheila will open it, Sol," she said.

Sheila took the bottle from Angel and peeled off the aluminum foil around the cork. She struggled on her knees to pull off the cork.

"Here, let me do it," Sol said.

"I said, Sheila will do it, Sol," Angel said.

Finally, Sheila yanked off the cork, the champagne bubbling out onto her breasts and down to her pants.

"Jesus, Sheila!" Angel said. "Didn't you ever open a bottle of champagne before?" Sheila didn't say anything. Angel said, "You made a mess all over yourself, Sheila. Lick it up."

Sheila shook her head. "I don't know what—"

"Yes, you do. Now, lick it up."

Sheila glanced at Sol who was staring at her and then she looked down at her breasts glistening with champagne. She put the bottle down on the floor. Then she cupped her hands under her pendulous breasts, pushed them up toward her lowered face, and began to lick the champagne off her breast with her tongue. Sol and Angel watched her. She heard Angel's voice, "Now, the other one." And then, finally, Angel's voice again; "That's enough." Sheila looked up. Angel held the three glasses by their stems in one hand. "Now, pour it before you lose it all," Angel said. Sheila picked up the bottle and carefully poured the champagne into the three glasses. Angel said, "Sol, tell Barry to slow down so we don't spill any more."

Sol leaned forward in his seat, close to Sheila kneeling on the floor, still holding the bottle of champagne. She turned her face away from him and stared at the window that reflected the inside of the limo. Sol tapped on the glass partition. "Hey, slick," he said. Barry ignored him. Behind him, Angel reached into her jacket pocket, took out a small pill, and dropped it into one of the glasses. It fizzled, then evaporated. Sol called out louder, "Yo, slick, you deaf or what?" Barry buzzed the glass partition halfway down. "Slow down," Sol said. "And buzz that window back up."

The big limo slowed in the heavy rain as Sol settled back into his seat. Angel handed him a glass, and then handed a glass toward Sheila.

"Sheila, honey, you want this, or what?" Sheila turned back from the window and took her glass. Angel raised her glass. "A toast," she said, "to a surprising evening."

Sol said, "That's a fuckin' fact."

They all touched their glasses. Sol took a sip while Angel watched him. Then she sipped her champagne. Sheila put her glass to her lips, threw back her head, and drained it.

Angel said, "Jesus, Sheila, you trying to be Julia Roberts, or what?"

Sheila grinned. "Cleansing my palate," she said. She reached up to hand Angel her glass and bumped Sol's hand, spilling his champagne all over his pants.

Angel screamed at her. "Sheila! For Crissakes!"

"Oh, I'm so sorry, Angel. I didn't—"

Sol said, "Hey, it's awright. No problem."

Sheila looked around for something to wipe up the champagne on Sol's pants. When she didn't see anything, she reached down to her waist, unhooked her bandeau top, and used it to sop up the champagne. She smiled up at Sol. "I wasn't using it anyway, Sol."

Angel stared at Sheila dabbing at Sol's pants with her bunched-up bandeau top. Finally she said, "That's all right, baby. At least Sol had a taste."

Angel took the glasses and the bottle and put them back into the refrigerator. Then she said brightly, "Now, where were we?"

Barry looked out the passenger window, squinting through the rain, trying to see the mile markers by the side of the road. The rain was so heavy, he could barely make them out. One flashed by. He thought it read Mile 23. Only a few more miles, he thought, until we get to the rest area close to the swamp. He looked through the rearview mirror into the backseat. Jesus, Angel was sucking the guy's cock! He couldn't see the other one—she must still be on her knees eating Angel. He looked back up at the fat guy, his head resting on the back of the seat, his eyes half-closed, the guy getting drowsy, weak. This is gonna be too fucking easy, Barry thought.

Sheila was on her knees, her face buried in Angel's pussy, her tongue working slowly, Sheila trying to hold back, not lose herself in it, trying to remember why she was here, forcing herself to concentrate on the rain pelting the window, the speeding limo, her sore knees on the hard floor, the pain in her hunched shoulders, the sweet, sticky, nauseating smell of champagne on her breasts, the cramps in her wrists as her hands held up Angel's bare ass so she could work better, licking Angel's pussy with her tongue, Angel moaning "Oh, Jesus, baby!" with pleasure, Sheila's breathing becoming more labored, her heart beating faster in her breast, Angel moaning with pleasure, Sheila's tongue working faster, the rain and the cramps and the speeding limo beginning to recede, Sheila conscious of nothing now but Angel's pussy in her face, the feverish working of her tongue, her mindless desperation to give Angel pleasure, her own body suffused with an exquisite pleasure of its own, the pleasure of a humiliation she had never known existed, surrendering to this woman who was driving her insane with a single desire, to give her pleasure, as much pleasure as was in Sheila's power to give her, even as Sheila hated her.

Angel stopped moaning, her pussy moving away from Sheila's tongue. Sheila looked up, wild-eyed, her breasts heaving. She saw Sol with his head resting on the back of the seat, his eyes glazed over, and she saw Angel hunched over him, sucking his cock, her legs pulled up under her on the seat, only a small patch of her pussy showing, Sheila's eyes fixed on it, thinking of nothing now but getting her tongue back on that pussy, giving Angel pleasure, the only thing that mattered to Sheila now, getting her hands on Angel's thighs, prying them apart, and then lowering her face. . . . Suddenly Sheila felt the limo slow down, turn, come to a stop. She heard the glass partition buzzing down. She saw Angel pull her head up from Sol's cock and sit up. She slid away from him toward the door, her bare legs still tucked under her. Sheila moved sideways on her knees to get closer to Angel. Sheila put her hands on Angel's thighs and looked up at her. She heard the sound of her own voice—but not her voice—a strange woman's whining voice, "*Please,* Angel!" But Angel didn't hear her. She was staring at the open space where the partition had been. Sheila turned her head in slow motion to see what Angel was staring at.

She saw a chrome .45 poking through the open window, and then Barry's long arm aiming the gun at Sol's head. Sheila screamed, "Sol!" and grabbed Barry's arm.

Sol opened his eyes to the sound of Sheila's scream that came from a great distance. He saw the blurred barrel of a gun pointed at him. In slow motion he reached a hand inside his sports jacket until he felt the .38 on his hip and he pulled it out with agonizing slowness as he heard the loud, echoing blast of a .45, saw the muzzle flash before his eyes, and felt the rear window shatter behind him, dropping bits of glass on the back of his jacket.

Barry yanked his arm free of Sheila's hand just as Sheila heard the sound of Angel's voice, "You fucking dyke!" She turned as Angel lunged down at her. Sheila raised her forearm hard against Angel's throat and then she brought up her clenched fist and slammed it into Angel's jaw. Angel's head snapped back against the passenger window. She lay slumped against the door, dazed.

Barry was squinting behind his tinted glasses, aiming again as the fat guy brought up his .38.

Sheila heard two shots ring out almost simultaneously, the shots deafening in her ears. She saw Sol drop his .38 on the floor and grab his shoulder. Blood seeped through his fingers as he began to slump forward until his forehead rested against the back of the front seat. Barry was smiling at the slumped form, his smile fading, his brows furrowing. He looked down at his chest. He saw the blood seeping through his white shirt, the blood, spreading wider and wider like a pool. Barry looked up at the fat guy's motionless form, raised a finger, "You cocksucker—" and fell forward, half hanging over into the back of the limo.

Sheila cried out, "Sol! Sol! You all right?" She pushed him back against the seat. His eyes were open, glazed, not from the bullet wound that only grazed his shoulder, but from the drug Angel had slipped into his champagne.

Sol muttered, "I don't feel nuthin', Sheila. I must be dyin'."

"You aren't dying, Sol. You're just not feeling any pain."

Sol looked at her like a worried little boy. "The truth, Sheila? I ain't?" And then his eyes opened wider and he muttered, "Sheila—the dyke."

Still kneeling on the floor, Sheila turned and saw Angel reaching into her purse, pulling out a gun, bringing it up in front of her. Sheila grabbed Angel's wrist and forced her hand over her head, the gun pointing at the roof, another shot ringing out. Sheila struggled to hold Angel's gun over her head while she searched with her free hand along the floor for Sol's .38. When she felt it, she picked it up and jabbed it into Angel's stomach. She felt Angel's wrist go limp and saw her gun drop to the floor.

"You going to shoot me, baby?" Angel said.

Sheila pressed the gun into Angel's stomach. "No. I'm not going to shoot you, cunt. But I should."

"I didn't think so." Then she said, "So you were in on it, too?"

"What do you think?"

"I think you're a hell of an actress, baby. That coy Mrs. Weinstein shit, the straight chick teasing a dyke. I tell you, you had me fooled." Angel sighed as if with an unpleasant thought. "I hate to bring this up, baby, but the blond muscle dude, he's your boyfriend, right?"

"Good guess."

"It wasn't much of a guess." Angel raised her eyebrows as if she'd just thought of something. "By the way, does he know?"

"Know what?"

"What a good actress you are."

"He knows."

"I'll bet he does. Does he know the other thing, too?"

"What other thing?"

"How much you like it. Or you going to tell him it was just acting?" Sheila didn't say anything. "You are a good actress, baby, but not that good. You may have been acting at the salon and at my penthouse and in my office, but you and I know you weren't acting when you were on your knees in this limo."

Angel smiled at her, the same smile Sheila had seen on the painting over her bed just before Sheila passed out from the pain.

Sheila heard the muffled sound of a gunshot, and felt her hand jerk back. Angel's eyes opened wide and her mouth opened as she tried to draw in a breath. She breathed in short, gasping breaths, made a gurgling sound, blood trickling from her lips. She reached out her hand and put it on Sheila's arm, gripping Sheila's arm tightly. Then she said softly, almost tenderly, "Don't blame me, baby." Her grip loosened and she fell back against the seat, her eyes still open.

"Jesus, Sheila!" Sol said.

"Come on, Sol. Let's get out of here!" Sheila opened the door close to the swamp and got out in the rain. She saw that she was splattered with blood. She reached into the limo and half-pulled, half-helped Sol out into the rain. He stood unsteadily. Sheila put her arm around his waist to hold him up. They began staggering in the mud, the highway on one side of them, the canal and the swamp on the other. Sheila's spiked heels kept sinking in the mud, so she kicked off one, then the other. She struggled to hold up Sol, almost a deadweight. "Stay with me, Solly," she said. She held him tighter as they walked more steadily now, the rain beating against their faces, bringing them back to where they were, moving away from a black limousine parked in the mud on Alligator Alley.

The lights of a car came up behind them, the car passing them, then pulling off into the mud in front of them. The front passenger-side door swung open. Sheila struggled with Sol toward the car.

Just before they reached it, Sol said, "Back there in the limo, Sheila. You was actin', right?"

"What do *you* think, Sol?"

Sheila opened the rear door and pushed Sol into the car. Then she got into the front seat and closed the door.

Bobby looked across at her, the blood splattered all over her. "Jesus, baby! You all right?"

"It's not my blood, Bobby. It's Angel's."

"Angel's?"

"The cunt surprised us. She was waiting in the limo for me. I couldn't do anything."

Bobby stared at her naked breasts splattered with blood. "You musta done something," he said.

Sheila looked down at her breasts for a moment without speaking, and then she raised her arms and folded them across her breasts.

From the backseat, Sol said, "Nuthin' happened, Bobby, wasn't supposedta to happen." Sheila glanced in the rearview mirror and saw Sol's eyes staring back at her. "Reggie's taken care of." Sol said. "I capped them both."

Pat Jordan is the author of the classics *A False Spring, A Nice Tuesday, Black Coach,* and most recently the crime novel *a.k.a. Sheila Doyle,* as well as a contributor to numerous national magazines and anthologies. He lives in Fort Lauderdale, Florida.

10/3